P9-DXK-840

Blue Asylum

Books by Kathy Hepinstall

THE HOUSE OF GENTLE MEN

THE ABSENCE OF NECTAR

PRINCE OF LOST PLACES

BLUE ASYLUM

Blue
Asylum

A NOVEL

KATHY
HEPINSTALL

Houghton Mifflin Harcourt
BOSTON   NEW YORK

For information about permission to reproduce selections from this book,
write to Permissions, Houghton Mifflin Harcourt Publishing Company,
215 Park Avenue South, New York, New York 10003.

www.hmhbooks.com

Library of Congress Cataloging-in-Publication Data
Hepinstall, Kathy.
Blue asylum : a novel / Kathy Hepinstall.
p. cm.
ISBN 978-0-547-71207-9 (hardback)
1. Plantation owners' spouses — Virginia — Fiction. 2. Psychiatric hospital
patients — Fiction. 3. Asylums — Fiction. 4. Virginia —
History — Civil War, 1861–1865 — Fiction. I. Title.
PS3558.E577B58 2012
813'.54 — dc22
2011029653

Book design by Brian Moore

Printed in the United States of America
DOC 10 9 8 7 6 5 4 3

For Keith

Blue Asylum

1

WHEN IRIS DREAMED of that morning, the taste of blood was gone, and so was the odor of gun smoke, but her other senses stayed alive. The voices around her distinct. The heel of a bare foot between her ribs. The pressure of the pile of bodies on her chest. Was this what the others had felt too, as they died around her? Her dream followed the reality so well that when the bodies were yanked away from her, one by one, the weight released and the darkness cleared, and she jerked upright, gasping, on the floor of a jail cell in Fort Lane. She'd been given a blanket and nothing else, not even a pillow, for she had been judged insane even before the trial began, and her jailers followed the logic that the mad shunned the comforts of the rational. When she awoke on the floor, on that cold blanket, she thought first of the man who had murdered those innocent people by the barely crawling light of dawn, but her rage held down something deeper, something that searched for oxygen to speak.

Her trial lasted less than an hour. The judge didn't want to hear her story. None of it mattered: The wayward turkeys that ran into the woods. The porcelain tub full of bloody water. The pale, blue-eyed baby. The two small graves. Her fate had already been decided. She was convicted and sentenced and put on a train to Savannah with an armed guard, from there sent on a series of trains going west, and when the tracks ran out she was taken by open-air coach to the port at Punta Rassa.

On the last leg of her journey, she set sail for Sanibel Island on the *Scottish Chief,* which also carried a hundred head of cattle. She had been allowed to bathe and put on a traveling dress with ornamental braids and her best spoon bonnet. She had even been allowed to bring her best clothes with her in a steamer trunk. But she had not been allowed to tell the story that would have excused or at least explained her actions.

The ship was stifling hot. The scent of the cattle rose up from the hull below her, their excrement and fear. She smoothed her hair and tried to steady her breathing. She looked out to the calm flat sea and tried to be just as calm and flat herself, so that others could see there had been a mistake.

This feeling of hatred for her husband, Robert Dunleavy, had to be contained. The judge had seen it, and it had influenced him. Frightened him, even. Wives were not supposed to hate their husbands. It was not in the proper order of things. And so she worked on this too, buried the hatred, for now, in an area of Virginia swampland where the groundwater was red.

The lows of restless cattle came up through the floorboards. They would go on to Havana, where they would be slaughtered.

"How much longer?" she asked the guard.

"Not long."

The ship churned slowly through the water. A large bird dived at the surface and came back up with a struggling fish. She nodded, her lids closing, and took refuge in a gray-blue sleep.

She awakened as the ship was docking.

"We're here," said the guard.

She stood and he bound her hands in front of her with a silk scarf.

"I'm sorry," he said. "Regulations."

He took her wrist gently and led her out to the gangplank, where she paused, amazed at the sight. Beautiful white sand beaches stretched into the distance. Palmettos grew on the vegetation line, and a sprawl of morning glories lay, still open, on the dunes. Coconut palms flanked the perimeter of the building itself, a huge two-story revival with Doric columns and tiered wings that jutted out on either side. A courtyard had been landscaped with straight columns of Spanish dagger. On the building, a sign:

SANIBEL ASYLUM FOR LUNATICS

A judge had signed the order. A doctor had taken her pulse and looked into her eyes and asked her a series of questions and confirmed that yes, something in her mind was loose and ornery, like a moth that breaks away from the light and hides instead in the darkness of a collar box. The heat made her shudder. Her dress was wet in the back. She moved her eyes away from the sign and noticed a blond boy and a large Negro man fishing in the surf. Both of them stared at her. The man was so black he made the pale boy beside him look like a ghost. The boy kept touching something on his cheek.

"Time to head in, ma'am," the guard said, and for just a moment she thought of hurling herself into the water and letting the folds of her traveling dress pull her down to the bottom. She shook off the thought, steeled herself, and gingerly made her way forward, difficult as it was to balance with her hands tied in front of her.

The blond boy, whose name was Wendell, had been fishing for snook with the chef, a freed Negro from Georgia, who was using his prized snakewood baitcaster. The chef was fishing and talking, fishing and talking, fishing and talking, a rhythm he had perfected through the years. His topic of conversation, on this morning, was his castor bean garden — his latest attempt at growing wealthy overnight—and he would have succeeded already if a rare frost hadn't killed the plants this past winter. Federal prisoners in Tortuga were dropping dead left and right from yellow fever. The treatment: castor oil. His new batch of castor beans was hardy, and although they covered just a half-acre at present, he had plans for expansion.

Overhead, a brown pelican circled.

"Of course I don't wish yellow fever on any man," the chef said.

Wendell wasn't listening. He'd just caught a glimpse of the ship. "It's a side-wheeler," he announced.

The chef pressed his lips together, annoyed by the interruption. He followed Wendell's gaze. "*Scottish Chief*. That's Summerlin and McKay's ship. It's probably taking more cattle to the Bahamas."

The side-wheeler steamer approached the dock.

"Why is it stopping here?" Wendell asked.

"I heard we got a new one."

"Oh?" Wendell cocked his head slightly to one side, his way of showing intrigue. "Maybe it's a really crazy one." Those were Wendell's favorites; lunatics were captivating, and the crazier the better. He had lived around them all his life, because his father was the superintendent and chief psychiatrist of the asylum. Wendell believed he was crazy himself, and it was only a matter of time before it was discovered in him and he was locked away with the others. He watched the boat, his eyes wide and drying out in the sea air. The end of his cane pole dipped downward.

"Look, boy," said the chef. "You got one!"

The pole jerked and danced in Wendell's hands. He pulled back too hard. A weighted hook, still with half the bait on, came flying and landed in Wendell's cheek. He sucked in his breath as the hook stuck fast, the fishing line trailing off into the wind. Blood ran down in a trickle from the new puncture. He was hooked good now, good as any fish.

"You did it again," the chef muttered, shaking his head as he cut the line to free him. "Third time this year. You must have a magnet in your head somewhere. Go in and find someone to cut that hook out of you."

Wendell wasn't listening. His head was cocked again. The fishhook dangled from his cheek. A woman had appeared on the gangplank. Slender and pale, chestnut-colored hair gathered in a chignon. Properly attired in a dress and white gloves. A single white feather adorned her bonnet. Her hands were tied in front of her.

"She looks just like any other person," Wendell said.

"Lunatics have a way of blending in, like green snakes in the grass. Go on in, now. Your blood is scaring off the fish."

"She can't be crazy!" Wendell insisted.

She seemed to hear him, turning her head toward him, staring at him a long moment. He froze. The trickle of blood slowed and dried in a new breeze.

"You best stay away from the patients," the chef said. "Remember what happened before, with Miss Penelope."

The hook had stung a bit, but the name hurt him deeper. The chef's baritone had evoked it without warning. The name had a barb on it, too. Instantly he remembered Penelope's freckled skin, her long red hair, which she refused to tie back, her crystal-blue eyes and perpetual half-smile, the doll in a pinafore dress she carried around with her. His father was not inclined to tell him anything about the patients and had instructed the nurses and guards to be equally reticent around the boy. So Wendell gleaned information by eavesdropping on fragments of conversation. Penelope was from New England and suffered from a sadness of indeterminate origin that had evidently driven her, one night, to attempt to hang herself with the sash of her nightgown. After the finest doctors in Boston had failed to conceive of a cure, her family had sent her to the island in the desperate belief that sunlight and the fragrance of tropical flowers could restore some kind of radiance to her sad, addled brain. She was seventeen years old, and had God not killed her, she could have grown to be an old woman, and Wendell an old man, so old that the gap in their ages would mean nothing.

Wendell looked back at the woman on the gangplank. He stroked the hook in his cheek until another bead of blood appeared and ran down to his chin. He wiped off the gore, looked at it.

Penelope.

The name still hurt him. No one had cut it out of him yet.

Iris stepped off the gangplank and onto dry sand, the short heels of her leather boots crunching in it. Above her, white birds circled, shrieking down at her. A tear slid down her cheek before she could stop it. Annoyed, she bent her head and shrugged her shoulder to wipe the tear away. As she approached the courtyard she saw what wasn't visible from a distance. The windows had bars on them.

A dozen people milled about the courtyard, guarded by attendants in white uniforms. One young man sat alone at a small round table set up near the steps. He had high cheekbones and was dressed in army-issued pants, a white shirt, and a thin coat. He wore a slouch hat. A checkerboard sat in front of him, set for a game. He looked up as she approached him. Something about his gaze was comforting. He glanced at her bound hands and nodded, as though remembering his own hands had once been tied that way. The man did not seem insane. Only deeply sorrow-ful. And if sorrow were a diagnosable offense, perhaps she was mad after all.

The man at the checkers table, Ambrose Weller, had watched the new patient come down the gangplank and make her way through the sand. He could tell she was a stranger to the coast, some genteel woman from further up South, completely out of her element. The way she moved, so dignified and calm, as though on a Sunday walkabout, reminded him of graceful sea birds he had seen after a storm, washed up on the beach, wings broken, wounded, and yet still attempting the gait characteristic of their species.

He had arrived on the island screaming and cursing, four strong men restraining him. He had to be carried all the way to his room and tied to his bed, dosed with laudanum until the vi-sions faded into the sweet syrup of delirious forgetfulness, and his mind finally let go of its torments in the same reluctant way a child surrenders his playmates to the call of his mother.

He thought about the woman, remembering a time when he could, clearheaded, desire one. Then some bolt of memory re-minded him that nothing was the same anymore. Dr. Cowell, the psychiatrist, had told him that the secret was not so much in for-getting as in distracting oneself. Think of the color blue, the doc-tor had suggested. Blue, nothing else. Blue ink spilling on a page. A blue sheet flapping on a clothesline. Blue of blueberries. Of water. Of a vase a feather a shell a morning glory a splash on the wing of a pileated woodpecker. Blue that knows nothing, blue of blank recollection, blue of a baby's eyes, a raindrop in a spider's web, a vein that runs from hand to wrist, the moon in scattered light, the best part of a dream and the sky, the sky, the sky . . .

2

ELEANOR BEACON, who was from a prominent Irish family in Baltimore, suffered from an uncontrollable and persistent imagining of the pains and sorrows of every creature on the Earth. She would not eat breakfast, as the slab of bacon was once a pig who cringed at a falling ax, and the eggs evoked a vision of the crestfallen hen, her future chicks stolen right out from under her. At night Eleanor imagined kittens calling to her from the bottom of imaginary wells; dolphins performing tricks in solitary waters with no one to clap; orphaned fawns, stepped-upon ants; birds that crashed into windows, turtles left on their backs by merciless children. Dr. Henry Cowell, head psychiatrist at the Sanibel Asylum, had worked with her patiently and had made considerable progress. But now she was back on the subject of that patient horse she used to see in Baltimore, pulling a carriage full of rowdy tourists in the heat of the summer.

Dr. Cowell was no stranger to the madness of women. In fact, he specialized in their treatment. But now he was growing tired of lunacy in general and Eleanor Beacon in particular.

He sat behind his desk and fondled the gold pocket watch that hung from his waist. Ten minutes left. Ten minutes of arguing that the natural world was a wound whose scab could not help but be broken. Jellyfish evaporated on the beach, dogs died under the porch, hermit crabs ate crustaceans and themselves were eaten by raccoons, which themselves might fall prey to an osprey. The circle of life was not a mad killer. It simply was round.

"The horse was doing its job," he said. "Horses have roles, just like people. Men have roles. And so do women. You have a role, Mrs. Beacon. Your role is back home at your husband's side."

"My husband is cruel. He kills spiders that are minding their own business."

A knock at the door. A nurse entered. "Dr. Cowell, the boat with the new patient is approaching the dock."

Dr. Cowell was grateful for the interruption. He nodded to the nurse, his signal to lead the patient away, even though the session was not quite over.

"The tourists were fat," Eleanor insisted, as she rose from the chair, clutching her handkerchief. "That poor, poor horse."

"Roles, Mrs. Beacon," he said. He turned toward the window, loosening his cravat as the door closed. This time of morning the sunlight was perfect for clarity but not steep enough to make him squint. His office was situated on the second story of the asylum, just above the foyer. The spiral staircase leading up to it lent the perfect sense of grandeur and dignity that should accompany any audience with him. He could gaze out the window, as he did now, at madness on the ground level — so much more tolerable from above, lunatics sunning themselves in the courtyard or collecting shells on the beach under the watchful eyes of the guards.

His son, Wendell, and the black chef fished side by side, knee-deep in the blue water. The doctor himself was too impatient to fish, too easily burned by the sun, too tempting for mosquitoes and the biting midges that plagued him when the winds calmed. And yet he felt a stab of envy, watching the two of them, their rapport obvious by their postures and how closely they stood. He wished he could be a chef, he thought, as a wave of self-pity washed over him. How simple and predictable a job that was. The equation of salt to meat never varied; there were no surprises

9

or screams or delusions involved in the thickening of custard or the steepening of broth.

Trained in his native England and influenced by the benevolent reformists of the York Asylum, the doctor was accustomed to establishing a rapport with a patient and then calmly building a case against their lunacy, guiding them back to their senses by dint of logic and persuasion. He dazzled himself with his own arguments, taking as his greatest satisfaction those moments when he could see the rational part of a lunatic, hidden so far, reveal itself in his office. He then nurtured that part, fostered it, treated it like the chef treated his precious castor bean plants. And only in the most desperate cases did he employ the application of cold water to startle patients from their madness. It was not punishment. It was merely a somatic incentive that, when judiciously applied, could be very effective. It didn't hurt them — no, there was never a mark on the lunatics. Their screams, he cautioned the staff, were not screams of pain, but merely the sound put off by their sudden leap of progress, like a puff of steam from a locomotive engine as it takes its maiden voyage to the west.

A side-wheeler came into view, churning blue water on its way to the dock. The new patient, Iris Dunleavy, was due to arrive this morning. The sun moved a tiny bit higher and shot a ray through the window. The doctor shielded his eyes, deep in thought, waiting as the ship docked and the woman came into sight. She was comely, to be sure, and dressed in the manner of a respectable woman.

A strange and special case. She was a plantation wife and, according to her husband, had started the marriage dutiful, obedient, and loving, but in the past two years had undergone a rapid transformation, becoming hostile and combative, and her acts of defiance culminated in an insult so deranged and spectacularly public as to cause the poor husband a terrible amount of shame.

As it was, the man desperately wanted his wife back — or, at least, the wife he'd once known.

Dr. Cowell was well regarded for his success in calming the most hysterical of women. His paper on the relationship of female lunacy and the suffrage movement in America had attracted widespread critical acclaim and had led to his first American assignment as the assistant to the chief of psychiatry of Pennsylvania State Hospital for the Insane. Now he was his own man, on his own island, his fame such that Robert Dunleavy, the plantation man, had sought him out specifically to treat his wife and had been more than willing to pay the hefty fee for her housing and treatment in one of the most exclusive asylums in the United States.

He watched her walk down the plank, her hands tied in front of her. She kept her head high, and though he could not discern her expression, she carried herself with a certain air of defiance.

The doctor turned from the window. He'd seen many a woman enter this place, head high, convinced of her rightness. He'd had great success in putting them back on the path to clear thinking and normal relations with their communities. She would be no different.

3

IRIS ENTERED a large foyer with the guard, the sand her boots had collected crunching against the stone floor. She stared at the furnishings: the rosewood benches, the seashell-patterned wallpaper, the lush colors of the oil paintings in their gilt frames, the dangling chandelier, the white marble staircase that spiraled up to the second floor. She wondered how such style could be wasted on the deranged, then remembered that she was considered deranged herself.

A stout woman approached them. She was not wearing a nurse's uniform but a simple alpaca dress and gaiters. She had the red, puffy cheeks of someone who used too much salt on her meat. A massive ring of keys was tied around her waist. Iris looked at the keys and recognized their authority. She had once worn her own ring of keys.

The woman looked Iris up and down, then nodded at the guard, who untied her hands. "I'm in charge of you," she announced. "Follow me." Her voice had a slight Irish brogue and not a modicum of warmth. She led her through an arched door into a great hallway, rooms on one side and a bank of windows on the other. Benches were set up against the walls. The hallway was nearly deserted save for an old woman in the near distance, who sat on a bench in widow's weeds, her arms folded, rocking.

The woman with the keys glanced back at Iris. "I am the matron of this asylum," she announced. "I have a lot of responsibility and I don't have time for problems. You've entered the women's ward. There are nineteen women here, and nineteen men in the ward opposite from us. Dr. Cowell believes in symmetry."

Iris followed her without a word, all the while rehearsing to herself exactly what she'd say to her once they were alone. Bits of sand fell from her dress as she walked.

"You are never to go to the men's ward under any circumstances," the matron continued, "nor are you allowed to bring any man into yours. But Dr. Cowell believes that your life here should imitate, to the greatest extent possible, life in the world of the sane and balanced. So you are permitted to sit across from one another at the table when you have your meals, and you are allowed to engage in polite fellowship with them during your courtyard time. You may play cards or checkers, although you are not allowed to bet on the games, not even using shells as currency. And you will be supervised at all times."

She swept a hand along the hallway. "All the corridors where our patients live are single-loaded, which is much more expensive than double-loaded, but the benefit is that the nurses are more able to supervise you, and the conditions are less crowded. Also, by having the rooms on only one side of the corridor, a nurse need never turn her back on a patient."

When they reached the room at the end of the hallway, the matron paused and fiddled with her keys. She opened the door and ushered Iris inside to a tastefully arranged room, with a cottage bed, a dresser, a small desk with a mirrored gallery, and a straight-backed chair. A large pitcher of water sat on a washstand. A porcelain bowl was placed on the floor between the stand's cabriole legs. The walls were painted Shaker blue.

"Every detail of this room has been designed by Dr. Cowell. He picked out the dresser design himself, in New Orleans. And the walls are blue because Dr. Cowell believes this particular color calms the mind."

A window faced the sea. It had no glass but was lined with bars. Iris stared out at the beach. The boy and the black man were gone. Only sea oats and calm water and circling gulls remained. The guard on the ship had treated her well. And even this woman, brusque though she was, did not speak to her as though she were mad. Perhaps they sensed she was different from the others? Iris turned from the window and kept her voice calm and steady.

"You seem like a kind and wise woman. And though your position here is one of authority over me, I would like to speak to you as one woman to another. There has been a mistake. I do not belong here. I am here simply for the act of defying my husband, who is a man of most indecent character."

The matron pointed at the desk. "The patients want to move the desk over to the window. That is not its place."

Iris took a step toward her, tried again. "I am sure that my family in Winchester has no idea what has happened to me, in the confusion of the war. If you could please contact my father, who is the minister of a Methodist — "

"Breakfast is at seven, dinner at one o'clock, supper at seven. Bells will announce all meals. If you are not on time, you will miss these meals."

"Please! Listen to me — "

"We have china plates here. A bowling alley. A billiard room. An icehouse, five milk cows, Cornish game hens. A citrus grove and a vegetable garden. And despite the embargo, we still manage to provide sugar on occasion, as well as beef."

Iris rushed to the woman and sank to her knees. All composure was gone now. She grasped at the hem of her dress, begging her to please listen, her tale spilling out in a crazy manner now. Any person entering the room would have seen a strict, stout woman standing with arms crossed, and a lunatic kneeling before her, wild-eyed, desperate, clingy, and hysterical.

The matron wrenched the hem of her dress free of Iris's hands. "Get up, collect yourself, and show some gratitude. Your husband paid thousands of dollars to send you here. He must love you very much, although I can't imagine why."

Iris let go of her dress. She stood slowly. Felt herself harden inside as she glared at the woman. "Love me very much?" she asked. "On the contrary, my husband hates me. And I hate him. He is one of the most vile people on this planet."

The matron fumbled with the keys at her waist.

"I have better things to do than listen to the rantings of a new lunatic." She found the key she was looking for and glared at Iris. "Do you know what happens to the stubborn ones, the defiant ones? The ones like you?"

"No, I don't."

"They get the water treatment. It stimulates circulation to the brain. The lunatics scream and moan and beg as they are dragged away to the water treatment room. When they're dragging you away, you won't feel so proud."

"What is the water treatment exactly?" Iris asked calmly, although her hands trembled.

The matron glanced at Iris's hands, saw the fear revealed there, and smiled. "You'll see," she said, and left the room.

4

HAD HE EVER loved her, even at the beginning? That question would never answer itself. It sat there like a fallen cake. Many suitors had come to her father's house to see her, back in those days she was single and free of care, but she was bored with the local boys. So familiar, so dull. Her childhood had been magical, hours spent in ecstatic loneliness in the apple orchard, dreaming of foreign lands and wild adventures. Everything was new, down to birdsong and grass blades. By the time she had reached adulthood, the town around her was like a grandmother who had used up all her stories and now simply rocked on the porch. The same flowers, the same streets, year after year. She longed for someone more exotic. A prince, a pirate. Her lofty expectations worried her father, a humble man of God. "I was a local boy," he told her. "And your mother was hesitant about accepting my marriage proposal. But she made a leap of faith in the direction of sincerity and has never regretted her choice. At least she has never told me, and I would be the first to know."

"Try to have an open mind, Iris," her mother counseled her. "I found your father just around the corner, and he turned out just fine."

So Iris tried but still could not concentrate on the earnest young men who came to court her. She would leave her body and float above the house, rising up into the clouds until the voices of her suitors were as faint as distant birdsong. At night, she heard her father's prayers for a suitable husband rising up through the gravity vent. And yet she could not will herself to fall in love. She had known every single young man in town since he was a boy, and there was nothing new about any of them.

Then one day at her father's church, the miracle arrived. His name was Robert Dunleavy, and he owned a large plantation in Virginia. He had traveled to Winchester to visit his brother. Iris glanced over at him as she sang "Rock of Ages," admiring his sideburns and his curly hair, but had not realized that she had been admired herself. Not until he sent word to her father that he wished to call on her.

He showed up at the front door, hat in hand, and they went for a walk through town, just the two of them, past the main square and the post office and the dry goods store—places Iris had known all her life but were now strange and new in his presence. He was exotic and surreal, an overload of color and music and light, akin to a circus that comes to town and pitches its tent right on your roof.

He talked about his plantation, Bethel, in a loving and respectful voice, as though Bethel was the name of his mother and not three hundred acres of choice Virginia land. She said very little, so intently was she listening to his tales. They returned home and Robert said goodbye and went back to Bethel and immediately began courting Iris's father with earnest correspondence written on lined French stationery, with cursive letters made from a quill pen that never dripped. He spent a good amount of time talking about his plantation earnings per year, his faith (Methodist), his ambitions (political), honor and probity and character and kindness. Yes, he knew that Iris's family was against slavery, and he was against it as well, but it was a necessary evil at the present moment, and he was looking forward to the day he would be able to free his slaves and pay them for their labor as sharecroppers.

In fact, he treated his slaves very well, new jersey clothes twice a year instead of once, a day off on Sunday and half a day on Saturday, a fireplace in half the slave cabins, and at Christmastime calico skirts for the women, tobacco for the men, and taffy for the children. What the plantation needed, what both he and his slaves needed, was the addition of a strong but loving woman. A woman like Iris, beautiful and pure of heart, humble, chaste, and kind.

Her father agonized over the dilemma. At night the sound of her mother's voice replaced his prayers rising up through the gravity vent. "Don't deny our daughter's happiness for your own piety and your own politics. This man could give Iris a good life. He wants to marry her, make her the mistress of his plantation, the mother of his children. What else will she do? Grow old and alone under our roof?" Eventually his wife's badgering won out against the milder, more contradictory and elusive counsel of God, and he gave his permission for Iris to marry Robert Dunleavy. And so it was that Iris fell in love, not so much with a man as with an exceedingly proper and literary courtship, one that left behind a stack of letters her father carefully bound with a length of cord and kept in the bottom drawer of his desk. She was also against slavery and found it both curious and terrible that one person could keep another in chains, but Robert did intend to one day free his slaves. He'd said it himself. And though she did hear the hesitation in her father's voice when he gave his consent for her to marry the man, she chose to ignore it. She was leaving this place for a new and exciting life. Exotic sounds, exhilarating colors. She didn't have to follow her mother's story and her grandmother's story like a fish follows the turns of a creek bed. She had been set free.

Iris was married in the spring of 1859, by her father, in her father's church that was filled with neighbors and friends. She left town beside her new husband in an open-air coach. A similar

coach would, five years later, take her to the port in Punta Rassa
to be loaded onto the *Scottish Chief* with a hundred head of cattle. Two rides engineered by a persuasive and powerful man.

As soon as the matron left, Iris tried the door. It was locked. She
tested the bars on the window. They were smooth under her
hand and held fast. The sounds of a quiet beach came through
the bars: the rattling of wind through the leaves of the coconut
palms, the pounding of waves, a group of willets cooing the same
sad song. How silly — how utterly insane, in fact — it seemed to
her now that Winchester had bored her so, and she could not
wait to leave it. Five years later, after all that had passed, she
would have given anything to be able to go back to the town she
thought she'd outgrown.

According to a folded note slid under her door, she was to
meet with the psychiatrist, Dr. Cowell, at four in the afternoon.
Surely he would release her, if she made a good case for herself.

She stripped down to her petticoats and chemise and bathed
herself with water she poured into the porcelain bowl. She rum-
maged through her steamer trunk and put on a pleated dress,
simple but elegant. Certainly not the garb of a madwoman. She
combed her hair and retied the chignon. She stared at herself in
the mirror. It was hard to believe that she was still intact. Skin still
porcelain, cheekbones high and balanced, eyes calm, chestnut
hair thick and healthy and neatly gathered. She could have been
any other lovely, mannered woman.

Just before four o'clock, a pleasant-faced nurse knocked
briefly and entered the room.

"Doctor Cowell will see you now," she announced, and led
Iris down the hallway and through the main building, up the
winding stairs in the lobby and into another foyer, this one fea-
turing a conversational sofa and a big window with a brocade

curtain. The nurse gestured to the sofa and went back down the stairs, leaving Iris alone. Almost immediately, the door opened, and the doctor came out of his office. He was a tall, graceful man in a ditto suit. Dark eyes peered at her behind spectacles with wire frames. He wore a chin-strap beard that left his upper lip bare and thin. He had a long jaw line and heavy brows. A muted gray cravat was fastened around his neck. A gold watch swung like a pendulum from his waist.

She stood up to shake his hand.

"I'm Dr. Henry Cowell," he said in a British accent. "And you are Iris Dunleavy." He said her name with a certain confidence, as though Iris Dunleavy was a condition he was sure he could remedy. He ushered her into the office, swept a hand toward a balloon-backed chair, and took a seat behind his desk, where a clock with fleur-de-lis crowning showed the time as exactly four o'clock.

She sat down and smoothed her dress.

"Did you find your trip pleasant?" he asked.

She let out a short, bitter laugh. "I came down here on a blockade runner full of cattle."

He spread his hands. "I'm so sorry, but I'm afraid we're at the mercy of the Federal army. They are blocking so many of our ports. You would have had a shorter trip had you taken the new Florida Railroad, but they've blown up thirty miles of track." He knit his fingers together, looking at her. "You live in Virginia and you are married to a plantation owner, Robert Dunleavy."

"Yes."

She moved her gaze to the window, looking out at the waves and the dunes and the coconut palms and the blue sky. She had something to say and it had to be delivered in her best voice. The one she'd used to say her marriage vows. That calm, that certain.

"I am not a lunatic. I am the victim of a terrible campaign of outright slander by my own husband."

The doctor nodded. "So you are not mad? Your husband is mad? Is that what you are telling me?"

"No, as far as I know his evil cannot take refuge in madness. He'll stand before God one day naked of that excuse. He is simply a terrible man, a brutal slave owner, a liar, and a killer." She tried to keep her voice steady. "I've been sent here as punishment."

"No, there is no punishment within these walls, for you have done nothing wrong. You have simply become confused. Your sensibilities have given way to hysteria. My only desire is to help you return to your right mind."

He paused, fooling with his watch and then looking at the desk clock as if to see if they were aligned. "My grandfather was a Quaker from Leeds. He helped build the York Asylum in 1796. You see, the Quakers are a compassionate people. They don't like war, even a war fought for the soul. They believe in a gentler path to restoration. You can see their influence in your country. At Hudson River State Hospital, they offer sleigh rides. At McLean, plays and concerts. Pennsylvania Hospital has rowing facilities and a museum full of stuffed birds. The environment, you see, is part of the cure."

"What is the water treatment?"

He raised his eyebrows. "Who told you about the water treatment?"

"The matron of the asylum."

"That is nothing for you to worry about. It is rarely employed."

"But what is it?"

He sighed. "It involves dousing the patient with ice-cold water for a period of time. Something about the temperature and pressure of the water seems to effect a strengthening of the rational mind."

"It sounds like torture."

"Some of the more hysterical patients call it that." He seemed to choose his words carefully. "But it's imagined pain. And besides, one could argue that insanity is itself unfathomably painful. It is, isn't it?"

"That's what I've been trying to tell you. I am not a lunatic. I no more belong here as a patient than you do, and if you contact my family in Winchester—"

"Your family will be contacted in due time, Mrs. Dunleavy. In the meantime, I have the sworn statement of a doctor, and the orders of a judge. And even if I did not, you would still be incarcerated purely on the basis of your actions. I'm not saying that you've done this deliberately, or maliciously, Mrs. Dunleavy. But you've embarrassed your husband. Humiliated him, here in such a pressing time, when the war is taking such a toll."

"You don't understand."

"Mr. Dunleavy could have put you in Georgia's state asylum, in Milledgeville. It would have been much less expensive. But it's a terrible, degrading place. He cared enough about you to want for you the very best."

Iris felt her face growing hot. She had to reach this doctor. Make him understand and believe. She summoned all her self-control, loosened her fists into hands again, and told him the story . . . the abridged version, calm and steady until she reached the part about the baby, where her voice choked and she had to stop and compose herself. In doing so, she glanced at the doctor and saw what was in his eyes. He was a man who had already made up his mind and was now listening to her not to gain information, but to bide his time or silently prepare his benevolent riposte. She folded her arms. She would say no more. She could not protect the baby but she could protect his story from nonbelievers.

"Please," he said. "Go on."

"Why should I continue? Clearly you see no truth in it."

"I believe that you see it to be truth."

Someone knocked on the door, startling Iris. The doctor sighed. "Yes?" he called.

The door creaked open and a nurse peered inside. "Dr. Cowell, your wife needs to speak with you."

He pressed his lips together. "Tell Mrs. Cowell I'm busy."

"She says to tell you it's very important."

He took off his glasses and fiddled with the sliding temples. "Tell her," he said in a measured voice, "that I am evaluating a patient and I do not wish to be disturbed."

"But Dr. Cowell, she sounded quite —"

"Tell her!"

Iris jumped. His tone, up to now, had never varied from the calm and the palliative. The nurse beat a hasty retreat, slamming the door, then opening it again and closing it gently in nervous apology.

The doctor closed his eyes briefly and put his glasses back on. "You'll have to excuse my wife. She's been in quite a bad mood because the war has cut off her supply of French boots and India lace, not to mention her favorite cold cream, although the chef does make a fairly good approximation of it with almond oil and rosewater."

Iris said nothing. His mind was already made up. His switching the subject to his wife's sorrows over lace and cold cream only further proved how little regard he gave her story. She stared at the blueprint of the building on the wall, imagining windows without bars, doors without locks. If she could not convince him to let her go, she must take the burden to escape on her own shoulders.

"I promised your husband," he said, "that I'm going to make you well again. And I am making you that same promise."

"And what will the proof be that I've recovered?"

"When you're well, you will understand the consequences of your actions and regret your misdeeds."

"Never. I will never do that."

Another knock. His lips tightened. "What *is* it?"

The door opened again, revealing the same nurse, whose voice now quavered as she spoke. "I'm so sorry, she still insists on seeing you right now."

"I thought I told you to —"

"I did but she says it's a matter of great urgency and you must come to the cottage right away."

"All right! I'm coming! I'm coming! I'm coming!"

5

THE CALUSA INDIANS once lived on this island. Long-haired, fingernails like claws, frenzied dancers, avid fishermen, they lived among cacti, alligators, and century plants. Loved the shine of gold and silver. Believed in three souls: one in the eyes, one in the shadow a body cast, one in that red-faced, long-haired reflection rubbed across flat water. Sometimes a soul would escape a sick man, and the others would hunt that soul through the woods and bring it back, struggling, to the village. The white man could not defeat them with musket and sword, so they sent their diseases. Measles, typhoid. And smallpox. Red spots on the tongue, extending down the arms and legs. Terrible aches. Delirious fevers. The ceremonial mask, the fire dance, the prayer. All useless. What few survived fled to the Seminoles in the north, or to Cuba in the south. Their open-air huts rotted. Their language faded away. Only their middens were left — giant shell piles of their refuge.

Wendell had stood barefoot on these middens in heavy gusts of moonlight and imagined the savages, crazy with fever, crawling through the spartina grass of the sloughs. An old Cuban man who fished for sheepshead from the dock told Wendell the story, and the white boy who had no friends, whose accent was that of neither an English psychiatrist nor an Illinois fishwife but somewhere in between, took up the grudge as his own. The island had also driven him mad. Infected him like a virus.

The sight of the new woman that morning, silk-shackled and brave, and the mention of Penelope's name, had darkened Wendell's mood to the extent that he sought the fellowship of the angry spirits and asked the chef to borrow his canoe. He paddled slowly over waters the Calusa once ruled, gliding through the pass toward the bay side of the island, where the water was stained red by the tannins from the mangrove trees. He touched the tender spots on his face, the places the hook entered and exited after a nurse had pushed the point through and cut off the barb with a pair of fascia scissors. He didn't mind the pain. It was a small, stinging, boy pain, one of many he had endured. Shell scrapes, hobnail stabs, ant bites, even a peck on the shoulder blade from a heron with a broken wing he'd tried to carry back to the asylum. Those pains were dwarfed by this other pain. Guilty pain, restless pain, lonely pain. Pain of Penelope proportions.

Now on the jungle side of the island, he headed toward a shadowy inlet. It was in this wild solitude that the first symptoms of his madness had arrived. That very day he had shyly offered Penelope some hard candy, and she had kissed his cheek in gratitude. Later that afternoon, standing in the muck of the bank in his gloomy, secret world, facing the mangrove thicket, the memory of Penelope's kiss clinging to his face like a leech, he watched in horror as his right hand slid down his trousers. His eyes flew open wide. He had no idea his hand was going to do that, but the hand, magically skilled and confident, paid him no mind, and would have waived him off dismissively were it not so busy. Wendell could do nothing but surrender himself to its maniacal activity.

Penelope, said the sky, and the wind, and the jungle, faster and faster, until he was lying, spent, on the shore, her name a single exhalation of joy among the whispers of ancient songs.

He found it odd and exhilarating, until the morning a male

patient was discovered sitting on the low stone wall of the court-yard, performing the exact same act upon himself, and was immediately set upon by the staff and wrestled into a straight-waistcoat. Wendell froze, watching with horror as the man was dragged away. As the only boy on the island, he had no one even close to his own age in whom to confide, and to go to his father was out of the question. He considered turning to the asylum priest, Father Byrnes, who wore the same tow-cloth cassock and leather sandals every day. According to rumor, Father Byrnes had been a vagrant in his youth, a sad creature robbed of his senses by whiskey. One day he passed out, face up, in a thun-derstorm, and a bolt of lightning came out of the sky and struck him in the chest, melting his gold crucifix into his skin. After the rain stopped, he stood up, cured of his drunkenness by God, and became a priest in gratitude. Supposedly the gold cross was still embedded in his chest, but no one on the island had the courage to ask if it were so, or the audacity to steal a glimpse of Father Byrnes in a state of undress. Wendell hoped it was true and held this legend as evidence that a loving God existed somewhere in the heavens, and that this God could cure his own affliction with a single, violent act of mercy.

In the end, Wendell decided such an odd and disturbing mat-ter would be better discussed not with the priest, but with the chef. One morning when he and the chef were out fishing in wa-ters so calm they could see their own feet, he brought up the man in the courtyard.

The chef scowled. "That poor fellow. Crazy as a bedbug. But happy." Then he unleashed a volley of basso laughter that seemed to go on forever, and that was that.

Wendell tried to stop his mad habit but found that he could not, any more than he could eat half a licorice stick and leave the rest for later. Even the death of Penelope could not make him stop. He tried, could sometimes last for days, but his right hand was its own king, and one time, all it needed was the sight of two horseshoe crabs mating in the water.

He tied his canoe to a prop root, exciting a rookery of white ibis in the branches above his head. He made a shallow dive and swam underwater, where time bent funny like the legs of a heron. He stayed in the water so long his fingers wrinkled, and the sea hibiscus that had been orange at noon was red and dying by the time he climbed into his canoe and started back to the asylum. As the building came into view, he realized he'd neglected to tend the fire for the chef, who was preparing a roast that night. The chef would be angry.

Iris had spent the rest of the afternoon sitting alone in a corner of the day room. She had not tried to talk to the other patients, some of whom were quite proper, sipping valerian tea and playing chess or Old Maid. Others were clearly demented, holding themselves, rocking back and forth, or shrieking out random declarations. At six o'clock the patients were ushered back to their rooms to prepare for the supper hour. At precisely seven o'clock a bell rang, and they were allowed into the dining hall, where four long, great plank tables awaited them. Iris took a seat at a far table.

The men filed in from the other wing, and Iris caught a glimpse of the dark-haired young man she'd seen in the courtyard earlier that day. Now he was wearing different clothes — canvas pants with slash pockets, a vest, and a blue shirt. His hair was combed, and he had freshly shaved. His eyes met hers and he gave her a searching look. He took a seat at a far table. She was still watching him when she heard a female voice in her ear.

"Do you mind if I sit with you?"

The owner of the voice was a trim, small woman, with perfectly coiffed hair and pretty green eyes.

"Not at all," Iris said.

The woman gathered her bustles and took a seat across the table. She extended her hand and clasped Iris's with a sane amount of pressure.

"Lydia Helms Truman."

"Iris Dunleavy."

"You poor thing. You must be frightened out of your mind." The woman took a roll from the filigree basket on the table and began buttering it delicately. "I watched you in the day room. You're not the least bit deranged, are you? You're perfectly sane, just like I am."

Iris felt a wild surge of hope. Was it possible that she would have a comrade here within these walls?

"Be careful of the medicines they give you here," Lydia said. "Various opiates like laudanum and morphine. Or Dover's Powder. All designed to render you docile as a child."

Iris leaned forward. "Why are you here?" she whispered.

"Because I was a threat to my husband." Lydia also kept her voice low. "I believed that women should have a voice in government, and I said so publicly. In 1848, I helped draft the female Bill of Rights at the Seneca Falls Convention. Three days later, my husband had me taken to Utica. I found out later my husband dosed my tea with chloroform to dilate my eyes so that I would have a wild appearance. He had the sheriff and the doctor come over. The doctor felt my pulse and declared me insane. Imagine that, insane from a rapid pulse. How many men would be diagnosed insane at a horse race or a poker game?"

"I'm so sorry," Iris murmured, shaking her head. "This is an outrage."

"For the last sixteen years I've been shuttled from one madhouse to another. Utica, Philadelphia, that awful place in northern Maine. I've been subjected to tranquilizing chairs, bled, and beaten. My ovaries were removed at an asylum in Manteno, as I was suspected of having an excitement of the uterine system."

Iris covered her mouth in horror, yet found herself leaning closer to hear the rest.

"When my mother died, she left me a small fortune, which allowed me to be transferred here. I was told it was the best facility and the most advanced medical care in the country. But within these walls I've had the worst torture ever imaginable — and all in the name of sanity."

Iris could barely breathe. "The water treatment?"

Lydia's eyes grew hard at the phrase. "You've heard," she said flatly. "The matron of the asylum talked the doctor into giving me a treatment."

"I've met her. A most unpleasant woman."

"Look down at her ankles sometime. You will find them purplish and swollen. I've noticed, in my life, that the bigger a woman's ankles, the more hateful her personality. She took offense to something I said or did last year, and next thing you know, I was strapped to a chair and freezing-cold water was poured on my head from a spout in the ceiling for over an hour." She shuddered at the memory. "Perhaps it sounds merely uncomfortable, not painful, but the truth is, after ten minutes the water drops begin to feel like knives stabbing down into your head. It was the most exquisite pain I've ever suffered."

The woman's tale of torture by water unsettled Iris, yet her heart felt lighter for the first time in weeks, just to have a fellow misunderstood soul with whom to take solace. "Are there others like us here?" she asked.

"Yes, there are a few. But some are quite mad. For example . . ." Lydia nodded slightly to the left. "Do you see that woman over there in the ivory dress? She swallows things. Buttons, nails, coins." She pointed to another woman. "And that woman went mad after she had her ninth baby. Couldn't take care of him. Tried to drown him in an apple barrel. Poor thing. And that woman . . . hears voices all the time. Can't sleep for them taunting her, calling her stupid and plain. That man thinks his loneliness will eat him. That man thinks Sunday is a wolf. And that man"—she nodded toward a distinguished-looking fellow with black patches over both eyes being guided into his seat—"tried to shoot himself in the side of the head with a Colt .45 pistol. He faltered at the last moment. His hand shook, and he blew his eyes out instead."

"That's terrible! Why did he want to die?"

Lydia shrugged. "They say he did it for love. That his beloved tortures him with the memory of her scent."

Iris stole a look at the dark-haired man, who had just taken a roll out of the basket and put it on his plate. "How about that fellow over there?"

"Oh." Lydia shook her head. "That's Ambrose Weller. You don't want to be anywhere near him."

"What's wrong with him?"

"No one knows for sure. Something happened to him in the war, I suppose. He'll be fine for days or even weeks, then something sets him off and they have to give him laudanum and tie him to his bed."

Just then, the man caught Iris glancing at him. She quickly looked away.

"He's handsome, though, isn't he?" Lydia observed. "It's a shame, what the war is doing to our men. No end in sight, though. No end in sight."

"With whom do you sympathize?"

"Neither gray nor blue. It doesn't matter here, what becomes of the Union. Not to these people, split within themselves, and not to me, fighting a lonely war all my own."

"You're not on your own," Iris said, and for a moment the two women smiled at each other. Lydia reached over and touched her hand.

"That's a nice ring you have," Lydia said, glancing down at her finger.

"Oh, that. It's made of white pyrite and amethyst. A gift from my grandmother."

"May I see it?"

Iris slid the ring off her finger and handed it to Lydia. "It's beautiful," she said, and popped it in her mouth, swallowing it with a hearty gulp and chasing it down with a gulp of water. Iris stared at her, disbelieving. Instantly, a nurse appeared at the table. "Lydia, did you just swallow something again?"

"Of course not! How could you say such a thing?" Lydia protested. As she and the nurse argued, Iris picked up her plate and moved to the next table, down a few seats and across from where the dark-haired man was eating. An attendant came by and set a bowl of cool cucumber soup on the plate in front of her. She took a deep breath and started to eat. If she was to escape, she needed her strength.

The superintendent and his family took their meals on a walnut dining table in their private cottage behind the asylum. Wendell slid into his seat, freshly washed, his hair combed, dressed for dinner. He was still subdued from being scolded by the chef, who was frantically trying to cook the roast beef in time for supper over the fire Wendell hadn't tended.

"See what you've done? It's gonna be too rare," the chef had said, scowling.

"Some people like it rare."

"I don't need your sass right now."

Wendell's parents had been arguing. He could tell that by the slight red tinge to their faces and the way they avoided one another's glances. Wendell had his own worries. The red lagoon's calming magic had failed him, and no amount of sea horses or skittering crabs or amazingly bright pinfish could banish the memory of Penelope. Wendell's resolve had broken, and on the way back to the asylum, he had paused the canoe in calm water and fondled his privates until the memory of her turned unbearably hot and painful . . . then a cool broken rush, a sweltering of shame, the sky turning pink.

His mother had applied a bit of rouge, badly. It showed on one cheek as a circle, on the other as something vaguely ovoid. Wendell, who was used to the perfection of color found in the native birds and fish, wanted to lean over and undo the whole terrible job with his napkin.

"I had a new patient! I wasn't to be disturbed," his father suddenly said. "Could you not have waited a few minutes? Is that too much to ask of you?"

"I had a terrible headache. You would leave me in agony, when a teaspoon of laudanum would have eased my pain?"

"A teaspoon of laudanum seems to cure so many of your problems," he responded darkly.

"This new patient," Wendell said. "What is her name?"

His father looked at him as though noticing for the first time he was at the table.

"What happened to your cheek?"

"Fishhook."

"Again?" his mother cried. "You are not to fish anymore. It's too dangerous. You could put your eye out. And what if you stepped on a stingray? And the currents. There are strong currents that can sweep you away . . ."

"The patient?" Wendell asked his father again.

"Iris Dunleavy. A plantation wife from Virginia."

"What's wrong with her?"

"Hard to say, since I was not able to finish the interview." He shot a quick dagger at his wife. "And regardless, you know I can't discuss specifics about my patients. But let's say that she came to feel contempt for the efforts of her generous husband to make a good life for her and demonstrated this contempt in a most shocking way."

"Perhaps," Mary said, "this woman's husband didn't care for her at all. Perhaps he merely fancied himself a good husband, when in truth he was cold and insensitive and thought only of himself."

"Perhaps the husband did everything he could and was met with defiance at every turn. Perhaps the husband had no other choice but to send her away."

"Perhaps the husband puts on a façade for the community but behind closed doors is a controlling, hateful man."

Wendell's parents stared each other down. He sighed. A grain of sand had found its way into his soup. It crunched between his teeth.

Iris had worn that ring all her life. Now it was gone forever, and her finger felt desolate without it. She glanced at the dark-haired man, who was sipping a glass of water. She couldn't believe this quiet man was a raving lunatic. He took another sip of water, studied the new level of it in the glass, set the glass down. He seemed deep in thought, lost in some land that may have been green with summer or brown with winter. The angle of his face and the glow of candlelight emphasized the high bone of his cheek, as though a sculptor's knife had carved it out of the pale clay of a hopeless war.

Attendants in white uniforms came around to collect the soup bowls, and others brought in the roasts. One of them approached their table and set the roast down in the middle of it. Immediately the aroma rushed into her nostrils, and it gave her a frisson of pleasure even as she thought of the doomed cattle that had been her fellow travelers.

The chef came out. Iris recognized him as the black man who had been fishing with the boy when she was led off the ship that morning. His long, pearl-handled knife glittered in the light. He strode over to their table and began to carve the roast. The meat was too rare. Blood ran out the side, spilling over the plate and gathering in a dark pool on the white tablecloth. Iris moved back in her chair. The blood of a steer had a different smell from the blood of humans, but the sight of it, pooling under candlelight, made bile rise up in her throat.

"Damn boy," the chef muttered. He put down the knife and huffed out of the room.

The dark-haired man looked at the blood. He had started to taste his soup, but now he let the spoon fall back into the bowl. Bits of cool cucumber spattered on his face. He shook his head slowly, moved his lips. He was whispering something, and she could not help leaning forward and cocking her head to hear the words.

"Blue. Blue like a marble. Like cobalt glass." He shut his eyes. "Like ice in a beard."

He opened his eyes and looked at her. "Like the stained glass windows of a church." He picked up his spoon and tapped it against the tabletop, harder and harder. An attendant material- ized, leaned down toward him.

"Can I help you, sir?"

"Don't touch me. Don't touch me, don't touch me."

"Give me the spoon, sir." The attendant took hold of it and tried to wrest it away, but the dark-haired man held fast.

"Let go," he said. "Let go, let go, let go!" His voice had risen to the point that a man babbling next to him fell silent and stared. Iris couldn't move. She was riveted to the scene playing out in front of her.

Another attendant appeared in the midst of the wrestling match over the spoon and seized the patient by the arm.

"DON'T TOUCH ME!" he screamed. "Don't touch me don't touch me take your hands off me—"

"Don't touch him!" The old man who sat beside her shouted. The other patients began shouting too, incomprehensible things, some pointing at the attendants, some at the windows or each other, reacting not so much to the situation, perhaps, as to the energy in the air. It was chaos; they lusted for it and would not be denied.

Ambrose Weller jumped out of his chair, knocking it over as he fought against the men who tried to restrain him. They wrestled him to the floor, pinning down his arms and legs, but still he struggled, screaming, "Get the doctor! Where is he? Dr. Cowell! Dr. Cowell!"

6

AMBROSE KILLED HIS first man in filtered sunlight, so close
he could see his enemy's face. He was in a wood lot managed by
the Mennonites. Bluebirds had flown away, squawking, and the
other animals had disappeared down burrows or into the holes
of trees. Even the ants had towed their white eggs into passages
made in rotting logs. The animals in that cool, brief forest were
accustomed to the sleepy sound of an ax in red oak, and not the
energy of war.

Ambrose took a step. His shoes had been made with the
leather from an artillery case. Walking in the rain had stretched
them so that they slid on his heel, and the bottom of each shoe
had a hole in it. He planned to throw away the shoes entirely
when the holes had grown to the size of cherries, had abandoned
that plan in favor of plums, then peaches, then apples, as there
were no other shoes to take their place. It was still early in the
morning and the light was weak, but the forest seemed unbearably warm to him, perhaps because of the fog of gunpowder sitting among the low branches, or the Enfield rifle whose barrel
had blistered his finger when he'd paused to reload. Only his feet
remained cool.

An artillery shell had burst too close to his ear a few weeks
before, and as a result the war made an ocean sound as it filtered
through the branches. It didn't bother him on open land, where
the enemy could be seen. But here in the woods it crippled him.
He saw a shadow move and caught the hint of a blue uniform.

Branches parted, the shade thinned, and the Union soldier stepped into clear light, trying to lift his gun as Ambrose fired. The soldier sank to his knees, his hand flying to a place on his chest that wasn't right anymore. The man looked down at his hand to watch the blood spurt through his fingers. Pain had not found him yet and thus allowed him, in his final seconds, to have the fascination of a boy. Finally he closed his hand and fell backward, where he lay still on the ground, still clutching his rifle.

Ambrose knelt and retrieved the weapon. It was an Enfield, like his own. He was tempted to go through the Yankee's clothing and find food, as other soldiers did. Ambrose could take a man's gun, but he couldn't take his food or his clothes. Something was sacred about those items. He held the gun, still kneeling, not knowing how to feel. He wondered what his father would say to him right now. He would be dead set against tears. Or trembling. He would say, *Get on with it.*

Ambrose looked down at the rifle in his hands. He murmured to himself sternly until his hands steadied and the shiver that ran through the rifle ceased, and everything was motionless again. Ambrose, the dead soldier, his hands, the rifle. That's what war was. A great motion and then a great stillness in which the winner crouches and the loser lies facing the sky.

He rose to his feet and walked through the woods. Came out the other side and fought the rest of the day on a sunken dirt road that years later would bleed again every time it rained.

Sharpsburg. Where he killed his first man. He remembered thinking, *I am going to be fine.*

7

IT WAS EASY to believe, on a day like today, that the island owned a separate sky than the rest of the world. The purest blue available in the universe. And the whitest clouds. She walked barefoot in the sand, hiking up her dress. She cast back a glance to see her footprints trailing out behind her. Yes, she was still real and still solid. A human being with weight and mass, one who could leave depressions in dry sand. She noticed a flower that looked like yellow jessamine growing out of the dunes and thought of Winchester, for at this moment, that same flower would be blooming along the fence in her father's yard. She'd grown up with yellow jessamine, but by the time she'd married Robert and moved away, she'd taken it for granted. Now the memory of it made her ache. Rows and rows along a fence post she could follow all the way back home. In order to stay sane, she would have to take stock of things familiar, like the Big Dipper she glimpsed through her bars at night, a constellation from childhood that had stayed with her, like a permanent tooth.

Other patients milled about, looking for shells, or wading ankle-deep in the water. One old woman, barefoot and in a yellow dress, held her arms out in front of her, swaying in the sand. Eyes closed, head tilted back. She had the smile of someone who has just tasted the perfect grapefruit. Iris watched her, intrigued. The old woman didn't look demented. Just too happy to be well.

"She's dancing." Iris turned to see Lydia Helms Truman standing before her in a white sundress and matching bonnet.

39

The small, green-eyed woman was as immaculately groomed as the night she'd swallowed her ring. She nodded at the woman, who had begun to turn in slow circles, her feet marking out a circular pattern in the sand. "Her husband of forty years, the love of her life, died of pneumonia several winters ago, and she cannot admit the loss. He is real to her, plain as day, as I am to you. She will not touch her food unless another plate is set down for him. Strange thing, madness, isn't it? It tortures some, soothes others. She looks happy, doesn't she? I could only have wished for such happiness in my own marriage. Perhaps I erred in choosing a visible man, when it's the invisible ones who are sweetest." She smiled at Iris, who found herself smiling back. The woman sounded so eloquent and reasonable, so full of gentle humor, that Iris was momentarily lost in confusion, imagining for a split second that perhaps she had been mistaken, that her memory had been faulty . . .

"I have something for you." Lydia reached into her pocket and drew out a silk handkerchief. From the handkerchief she removed Iris's ring. The amethysts glittered in the sunlight.

"I heard you were missing a ring. I found this in the day room. Does this belong to you?"

Iris shook her head. "No, no."

"Are you sure?"

"Yes! I am very sure." She backed away from Lydia's proffered hand and moved past the dancing old woman down the beach. She walked quickly until she had made a good distance from the two women, then slowed her pace and followed a meandering trail left by a gopher turtle. The urge to flee rose up inside her, clear as a voice calling over water, and she remembered the flight from her husband, traveling over broken ground, fording rivers so the dogs would lose her scent. Making progress in the nighttime. Taking cover in the day. Stealing meat from smokehouses.

She looked over her shoulder and spied two male attendants in the back of the courtyard, They talked earnestly to each other, unmindful of the milling souls. And she thought to herself, *I can just keep walking.* Warm sand under her feet. A sharp clean scent blowing down from the citrus groves higher on the beach. Morning glories still open on the dunes, hermit crabs dragging their shells.

She would worry about food and money and clothes later. Right now, just one foot after another. She walked faster and faster, her breath growing jagged, a salt rush in the back of her throat, palms sweaty. So many footprints now separating her from the others.

A hand on her arm.

She froze.

A quiet, Southern drawl in her ear. "Ma'am, I think you've lost your way. Perhaps you'd like me to escort you back."

Iris let her breath out. She'd been caught. She followed the guard back silently. Lydia and the old woman were gone. The guard left her in the courtyard, shooting a warning look over his shoulder as he walked away. She rested her elbows on the low stone wall and looked out at her footprints, the ones going away and the ones coming back, accompanied by the prints of the guard's heavy brogans.

"It's not so easy, is it?" A familiar-looking boy with straw-colored hair stood on the wall, wearing faded overalls rolled up to the knees. She studied him only a fraction of a second before she placed him. That was the boy who was fishing with the chef when she first came to the island. Up close she could see the freckles on his face, and two pinprick black scabs on his cheek.

"No, it's not."

"Even if you get past the guards, it's dangerous out there. Alligators and rattlesnakes. Wild pigs, too. And some people say there are still pirates hiding out on this island. And if the pirates or the gators or snakes or the pigs don't get you, the mosquitoes will eat you alive."

She liked the way the boy addressed her, without the studied distance of the nurses and attendants. She scanned the beach again, where the wind was calm and her footprints were still perfectly formed.

"Has anyone ever escaped?" she asked.

"Somebody tried just last year. He collected feathers and made himself a set of wings. He jumped off the top of the asylum. Landed on his head and broke his neck. He's buried out back. My name's Wendell." He stuck out his hand.

"Iris Dunleavy."

They shook.

"Sorry, I've got sticky hands," he said. "Taffy."

He looked about twelve. His accent was strange. She couldn't quite place it. He motioned her to follow him and walked to the edge of the water. He stood watching the waves coming in and out, adjusting his position so that the water never lapped beyond his toes.

"Are you crazy?" he asked.

The question flew at her so open and direct that it took her aback. "No," she said after a moment.

"You must be crazy, because you're here."

"You're here, too."

"I'm here because my father runs this asylum."

"Your father is Dr. Cowell?" That explained his strange accent. A vague lilt. Something handed down from Britain.

"Yes. I am his son. Help me look for shells." He moved into the tide line, scouring the sand as she watched. "Best time is after a storm." He picked up a shell and showed it to her. "See this? It's a coquina. It's common. What you really want to find is a junonia. It's brown with black checks. It is the rarest of all. I've only seen them in books."

He dropped the shell and went back to searching, intense and quiet, bent low to the ground, his hands clasped behind his back.

She caught up to him. "Tell me. How long are patients kept on this island?"

He shrugged. "Depends. Some people stay forever."

"Forever?"

He nodded. "It's a very long time." He straightened and stared up at the sky. "But how did they know you were crazy? What exactly did you do?"

"I told you, I'm not crazy."

"My father thinks you are, and so you must be."

"Your father is wrong."

He looked somber. "My father is never wrong."

That night she found a shell on her windowsill. The color of a peach. Perfectly smooth. She wondered how long he'd searched the tides to find it. She held it in her hand, up to the moonlight that came through the window and left the shadows of the bars across the stone floor.

Some people stay forever.

The next day, as she milled around the courtyard with the others, the sharp gazes of nurses and guards taking away the feeling of leisure, she saw Ambrose sitting at the checkerboard table. Looking at him now, so calm and contemplative, hands at rest, face shaded by his hat, it was hard to believe the madman he'd been just a few nights before, screaming and calling for the doctor and wrestling the guards. She surprised herself by walking up and sitting down across from him. He looked at her, and she caught a glimpse of something in his eyes she recognized. Some tiny thing swirling in that young infinity that makes a human life. A thought, or memory. It had no shape or color, and yet instantly it registered. The ghost of kinship.

"You're Mr. Weller."

He stood awkwardly, removing his hat to reveal a mass of black, uncombed hair. "How did you know?"

"I was informed by an acquaintance, who later swallowed my ring."

He stared at her, then chuckled. "She swallowed your ring?"

"Yes. The same night you —"

He stopped laughing. "Yes. That night. I've taken my meals in my room since then. Dr. Cowell believes I'm ready to try open dining again." He fiddled with a checker piece. "I'm very sorry if I frightened you."

"No harm done." She put out her hand. "I'm Iris Dunleavy."

She studied his face as they shook. He had the look of a man who had just risen from a sickbed, all pale and tangle-haired, razor stubble thick on his cheeks.

He noticed her looking and touched his face. "I'm sorry I haven't shaved. They won't let . . . I'm not supposed to . . ."

"You look fine." A grasshopper materialized out of nowhere, briefly alit on a stacked pair of red checkers, then bounced away, vanishing as fast as it had appeared. She liked watching the grasshopper come and go. The universe pulped into that simple moment.

"Were you in the war?" she asked.

"Yes, I fought in the Stonewall Brigade . . ." His voice trailed off, and Iris almost apologized for raising the subject. "But Dr. Cowell says I mustn't dwell on it. Instead, I'm supposed to think of the color blue. Sometimes it fails me. But I'm growing stronger, day by day."

The whole idea seemed stupid to her. But she said nothing.

44

He was so fragile, and she did not want to disparage anything he believed in, even a color.

"Dr. Cowell says you have to be the master of your own remembering," he said.

"That sounds like something he'd say," she said, trying to keep her voice neutral. Master of her own remembering. And yet the doctor did not believe her memory. It was copper next to her husband's gold.

8

WHEN SHE HAD first arrived at Bethel, Robert didn't show her the main house first, or the slave quarters, or the gardens, or the seemingly endless field of tobacco that stretched into the distance. Instead he took her to a small fenced area near a copse of cedar trees. He opened the gate and ushered her inside, where nearly two dozen tombstones were arranged, each with its own inscription. The stones were of the finest granite, the landscaping immaculate. The shadows of a perfect texture. The ground smooth and clean of leaves. This was where the generations of his family had been laid to rest. He took her hand and led her to a space by the back fence, where a cherry tree stood. A blanket of pale blossoms covered the two graves under the branches. She leaned in, read the names on the headstones: Lucille Dunleavy. James Robert Dunleavy.

He stood between the two graves, put his arm around Iris. "Mother, Father," he whispered. "Here she is."

At first, she imagined the slaves were happy. They sang and laughed and chased each other around in the evenings on the way back from the field. It was only after a long span of time that she noticed their seething resentment. They did not work to help the farm flourish or to grow the tobacco. They worked because they were prisoners and had no choice. By the time she understood this, she was a prisoner too.

"A prisoner?" Dr. Cowell said. "Why would you say that?"

His long fingers intertwined. Any moment he was going to take the folded handkerchief out of his pocket, shake it out with a quick flourish, remove his glasses, and polish them. She had seen him twice and was already weary of his habits.

"He kept my family from seeing me. He intercepted my letters."

"What makes you think so?"

"My father, especially, would not suddenly cease all correspondence with me. It made no sense."

"Why didn't you seek help from someone? The sheriff or the pastor of your church?"

"My husband was friendly with the sheriff. And he was an elder at the church."

Dr. Cowell nodded, a gesture she had learned did not necessarily connote empathy or understanding. It was as though he were nodding in agreement with the thought he was about to present. "Your husband was an esteemed member of the community, active in the church, in good standing with the sheriff. Think about this with your rational mind. Does he sound like a criminal, Mrs. Dunleavy?"

She sighed. Nothing she told him mattered at all.

After the hour ended in silence and the woman was gone, the doctor put on his glasses and tried to go over his notes, but he was finding it increasingly difficult to read his tiny, neat handwriting. He had ordered some new glasses, but the war was preventing them from reaching him. His failing eyesight was just one of the things that annoyed him lately. Another was the bags under his eyes he saw now whenever he looked in the mirror. This island was taking his youth, little by little. Were he not trapped here, with the lunatics and his moody, attention-demanding wife and son, he'd have been able to remain a younger man.

A knock at the door. It was time for his last appointment, a man who was convinced his feet were too heavy, who often could be found frozen in mid-step in various places around the asylum. The hour passed swiftly, although the man took so long dragging his feet out of the office that the doctor was compelled to give him a gentle shove through the doorway.

It was the doctor's habit to walk down to the beach just before sunset and watch the birds coming in to feed, and the sky turning deeper shades of blue. Now he was finally rid of his patients, at least for the time being, and could indulge in a few moments of contemplation before he was expected back at the cottage. He loosened his cravat as he walked toward the shore. His coat jacket flapped in the wind. Wind was good, for the midges, biting specks of torment, didn't attack on windy days. The woman, though, was getting under his skin with her short answers and defiant posture. Such defiance would be an impediment to any sort of progress he could make with her.

Women, he decided, became unhappier the better they were treated. He pitied her husband and wondered what tricks of perception, what prayers, what gin had got him through daily life with her. He reached the water's edge and let the toes of his shoes sink into the border of the wash. The water lapped at his feet. He tilted his head back, closed his eyes, and listened to the ocean rush of sound that reminds of tomorrow's approach. It was a sound that bowed to no other, neither bell, nor cannonade, nor bugle, nor a man's beating heart.

Under the moon the sand on the beach shone ghostly white. In the swamps, crocodile eyes shone red. A light breeze came through, just enough to take the fragrance of the spring flowers and make it sweep through everything like a collective wish.

It was a good night to be a boy.

Wendell, as was his custom, had slid out of his window once his parents were asleep. Now he lurched under starlight through the sand. He had designed and whittled out of thin board two enormous pawlike feet, spent two more weeks on the delicate task of whittling claws for them, then another two days figuring out the best way to tie them to his feet with leather laces. One of the claws had fallen off on a test walk, but the others were holding out. For once no thoughts of Penelope or his own insanity crowded his mind, for tonight it was filled only with the exhilaration of seeing his careful plan put into action.

He paused, turned, and looked back toward the asylum. All was quiet. No one had seen him, save for a hawk that swooped low, found the boy too big to carry off, and rose back into the sky. Wendell continued his awkward gait, lifting his feet carefully, pausing only to clear his claws of bracken.

He reached the edge of the chef's prized castor bean patch. He smiled, set a single foot in, then another. Looked behind him to make sure the prints were registering in the celestial light. By day they would be even more impressive.

9

AMBROSE LOOKED UP at her and smiled as she approached him. They had played checkers every day for a week, saying little, concentrating on the game. Several of the checker pieces were missing.

"What's happened?" she asked.

"Well, I'm not making accusations, but Lydia Helms Truman was seen hovering nearby the checkers table yesterday, and this morning she was in the infirmary."

Iris studied the board. "I suppose it could be worse. We could have been playing chess."

Ambrose burst out laughing and she flushed with pleasure. They kept smiling until their eyes lingered upon each other too long. Ambrose said, "Well, I suppose we'll just have to play with fewer pieces."

The red checkers were warm to the touch. She pushed one out into a square and waited. She'd often played checkers with her beloved father on the porch during her transition from tomboy to young woman. Ambrose himself had an ordinary, familiar way about him, so much that he could have grown up next door, and she felt comforted by his presence, as though the bucolic childhood she'd left behind so hurriedly had been handed back to her.

He stared at the board, still contemplating his move, as her eyes skirted the edge of the beach.

The boy, Wendell, was fishing in the surf with the chef. He

turned and caught her eye, and their gazes locked for a moment. She had noticed him passing by when she and Ambrose played checkers. The expression on his face was not entirely approving. The boy went back to fishing.

The patients were allowed to swim once a week under close supervision. Wednesdays were reserved for the women, and Thursdays for the men. Iris stood at the ocean's edge and let her cotton robe fall to the sand, revealing her two-piece suit — a bathing gown and pantaloons.

"Iris Dunleavy." The Irish brogue was harsh and unloving. She turned, surprised to see the matron there, as she was sensitive to sunlight and rarely went outdoors. The matron squinted at her. "What do you think you're doing?"

Iris blinked. "Doing? I'm swimming. Aren't I allowed to swim?"

"That's not what I'm talking about. Apparently you were silent during much of your session with Dr. Cowell. Too good to speak to him, are you, Mrs. Plantation Wife? Do you know what happens to defiant people here? They get the water treatment. Then they're not so defiant anymore."

Iris started to say something conciliatory, but the matron turned on her heel and stomped away. Iris hesitated, then turned and stepped into the frothing water. She had been to the beach, once, when she was seven years old. Despite the plenitude of ponds and rivers right around their hometown, her father had taken the family on a long trip all the way to the ocean for her baptism, a ritual repeated in his family for generations. Her father said a prayer as he lowered her head into the sea. She opened her eyes underwater and fish rushed by, in every color, it seemed, and in all directions; the sun was blurry overhead and her father's prayer had flattened out on the surface and could not reach her. He pulled her out of the water and held her up so that she was as tall as he was. The next wave knocked them both down, and they came up laughing.

She liked the God she met that day. A playful, saltwater God. And this meeting, she knew, was the way her father planned it for her. Every father wants a daughter to meet the right God, and the right man. Perhaps her father had failed with both.

She waded in farther and let the water reach her chin, then took a deep lungful of air and sank down until her knees touched the sandy bottom. She opened her eyes. The very same fish she saw as a little girl swam by her, and time hadn't erased a single color. They were all accounted for, silver, red, blue, and green. Bubbles escaped her mouth. Fernlike plants swayed back and forth. Time had vanished. It was bobbing on the surface where her father's voice used to be. Other women had waded in, and their bathing gowns had floated up around them, giving them the appearance of jellyfish. Nothing could bother her here — no matrons, no doctors, no bells — and that thought appealed to her so much that she stayed down even as her lungs began to ache. Finally, when she could no longer hold her breath, she let it out in a spray of bubbles, swam up, and caught the sea between waves.

She thought of Ambrose later that night, as she lay in bed and listened to the night sounds. The younger man intrigued her. What was broken in him felt liberating. She had suffered under two controlling men — a husband and now a doctor — and the fact that he spent all of his effort trying to control his own demons was inviting. Her father would like him. She closed her eyes and just as she imagined Ambrose's hand moving toward her father's to shake in greeting, she heard her name. She raised herself up in bed to find the boy, Wendell, staring at her through the bars of the window. With his hair disheveled and moonlight shining down in his big eyes, he reminded her of a raccoon. Behind him the beach was quiet save for a lulling breeze.

"What is it, Wendell?"

"I have to speak with you; it's important."

She got up and put on a robe. She approached the window and rested her face against the cool bars.

"You need to stay away from that man," Wendell said.

"What man?"

"The one who plays checkers with you. He's dangerous. You never know when he's going to have a fit."

She felt suddenly angry at the boy's impertinence. Showing up like this, uninvited, imposing his own opinion. Just like his father. But his eyes were so sweet. He meant well. "I appreciate your concern, Wendell. But I'm a grown woman, and I can take care of myself. Why don't you go to bed now? You must be tired."

"But—"

"Good night, Wendell."

10

WENDELL STOOD ON the roof of his cottage house in a swell of moonlight, shells piled at his feet and a homemade bat across his shoulder. Conch, whelk, olive, pen, tulip, cockle. One by one they cracked off the end of the bat and sailed into a flowering yucca that grew past the other side of the roof, or burst into a spray and flew in all directions. He felt wounded by Iris Dunleavy's dismissal. He was just trying to warn her, because he liked her. She was different from most of the other patients. Sharp eyes and a quick temper and a stubborn will. He didn't love her the way he had loved Penelope, but he felt the same wish to protect her. Iris didn't understand how things could turn. He'd seen it before. Dangers would come up in an instant. Life could perform its cold-blooded acrobatics in the blink of an eye, resulting in sudden and irretrievable loss.

Penelope.

His father had noticed his fixation on the young woman and had taken him aside one day. "Wendell, it's a fact of nature that some birds have to stay in the shallows because their legs are so short, and other birds — like herons or the great egrets — have longer legs and can go into deep water." His father had tapped the side of his forehead with two fingers. "Penelope wasn't built for deep water."

Wendell was bewildered by the metaphor, and it only endeared him further to the addled girl.

The chef was more direct. "Listen," he told Wendell one day

when the boy was helping him pull weeds from the castor bean garden. "Miss Penelope, she's not for you. You stay away, hear?"

"She's nice."

"Nice, sure, but crazy as a loon. Whooo-whoooo-whoooo."

He wanted to tell the chef that he was crazy too, in fact a depraved private-fondler of the lowest order, but he had kept the confession to himself.

The first time he set eyes on Penelope, she was standing on the beach, keening and pointing out at the water. Three guards hovered near the girl. Wendell had been looking for shells, but he abandoned the task in favor of this new intrigue. He moved in closer to the spectacle, putting himself within earshot.

"Save her!" Penelope cried, still pointing at the waves. Wendell squinted. A doll bobbed out in the waves.

"We're not going in there," a guard said. "You're the one who threw her in. Why did you throw her in?"

"Because she's crazy?" another guard suggested, and the three of them laughed.

"She's drowning!" Penelope took off toward the waves, running awkwardly, her feet sinking in the sand. The guards grabbed her, pulling her back.

"Where do you think you're going?" one of them asked. "You're not going anywhere!"

Penelope struggled in their arms. "Let me go! Please! I'm her mother!" Her voice was so wounded, so desperate, that Wendell ran down to the water's edge and kept going, forgetting even to remove his shoes.

"Hey!" the guards shouted. "Hey!"

But he was already fighting the waves, the water soaking through his clothes, his shoes sinking into the soft ocean floor. He pulled his feet from the sucking grasp of the sand and began to swim, water going down his throat. Coughing, sputtering, he forced his arms and legs to move, the waves pushing him back, but finally he reached out his hand and touched the fabric of the doll's dress.

He turned around and swam back to shore, the doll held tightly under one arm. As he staggered out of the water, he held the doll above his head and Penelope, who had collapsed in a heap in the sand, now stood and clapped.

The guards scowled at him.

"You're a fool, boy, diving in after some stupid doll with all your clothes on."

Wendell handed the doll to Penelope and spat a mouthful of briny water onto the sand. He glared at the guards. "Go away, or I'll tell my father you were mean to her."

"We're not afraid of your father," one of them shot back, but he slid a glance at the other two, and the three of them turned and shuffled back toward the asylum.

Penelope had sunk to her knees and set the doll down on its back, its crystal-blue eyes sparkling in the sun. Wendell knelt next to her as she gently removed a sprig of seaweed from the wet yarn of the doll's hair. His hair was plastered to his head. He could feel rivulets of water running down his body, down his arms, and off his fingers, starting two dark pools in the sand. He watched as the girl leaned forward and kissed the doll's cheek, then straightened out the wet petticoats under its dress.

"Why did you throw it in the water?" Wendell asked.

She turned to him, her expression ferocious. "I didn't! *They* threw her in the water! But no one will ever believe me."

"I believe you."

Her lashes were red. Red and very long. He would remember that always. The length of her eyelashes and their color in the sun. Like a flame.

More water dripped down his body. The sun was high over-head, but he shivered in the sea breeze.

"What is your name?" she asked.

"Wendell."

"Randall?"

"Wendell."

"Randall, I'm Penelope. I'm seventeen years old. I tried to hang myself with the sash of my nightgown. I like the way rabbits jump."

He didn't know what to say in response to that, what informa-tion to give. He thought hard. "I like shells," he said at last.

She touched the doll's lips. "I saw a girl who drowned. She lived down the street from me. She fell into a dairy pond. I was there when her father and her uncles dragged her out. Her father started to cry and they let her lie down in the grass. He closed her eyes with the tips of his fingers. Like this."

Gently, she closed the doll's lids. She moved her hand away and the doll's eyes sprang open with a tiny squeak, the eyes crys-talline once again. "Her father said her name so sweet and cov-ered her with a quilt. When I die, I want someone to be nice to me that way. Say my name, and cover me with a quilt."

Wendell could feel his hair drying. The slight tickle as sprigs of it stood up one by one. It all seemed to mean something just beyond his grasp. If he thought hard enough, he was sure he could figure it out. He and Penelope looked out at the sea to-gether. When he finally stood up, his clothes were dry and his pants were stiff in the knees.

Wendell tossed another shell into the air and swung the bat with all his might. He was rewarded with a pinging sound as the shell sailed away into darkness. This new woman, Iris, seemed so sad and yet so dignified. He had seen every variety of lunatic in his short life, but never one who so yearned for escape. Like himself. He had to protect her, had to show her never to lower her guard. He had been fine until he fell in love. Watching Iris with the soldier, he had seen her faraway smile and knew she had no real understanding of the man who sat across from her.

The world was cruel and sudden. This he knew for sure. Relax for a moment, breathe in the scent of a rose, rest in the shade, pet a dog, take a sip of lemonade, fall in love with a dreamy-eyed girl or a haunted-faced man, and you are just waiting for the other shoe to drop. Buzzing around the lemonade, you'll find flies. Follow the flies and you'll find death.

Wendell threw down his bat. It hit the roof with a loud thump and rolled off into the darkness.

Mary Cowell's eyes flew open. She sat straight up in bed and shook her husband awake.

"Did you hear that?"

"Hear what?" Dr. Cowell mumbled.

"Something's on the roof!"

"Nothing's on the roof. For God's sake, go back to sleep."

11

THE WINDOWS OF the office were open, exposing Ambrose to early morning sounds, birds and waves and the low horn of a sloop approaching the wharf. The doctor had on a new cravat. Something seemed to bother him about it. He kept pulling at the knot. Ambrose watched him, his legs crossed politely. The doctor intimidated him with his British accent and his mannered ways.

"I notice you've been spending time with that woman," Dr. Cowell said.

"Iris?"

"Mrs. Dunleavy, yes."

"We play checkers."

"And you have conversations?"

"Yes."

Something about that answer seemed to rankle the doctor. "About what?" he asked, his tone suddenly sharp.

Ambrose's foot began to jiggle. He wasn't sure what he had said wrong. "Everyday things."

"She's a married woman."

"I know."

The doctor began to wind his pocket watch. He seemed troubled by something that winding it only halfway cured. "We encourage conversation between ladies and gentlemen here. The social structure of the outside world is emulated, in the hopes that you may return to it. So you've done nothing wrong. My concern is that you might start forming an attachment with her based upon some idealization of the situation. The truth is, the only reason that you find yourself in proximity with her on this beautiful island is that you're both thoroughly mad."

Ambrose looked away. Thoroughly mad. The British accent made the words more damning. He didn't feel mad. Not at this particular moment.

"Do you find her comely?"

The question sounded accusatory, and Ambrose retreated. The doctor was making him feel stupid. Stupid and slow and completely outmanned. He found her attractive, to be sure. Beautiful and rare as a good night's sleep.

"She isn't plain," he said in a measured voice.

"A woman's a very complicated distraction. In order to concentrate on your path back to wellness, I would urge you toward the simpler things. Colors and shapes. Warmth of the sun on your face. Taste of citrus. Texture of sand."

Ambrose nodded slowly.

"You've made quite a bit of progress."

"And I'm so grateful, you know I am. I think you're a genius."

A brief look of pleasure came to the doctor's face.

"Can I still sit with her at the checkers table?"

The doctor thought about this several moments. He took his handkerchief out and began to polish his glasses. Ambrose's foot jiggled harder. With an effort, he steadied it.

"I suppose you can," the doctor said at last. "As long as that is all it is. Nice conversations with a married woman. It's therapeutic and yes, even a beautiful woman can be part of the cure. As long as you realize you have no rights to her, or she to you."

Ambrose left the office feeling chastened by the great doctor and determined to think of simple things. Blue of the sky. The smell of honeysuckle. Oranges. Yarn. Birds. Organ keys. Ears of a dog. Pages of a Bible. Soggy center of a sandwich.

Sunlight on a dress.

She was just easy to talk to. He had not enjoyed that kind of company since back in the war, after the new recruit, Seth, appeared during an unreasonable period of rain.

It fell from the sky in drops big as plum pits. Leaked through woolen uniforms, plastered hair against heads, and soaked the face of Jefferson Davis from the backs of playing cards. Horses shook their manes and tried to shake off their riders when thunder rolled. Drills continued during pauses in the deluge, but the rain would come again, preventing campfires and sending the temperatures plunging.

The new recruit stuck out his hand.

"My name's Seth."

"Ambrose." The boy's shell jacket was too wide in the shoulders and his belt was too loose, although he had cinched it to the very last hole. He said he was eighteen. He looked younger. Something about his unsteadiness and shyness of gaze drew Ambrose to him. The boy seemed always watchful, anticipating the approach of strangers even in a resting state, like the way a cat pricks up its ears before it opens its eyes.

"William," Ambrose said once to the old flag bearer, "you notice anything funny about that new boy?"

"Which one?"

"Seth."

"Looks too young to fight."

"Besides that."

William shrugged. "Hell, I don't know. I can barely tell what's funny about me."

12

THE SESSION WITH Ambrose Weller left the doctor with something under his skin. Something invisible and itchy. What was it? He had no time to consider the answer. He had to rush off on his rounds. The woman who swallowed things had gulped down three buttons and a pinna shell. The old man who didn't remember his name had a story to recount with no ending, one that kept maddeningly circling around and starting again. The man whose feet were too heavy was stranded in the day room, five paces to the door. The woman who was dreadfully afraid of sunlight was hiding under her bed. The man who thought Sunday was a wolf now thought Wednesday was a crocodile. And the man who was terrified that he was but a mote in a dusty universe was crying. It was only after the doctor had taken his midday meal of turtle soup out to the orchard that he was able to spend some time discovering the source of his dark and impatient mood.

He sat on a bench made of tabby cement facing the citrus orchard, sipping at his soup, going back in his mind to earlier in the day. He usually enjoyed his time with Ambrose Weller. No lunatic clung to his words so fervently or so faithfully carried out his advice. And his fits were, to be sure, lessening in frequency and severity. So far the soldier had never revealed the event that had so undone him, a fascinating mystery the doctor desperately wanted to solve. So far, no clues were forthcoming. But in the meantime, he found the soldier's progress and ardent devotion to be a source of great pride.

The turtle soup was musky and strong and slightly bitter, as though the turtle contributing its meat had its own surly vexations. He made a face and set the soup to the side. Perhaps, under all his professionalism, he was jealous that his most loyal patient was keeping company with someone else. And not just anyone.

A thought was coming around the corner, headed right toward him. Had he allowed its arrival, it would have diplomatically introduced the possibility that the attention Iris Dunleavy gave the soldier was the actual source of his jealousy. But the doctor was an expert in avoiding conclusions he found unsettling, so he chose to sniff the orange and lemon scent of the breeze that bore the thought and ignore the thought itself altogether. He took a swig of water from a hobnail cup.

"Dr. Cowell."

A nurse had appeared, one whose skittery demeanor always reminded him of the red-tailed herons that made such a fluttering drama out of nabbing a fish from shallow water. "It's your son, Wendell. He's run out of class again."

The doctor sighed. "In the direction of the woods?"

"Yes. Your wife is afraid he's up the tree again."

"Then he can wait until I'm done with my soup."

"But Mrs. Cowell says—"

"Please! Leave me be!"

"Very well," she said in a defeated voice, and left him. He hated when he had to talk his son out of his favorite sulking tree, a gumbo limbo that sat on high ground a half-mile from the asylum. The path into the woods ended after a hundred yards. He was going to have to pick his way through the swampy woodland, which harbored not only midges but alligators and water moccasins. He supposed it was too much to ask of his son to shinny up any of the worthy palm trees on the grounds of the asylum.

After a few minutes, he heard different footsteps approach him from behind, then stop. He knew his wife was standing behind him before she said his name, for since the nurse had come to get him, there had not existed the smallest chance of him finishing his meal in peace. She hadn't dressed for the day and she was still in her long robe and mules. "I have a migraine," she said in a querulous voice, "and I had to get up off the bed and drag myself out here to get you to do what you would naturally do on your own, were you a caring father."

"I am a caring father! But I will not be a party to rewarding our son for his dramatics. He's inherited his tendencies toward hysteria from you and I won't support them."

"There are dangers out there. Snakes and wolves and alligators and poisonous berries."

"You're exaggerating. He's always traipsing around the island alone."

"He is strictly forbidden to leave the property, and yet he comes and goes as he wishes. He's become simply uncontrollable."

"He's a boy. Boys are adventurous."

"How would you know what he is, Henry? You never spend any time with him. You're the worst father in the world!" Red blotches had appeared on her face. Tears would follow soon.

Dr. Cowell took a deep breath. He knew exactly how the next few minutes of his life would play out. He and his wife would argue back and forth a few more moments, she would let out a cry that would scatter the white moths circling a nearby yucca blossom, and then he would slog out to visit his son's sulking tree and he'd get dirty and hot and be bitten by insects and possibly pick up a rash as well.

Perhaps a rash. Perhaps not. See, Henry? he told himself bitterly. *There is still some uncertainty left in the world.*

The first midge bit him between the knuckles after he had passed through the citrus orchard and taken the short, overgrown path hacked into the forest of mangrove and buttonwood. He winced and slapped himself on the back of his hand. Gnats danced around his face as he trudged through the gloom, brushing sticky vines aside. Another midge bit his neck, another his cheek. He slapped himself in the face, felt the sting of his own assault, and swore softly.

The path ended and the woods thinned out. The ground turned swampy. Black mud covered his leather shoes. The cuffs of his pants were filthy. A mosquito buzzed in his ear. An alligator had eaten a Cuban fisherman on the bay side of the island last year. Dr. Cowell tried not to think about this story. Instead he whistled a soft tune to himself, one he'd learned as a child from his grandfather.

A rattling in the brush made him jump back, heart pounding, as a palm rat skidded past his feet. *It's nothing, Henry. Just the natural world.*

He collected himself and kept walking. This was the time of year when the alligators mated. Their salacious roars could be heard all the way to the beach. He needed to urinate and he was afraid the sudden mating call of an alligator might make him soak his pants. He considered stopping to relieve himself but was afraid of exposing that part of his body to the torment of midges. So he kept walking, trying to clear his mind of all that vexed him. His wife. His son. The lunatics. And that woman. Iris

Dunleavy. He said the name in his head, frowned because the name sounded light and sweet. *Think of something else, Henry,* and he pictured his grandfather, whittling on a stick, the shavings peeling off one by one and falling onto the floor.

Up ahead, the ground rose and turned to crushed shell. He was at the site of an old Calusa village. Atop the shell mound grew a huge gumbo limbo tree. He approached the tree and looked up. Wendell clung resolutely to an upper branch.

Dr. Cowell removed his sweat-soaked cravat. "What is the problem now?"

Wendell shifted on the branch, causing a measure of loose red bark to peel off and spin to the ground. He said nothing.

"You have given your mother a migraine and thanks to you, I have a bit of one myself."

"Mother had the migraine when she woke up this morning. I didn't cause it. I didn't do anything. Why do you always accuse me of doing things I don't do?" His face was flushing the same way that his mother's did.

"Why did you run out of class today?"

"I hate school. And I hate Miss Miller. She's not even a teacher, you know. She's just a bookkeeper. She doesn't know anything. She just reads to me out of a textbook. I can read to myself."

"She's the only teacher available to you and, as you know, my education put me where I am today." Sweat pressed through his cotton shirt. Another midge bit him in the crook of the arm.

"You tell me, Father, what the Pythagorean Theorem has to do with anything."

Another midge had somehow gotten under his trouser leg and made it halfway up his thigh. He bent down and scratched himself vigorously. His bladder ached. He looked up the tree again. "If you don't understand the Pythagorean Theorem, you will never understand Euclid's Proof."

"I don't care about a stupid proof!" Wendell bellowed. "I hate school and I hate Miss Miller and I hate this island! I'm going crazy here!"

"You're not going crazy."

"Yes, I am. If only you knew how crazy I am!"

The doctor scratched his wrist brutally and made a mighty, shivering effort to control his temper. "Please come down. I'm allergic to these bugs and they are eating me alive."

"There are no boys on this island. At least when you worked in Philadelphia I had friends."

Another midge bit him on the spine, and he arched his back in misery. He gave up then. Utterly surrendered. He would spend years and years valiantly fighting for his most demented of patients—the man, for example, who thought his shadow healed typhoid—but in less than five minutes, he conceded defeat to his own flesh and blood.

"If you come down now, I will take you shell collecting tomorrow morning."

"No, you won't. You always say you will and then you forget."

"I promise I will not forget."

Wendell was silent. Suddenly the doctor felt a bite and then a terrible itch inside his ear. The bastards had found his ear canal. He probed it with his pinkie finger as he added, "And I'll also give you a quarter."

"What would I do with a quarter?"

"You can buy licorice from the Cubans. My God, son, I'll give you a dollar, just get the hell down out of that tree, please please please!"

The branches quivered above his head. A bare foot slid down out of the foliage, then another, and the battle was done.

13

IRIS LIVED IN the big house with her husband and a retinue of slaves who did the housework and the cooking. If she walked out the front of the house, she would find the grid of apple and peach trees that made up the orchard, as well as the vegetable and herb gardens. A walk to the west down a path of crushed stones would take her to the stables, the drying house, the storage, and the barn. The overseer's house and the slave cabins sat at the back of the property. Beyond that stretched the tobacco fields. In the early years of her marriage, it was easy for Iris to believe that the flourishing plantation was halcyon even at crop level. Sun level, sweat level, dust level. But over time she discovered what being a slave meant, slowly and with starts and stops, in the same manner she had learned, long ago, to read and write.

She was given a set of keys to wear around her waist. The keys opened every door to every outbuilding and storage area on the property. She was charged with supervising the slaves of the household, overseeing a small garden, managing the smaller business affairs of the plantation, and entertaining guests. This last duty filled her with dread, for nothing in her simple upbringing in Winchester had prepared her for the life of Haughwout crystal and long candles and English scones with her tea. The other plantation wives seemed haughty to her. Remote. She remembered one gathering in particular, after the men had gone out on the front porch to smoke and the women were left talking among themselves.

Delores Spears lived out on Gabler Plantation, named for her grandfather and twice the size of Robert's. She told a story that night, inside by the fire, in her gauzy dress whose daintiness made the story more atrocious. "The overseer had to whip one of our slaves yesterday. He tried to escape. Peter called me out to the yard and Barney had his shirt off and was tied up to a poplar tree. Peter handed me the whip. He said the slaves thought I was too soft, too easy to manipulate. I had to make a point, he said."

Iris didn't know what kind of expression to wear on her face. The other women looked fascinated. "Go on," one of them said. "What did you do?"

"I took the whip. It was heavier than I thought. The slave looked around and saw me and he just looked at me. My husband said, 'Go ahead, Delores. Hit him.'"

"And then what did you do?" another woman asked.

"The overseer showed me how to hold the whip and snap it back, then forward, and I tried and I didn't even touch him. Knocked a twig off the tree, that's all."

Loud laughter rang in Iris's ears. She was very conscious of her own pose, awkward in it. Her smile felt strange, and so did the frown she replaced it with.

"So you didn't even hit him?" asked another wife.

"I missed. That whip is so heavy. It hurt my wrist." The women leaned in, hanging on her every word. "The overseer told me to try again. I closed my eyes and snapped the whip and it made the loud popping sound. I heard a sound. Not so much a scream but more a gasp. I opened my eyes and his skin was laid open, and the gash was filling up with blood."

Iris felt horror and revulsion. The women looked awed. One held up her glass. "To respect," she said. The others raised their glasses. All except Iris. The others gave her frozen looks. But she would not toast to a slave's blood.

Word about her actions reached her husband by the end of the party. During the carriage ride home, he wouldn't speak to her, and they rode in silence but for the noises of their own transportation: hooves against macadam, the breathing of the horses, the squeak of the carriage wheels.

"You were very impolite not to join the toast," he said finally. He kept his eyes straight ahead. His voice was cold and hard.

"Impolite? Those women are horrible! I could barely—"

He gave her a long, steady look. "You will write a note of apology in the morning. You were a guest in their house and it was not your place to sit in judgment of another person."

She'd been on the island for almost a month. Each day she would meet Ambrose in the courtyard and play checkers until the game was forgotten and they fell into an easy conversation that forgot the most recent years and went straight back to childhood. Before the war, before the damage, before they believed that they had a voice in their destiny, they were children. She was a pale, curious girl who made too much noise while eating celery. The fields behind their property grew wild with evening primrose and goldenrod. Near the cornfield on the east side of their property stood an apple orchard, and it was here that Iris made her sanctuary.

In the spring the leaves grew thick. The apples appeared late in the summer, slowly darkening into the kind of color that, when flushing through a boy's cheeks, means that he is shy. She sat in the branches, bare legs swinging, biting into the ripe apples, pulling flesh away. Apple cores dropped to the ground around the tree trunk. When she slid down to the ground, her bare feet landed in pulp.

Ambrose had tales from growing up in Charleston, and stories to tell of killing snakes and fishing, favorite dogs and bruised knees, a fascination with pirates, arrowheads in the riverbed, breaking a colt in thigh-deep water, lightning storms. He, too, had an apple orchard. He had climbed the trees and sat on a limb and rested his back on the trunk. He had eaten the apples and landed in pulp. As the days passed, their orchards grew together, and they sat on opposite trees, feet swinging gently. Rationally, she knew that she was an inmate in an insane asylum, people shrieking around her, the polite remonstrations of the guards, the pounding of waves, the maddening bells signaling the schedule. But it was easy to believe they were back in that orchard that not only welcomed their childhoods but all childhoods, and this, for the time being, was her only method of escape.

The courtyard was bright. Summer was upon them, with it a new season of birds and tides and fruit and flowers and loggerhead turtles dragging themselves up the beach, laying a hundred eggs so that one hatchling might survive the raccoons and the gulls on their way back to the horizon line.

The sight of Ambrose did strange things to her now, made her feel alive and strong, as though her home were just beyond the swell of dunes, reachable by an effortless stroll. She had to remind herself that he was a diversion, a puzzle of dark hair and an angular face that would help her pass the time until she could devise a plan for leaving. She'd been studying the layout of the asylum, the entrances and exits, the habits of the guards, which windows had no bars.

All systems have flaws. Marriages, governments, insane asylums. All she had to do was think a little harder.

They were halfway through a checkers game when they noticed a scuffle on the beach. A man wearing a frock coat and a stovepipe hat was standing frozen on the sand. Iris recognized him as Mr. Sinclair, the man whose feet were too heavy.

71

A guard shouted at him.

"Move! Move!"

But the man just kept shaking his head.

"I said move!"

"The poor man," Iris said. She stared at the guard. Something about his body language and harsh directives reminded her of someone else. She narrowed her eyes as the clues moved through her body and connected to a memory of the plantation. Clyde Sender. The overseer. He began to take shape in her mind, red-faced and stout. She blinked him away.

Just then the guard swore loudly and pushed Mr. Sinclair in the back. He fell flat, his hat falling off and rolling in the sand.

Ambrose stiffened and rose.

"Where are you going?" Iris asked, but he had already started toward the men. Something was different about his posture. A straightening of the shoulders. A coiling tension in the body. A deliberate stride. Ambrose approached them and helped Mr. Sinclair to his feet, brushed the sand off his coat, and retrieved his hat, handing it to him as the guard kept shouting imprecations at both men. Ambrose turned and said something to the guard that Iris could not discern, but it made the guard furious and he shouted, "Who are you to tell me how to act?"

Onlookers appeared out of nowhere — patients, fishermen, nurses, other guards. All of them drawn by the salty boiled-crab smell of rising tensions. Iris even spotted Wendell, watching from behind a tree.

The other guard moved closer to Ambrose and took a swing. Ambrose ducked and punched the guard in the stomach as the entire island gasped. Then the two of them were rolling in the sand, the guards shouting encouragement at their comrade and the patients screaming, "Get him, Ambrose! Get him!" Mr. Sinclair stood frozen in mid-battle, clutching his stovepipe hat.

Iris leaped from the checkers table and darted forward, desperate for a better view, just as she saw a squat, plump woman, who she imagined was Wendell's mother, come flying from the direction of the cottage, still in her dressing gown, to join Wendell behind the palm tree.

The flying punches liberated the mad. It was joyful as a church, this fight, joyful as a picnic, a choir, the Fourth of July, a fox hunt, sex — everything denied them on this island. They screamed like children. They were free, and these precious things denied them — curiosity, fair play, righteous anger — released themselves with alacrity. From out of nowhere, Lydia Helms Truman threw herself on the guard's back and clung there like a kitten as he swore and tried to buck her off.

A sudden hush came over the scene and the crowd parted as Dr. Cowell dragged his long shadow over the cobblestones and then the sand. "Stop it!" he said in a voice whose authority stopped the fight dead, and the guards came to themselves and separated the brawlers. Ambrose's eye was starting to swell. The guard had a split lip that dripped blood on his shirt. Lydia Helms Truman's dress was ripped.

"What is the meaning of this?" Dr. Cowell demanded. "Are you animals? Well, are you?" Dr. Cowell's wife wrenched herself free from behind the palm tree and fled in the direction of the cottage, Wendell right behind her. The doctor watched them, lips pursed, before turning to the fighters, who were trying to catch their breath. "I thought better of you. Better of you both."

Mr. Sinclair, who had remained motionless throughout the battle, pointed at the guard. "He started it."

"I don't care who started it," the doctor rejoined. "Everyone go about your business!" He addressed the guard. "You are dismissed from your employment here!"

"But, sir—"

"You heard me." He looked at the other guards, who were hovering about with guilty expressions. "Put him on the next boat. And this man . . ." He nodded at Ambrose. "Take him to his room."

"How about me?" Lydia asked, but Dr. Cowell had turned on his heel and started walking back to the asylum. The fight was over. There was nothing left but the humidity and the returning birds and the reluctant movement of scattering spectators and a man whose feet wouldn't move.

After the fight, Iris retreated to the edge of the shore and walked along the sand, taking solace in the sight of her footprints alongside those of raccoons and dune mice that were never seen full-on, just barely glimpsed as they darted for cover. She was both roiled and calmed by the scene she'd witnessed. She had thought Ambrose was fragile and soft—his insides like those of a sparrow's egg fallen from the nest. But no. This man had a warrior's steadiness and righteousness. She had seen no lunatic today—only someone in the mood to stand up for the helpless. She wanted to take this quiet soldier, broken in so many mysterious places, resilient in so many others, and put him on the plantation. Put him between the weak and the strong, the innocent and the murderers. Put justice where no justice was served. Take him back there with her. Give that bully that is history a bleeding lip.

14

AMBROSE GAZED AT the night sky through the bars, listening to the ticking of the Ingraham clock behind him. They hadn't tied him to his bed. He had not descended into the chaos of screams or the grinning authority of a laudanum sleep. He was himself, his face still flushed from the fight hours before, which had been ferocious and had left him with a throbbing eye and a clean sense of fair play. They had fought like men. Not a patient and a guard. Two raw tempers and two pairs of fists. No, the fight had not brought him back to the horrors of war but to a simpler time that predated them, when a fistfight was a solution, and so was a plowed field, and so was a kiss. Now, as the shadows of the bars made stripes on the white sleeves of his shirt, he thought of a night shortly before he'd gone to war when Celia, the girl he was courting, decided any man so heroic as to take up the Southern cause deserved a parting gift, one given spontaneously in a field behind the church where the going-away dance was held.

Halfway between a huckleberry bush and a dogwood tree, two feet south of a limestone rill. Nothing but patches of ironweed and a single black-eyed Susan too early for the season, towering behind Celia's head as they kissed, her hands rising up to help his fingers with hooks and buttons. So much lace, so much fabric. The bones of her corset. The silk of her pantaloons.

He fought to free her before she came to her senses. It was a race against the clock of propriety. Somewhere in the darkness his stern father was lighting an oil lamp and beginning a passage in the Bible, tracing it with creosote-blackened fingers. Farther away, armies settled in for the night, nursing wounds, drinking coffee as campfires burned, as banjos played and voices fed their singsong prayers to the stream of God's mercies. Still farther away, Davis paced and Lincoln rubbed his temples.

But none of that mattered, for Ambrose was taking time to be awed by the sight of Celia's bare white skin. Celia sighed and giggled, moaned and gasped, and they rocked against the ground, his coat under them both; her head slid closer to the stem of the black-eyed Susan as she closed her eyes and said his name in a broken way, half regretful, half defiant when she said it, *Ambrose, Ambrose* — his name achieved a crystal definition. In the distance they could hear the music of the dance where girls still shyly looked at boys. Her head reached the black-eyed Susan and bumped against it as they slid back and forth. The thick stalk broke and the weed fell by moonlight and Celia said *Ambrose* one more time and then it was over, a bookmark between his boyhood of sleeping in haystacks and hunting for catalpa worms and the ache of hard labor on his father's farm, swearing at a mule with a handful of words that hated Sunday — and his incarnation as a soldier. Smoke of battlefield, suppuration of wounds, clouds of breath, snow, ice. Freezing nights on mountaintops. Air too thin for shouting. Wind too strong for fires. Ground too hard for graves. Toes and fingers turning black. Stirrups frozen to boots. Fingers to soup ladles. Urine to tree trunks, in the pattern of sunbursts.

Celia sent him to war with a tintype picture. Never wrote him. Married his friend. Left him with that memory that had been buried, previous to now, by all that necessary blue.

15

"YOU KNOW THAT man is very ill," said the doctor. Someone had given him a haircut, and he'd switched to linen suits in deference to the heat.

"What man?" Iris asked.

"Ambrose Weller. He's very fragile."

She felt a sudden rush of pride. "He didn't look very fragile yesterday when he was punching that guard."

"It does not escape me that he had never fought with anyone until he started playing checkers with you."

"Ambrose was defending a patient who could not defend himself. His anger was justified."

"He is a lunatic and his anger is uncollected and irrational, like all his other emotions." The doctor seemed annoyed. His tone was less paternal today. He kept scratching one arm. "And I noticed you at the corner of the crowd, fascinated by the violence."

"I noticed your wife and son behind a palm tree, also fascinated by the violence."

The words moved his eyebrows into a stormy shape, and he seemed to be making a great effort to control himself. "I worry about your effect upon this man, and his effect upon you."

"You are worried about the wrong man."

That night she dreamed she was holding the baby, that pale and sweet-faced boy. The dream was heartbreaking in its lack of narrative. Whoever designed that dream—god or devil—knew the weight of a baby, knew the warmth. Knew how to break a heart with the realness of the moment—a bit of saliva on the lips, a tiny crust on an eyelash—so that when Iris woke up the next morning, her arms empty, she wept in the early light, and the flood of tears did not stop as she bathed and dressed. As she was making her bed, another tear fell and spread to the size of a dime. Just then, the door burst open and the matron swept in.

"What's the matter, poor dear?" she asked. "You look like you have been crying. Do you have terrible troubles, Mrs. Dunleavy?"

Iris ducked her head and went on straightening the sheet. She wondered how many lunatic women, on the cusp of recovery, were sent back to their scrambled selves after the matron made sport of them. The matron seized the sheets from Iris's hands and ripped them off the bed. "Your bed making is a disgrace. Make it again." She crossed her arms, her breath whistling out her nostrils.

Iris moved carefully, measuring out the sheet so each side was perfectly aligned, fluffing the pillow just so, tucking in the bedspread with the greatest care. She fought back the tears, finished the bed, ran her hand across a single surviving wrinkle, smoothing it out flat. She stood back.

The matron looked at the bed, as perfectly made as any bed in history. She seized the bedspread and pulled it off. The pillow went flying and landed like a heavy bird near the nightstand.

"Make it again."

Iris set back to work, hands trembling with anger, the urge to cry like a hard shoe pressed against her sternum. But she would rather die than have the matron claim responsibility for a single new tear. She finished the bed and the matron began to reach for the bedspread, then seemed to change her mind, perhaps tired of that particular game. She went around the room barking orders: "Straighten that picture. Dust that chair. Put your filthy shoes in the closet." She pointed at the water pitcher. "The handle should face west, not east. Fix it."

Iris did as she was told.

The matron looked her up and down, her pupils tiny black specks in the light. "You think you're better than everyone, don't you? You with your frilly dresses and your nice shoes. You're nothing. Your husband doesn't care for you. He sees you as you are: a faithless, selfish, pathetic woman who will grow old here. Old, and alone."

Iris did not remember the span of time it took to pick up the pitcher of water and pour it over the matron's head. One moment she was looking into those tiny pupils. A blink later, the matron's hair was soaking wet, water was rushing down her dress, she had a shocked expression on her face, and she had sucked in such a gasp of air that her bosom had lifted. Iris couldn't believe it. She glanced into the pitcher. Sure enough, it was empty. Something inside her had broken free and done the deed on its own. She knew she'd crossed a line and would pay dearly, so she allowed herself to live in the first few moments of the aftermath, there with the light pouring into her room, the steady dripping of water on the floor, the matron's shocked and staring eyes.

Iris could not move. Leather straps held her arms and legs to a straight-backed chair. A group of female attendants had come into her room later that morning. She had been forced to put on a dressing gown and a special pair of white slippers, and then she'd been taken to a room she'd never seen before. Now she was alone inside it, waiting. Her bare legs shivered. Her lips felt cold to each other when they came together. A terrible knot of fear had formed in her stomach. The tile floor of the room sloped down in the center, where a drain had been built. A metal chute loomed above her head. She tried desperately to steady herself, loosen that knot of fear so she could breathe a little better. She tried to imagine that she was no longer in that room but in her own bedroom back in Winchester, and the drain in the floor was the gravity vent from which her father's prayers rose. *Lord, let us remember that our trials become laughable in Your presence, let us laugh with You, Lord, laugh with joy over sorrows eaten by eternity, and all suffering and injustice left at the gates, for in the end there is nothing left but the elation of Your presence, when we are Your children come home . . .*

Something hit her head. It was hard and cold, like a frozen pea. She looked up as another drop fell from the lip of the chute and hit her in the forehead with a distinctive thump. She moved her head down again, preferring the water on her crown rather than on her face. She tensed her body and forced herself to stare straight ahead at the knob on the locked door. In the door was a window. The window was empty.

More water drops began to fall, each one of them cold and surprisingly heavy, as though a giant frozen fingertip were coming down to tap her, reminding her of something urgent she hadn't done. It was uncomfortable, painful enough for her to wince with each drop, but she thought, *This is endurable. I can stand this,* and found some comfort in this thought.

But the drops increased into a stream, growing more painful as the moments passed and the stream grew in power and volume. She closed her eyes, her entire body shaking, chilled down to her childhood prayers, her teeth gritted, hands clenched into blue-tinged fists as the water came pouring down. Her hair was freezing wet against her neck, her gown soaked. Rivulets of water ran down her body to the floor and down the drain with a metallic gurgling. The pain grew worse, as though nails were being driven into her head, and she struggled vainly against the straps that held her down. She began to panic, because the pain was approaching an unbearable state and she didn't know where to put it. There was no room for that kind of agony, and yet it came. Her head was breaking apart, her skull cracking. She felt hot blood pouring from her scalp, but the water rushing into the drain was crystal clear. It was too much to bear now and so she did not.

Screaming, she called out for her father, remembered desperately the soft warm water in which he had baptized her. Remembered the sun and the sky but the pain was too much, so she screamed for the God who lived inside her father, and when He made no answer and the pain grew even worse — intolerable pain, pain beyond understanding, the pain of literally coming apart on the level of bone and brain, pieces of herself breaking off invisibly to expose the hot nerves, red-tipped like flowers, she screamed and screamed and screamed and screamed, for as she was stripped down to nothing, to a specter, and as the room grew dark and she slipped into unconsciousness, she saw, at the window, the doctor's face come into view. Sad, it seemed. Concerned about whatever lump of nothing remained in the room.

16

IRIS WAS ASTONISHED, once again, to find herself alive. She lay in her bed, covered with warming blankets, her hair dry, her body restored. She moved a hand out from under the covers and touched her head. It was whole and unbroken; the skull that had come apart was back on tight; the mind within it was stunned but coherent. Afternoon light filtered into the room.

The doorknob turned, and Dr. Cowell entered, followed by a nurse. He drew up a chair to her bed and sat down heavily, balancing the chart on his knee while the nurse busied herself straightening Iris's blankets.

"How are you feeling?" he asked. His British lilt felt like a water drop against her crown, one of the early ones, not painful but still uncomfortable enough to make her wince.

"Can you send the nurse away?" she asked, surprised by the sound of her voice, as though she were hearing it for the very first time. "I need to speak to you alone."

The doctor hesitated. The afternoon light streaked across his glasses. He pushed them back on his nose and motioned to the nurse.

The door closed and he leaned toward her slightly.

"You are a fool," she said.

His eyes widened. He let out a little gasp.

"What?"

"A fool. An idiot. A moron. For no good reason, you have put me through the worst physical pain imaginable."

"But there's not a mark on you!"

"I saw you looking through the window at me before I lost consciousness. Did you not see the expression on my face? This is not treatment. This is torture. Punishment for my quarrel with the matron and refusing to flatter you like all the other silly maniacs. If it has improved the circulation of anything to my head, it is the realization that I am alone in this world."

"You're not alone, Mrs. Dunleavy."

She used all her strength to raise herself up in bed. "Get out. There are souls waiting for your incompetence. I've undergone your torture and there is nothing more you can do to me."

The doctor looked distressed. "I only did what I thought was right. I only wanted to help you!"

"Get out." She pointed toward the door. "Get out, get out, GET OUT!"

Wendell's eyes were wide. His mouth hung open. From his position beneath Iris's window, sitting with his arms holding his knees, his back against the asylum wall, he had heard everything. He could not believe it. He had known the inhabitants of the asylum — whether nurses or attendants or patients — to speak to the doctor only in the most respectful of tones. No one had ever called him such names. Not even his mother. The thought of his esteemed father being called a moron was scandalous and exotic and thrilling and wrong.

He had heard whispers about the water treatment. Penelope had gotten it once and could not walk upright for three days. And it was his horror over the thought of her enduring it again that had led to the biggest sacrifice of his life.

Penelope and Wendell sat facing each other over a half-finished sand castle. Her doll was propped nearby, facing them. The tide came in close to the hem of the doll's dress, then washed back out again.

"Was it really beautiful?" he asked.

"Yes."

"Show me," Wendell said.

"Show you?" Penelope lifted a flame-colored eyebrow.

"I want to know exactly how it felt." A sandpiper darted in and out of the waves.

"How old are you?" Penelope asked.

"Thirteen."

She contemplated this and nodded, as though this settled the matter. She cleared aside the barely begun sand castle so she could sit closer to him. Now they were knee to knee.

"Close your eyes," she ordered.

He obeyed. The surf and the cry of gulls. The creaking of an old palm tree growing behind the dunes. Penelope's breathing. He waited in the silence and then felt her warm fingers on his neck.

"My neck is sweaty," he said, by way of apology.

"Shhh." Her grip tightened. He felt a small pain from the pressure against his vocal cords, but nothing else, besides the ecstasy of her nearness.

"Hmmm." Her voice was soft. Her fingers shifted and tightened their grip, and all of a sudden, there it was. His head was suddenly full of breeze and blood. He felt dizzy. His thoughts sloshed together, swirling. His face grew hot. He tried to take a breath but discovered that, although he could not, he really didn't need to. Breathing was something he could put way on the back of the shelf, along with math. He opened his eyes a slit, and red light poured in. Red like blood, like Calusa waters. His head fell back; his mouth fell open. He was moving backward in the direction of sand, and the sleepiness that overcame him was something wise and still; he loved everything, he loved her, he had misplaced her name but loved whatever that was out there in the red darkness . . .

"What in the hell?" The rough voice of the chef was accompanied by the wrenching away of Penelope's fingers from his throat, and Wendell coughed and gasped, tears running down his face. His eyes flew open. The chef had him by the shoulders and was shaking a less perfect world back into him. Moment by moment he recovered bits of himself: reason, the memory of names and places, the boundary between his skin and the universe.

"Talk to me, boy!" the chef bellowed, continuing to shake him with one hand and tapping his face, so hard it hurt, with the other.

"Stop hitting me," Wendell managed.

The chef turned on Penelope. "Go on, git out of here. Take your doll and git, now, git, crazy girl!"

"No, wait!" Wendell croaked, but Penelope was gone.

"You've got her paw prints on your throat!" the chef exclaimed. "Damn girl nearly killed you."

"No, no, you don't understand. She was showing me what it feels like to hang yourself."

"Are you out of your mind? You let her strangle you?" He snorted in disgust. "You let a woman strangle you, no telling what she's gonna want next."

The chef got up, dusted the sand off his knees. "I'm gonna tell your father. That girl is dangerous."

"No! I told her to! I should get in trouble, not her."

"You're just a damn kid. You're twelve years old."

"Thirteen!" Wendell shouted. He threw himself at the chef, grabbing onto his trouser legs. "Please, please don't tell my father. He'll give her the water treatment and it hurt her so bad last time. She couldn't bear one more treatment. Please, chef, I will do anything. I will work in your garden and wash your vegetables and clean your fish and do your dishes, forever! Forever!"

The chef pushed Wendell hard with his foot. He fell onto his back in the sand.

"You're as crazy as she is," the chef said.

Wendell stared up at the sky. "I know."

The chef pointed a big black finger down at his chest. "All right. But if I ever see you near her again, I'm gonna tell your father what happened. You understand? Ain't gonna have no dead boy on my watch, even a stupid one."

17

THE COWELL BEDROOM felt stiflingly hot, so much so that the doctor and his wife were covered by a single sheet, and he had dared crack the window open at the risk of exposing himself to the biting insects of the nighttime world. A bare minimum of breeze came through the room, causing the oil lamp on the night table to flicker. The resulting draft carried the scent of Mary's bergamot lotion into the doctor's nostrils. On those rare occasions when she desired lovemaking, she always applied this concoction, specially made for her by the chef. The doctor hated the scent of bergamot but could never summon the courage to tell his wife her application of that supposedly inviting potion had the opposite effect upon his passions, and that when he performed the act, he did so in spite of the horrific aroma, not because of it.

He had been in a dark mood ever since the plantation wife had excoriated him in a most shocking and boorish manner, completely misunderstanding the compassion and years of careful study behind his water treatment. Wounded, he had canceled his afternoon appointments and remained under a storm cloud all through dinner. This romantic overture was his wife's way of noting his distress and comforting him without necessarily getting involved, and he would have partaken more or less willingly of this gift, but for the fact that she had evidently applied the lotion with an exuberant generosity, and he was still preoccupied with the earlier slight. How dare she, that lunatic, that inmate, that woman, call him an idiot and order him out of the —

Mary touched his shoulder. "Do you suppose Wendell is asleep?"

"I don't know. The boy stays awake at all hours, from the way he comes dragging in to breakfast."

She moved a little closer to him and stroked his arm. "You are too preoccupied. You have been working too hard."

"It's just that a patient shouted at me today. And called me terrible names."

"What do you expect, my darling? You work with people who've taken leave of their senses. Surely you aren't going to let this man upset you."

"*Woman.*"

She let out a high, girlish laugh that carried within it the odor of her teeth-cleaning powder. "Well, that is even more the reason to dismiss it. You are a famously recognized expert on the insane. She is probably jealous and intimidated by your knowledge and your fame."

"True," he conceded, taking the next deep breath through his mouth as she slid farther over and draped her arm across his chest. "I have one of the highest success rates in the country of restoring lunatics back into wives, fathers, accountants, farmers, soldiers . . . the list goes on and on!"

"On and on," she murmured, caressing his chest through his nightshirt.

"And many, many people have benefited from the water treatment. Do you know that I have, in fact, received several grateful letters from former patients that name the water treatment as the turning point in their recovery?"

He sat up in agitation. Her hand slid off his chest and made a small thump on the mattress. "She called it torture! As though I were some kind of monster!"

Mary sighed and slid back over to her side of the bed. "I'm going to sleep," she announced, and blew out the lamp, leaving him in darkness, but he barely noticed. He wasn't even in the room. He was in Iris's room now, in his mind, in the fading light of afternoon, and she was screaming at him.

Get out! Get out! Get out!

18

THE NEXT MORNING, Iris made her way slowly to the dining room and took a seat, nodded at the attendant who appeared to pour her coffee, then ordered grapefruit and a poached egg. Her movements were unsteady, her voice soft and halting. She added cream to her coffee and took a delicate sip. The unbearable pressure of the water had shaken up terrible memories.

Mattie was first to die. Old Mattie, whose index finger was bent from so much sewing. Iris Dunleavy heard the pop of the gun and then Mattie's gasp, unmistakable. The same one she made when lighting the coal stove and the match burned her hand, or darning a sheet and the needle came too close. Or when something in her back caught while she tried to lift a baby. It was that sound, only deeper, sharper; it had no ending as it rose into the cool springtime air of Virginia, with its tulip trees and willows.

Mattie first. Then the others. Bunched up together, pinned into a tiny clearing in a thicket of cypress trees, one by one, they fell on the ground, crowded so close they took Iris down with them.

Underneath the bodies, there were no thoughts and her senses flourished. Cold soak of groundwater on the back of her head. Acrid smell of gunpowder. The early light gone. The air pitch black under the sweaty weight of the dying. Moans, gasps. An unfinished prayer. The death throes of one made the whole pile of them shudder. Someone's blood ran into her mouth.

"Oh, my dear friend." Iris looked up as Lydia Helms Truman slid into the seat across from her. "Those terrible brutes. What have they done to you? Your screams could be heard echoing down the hallway. I begged the matron to stop it. She ignored me. As she was walking away, I bit her."

Iris felt herself smiling, even though she did not feel happy. It was as though the smile had flown away from the vision of the massacre like a bird. "Lydia, you shouldn't have done that! Now the matron will be after you as well."

"Oh, she is. She immediately signed the form requesting the water treatment for me as well. Then she limped off to get her ankle tended to. I saw one of the nurses tear the form into little pieces and put it in her pocket."

An attendant appeared at the table.

"Doctor Cowell wants to see you in his office immediately," she told Iris.

"But I haven't had my breakfast."

"Let the poor woman eat!" Lydia protested. "Think of all she's been through!"

"Now, you calm down, Mrs. Truman," said the attendant. "You are in enough trouble already. We'll save breakfast for her."

Iris rose from the table. As she started to follow the attendant, Lydia reached up and seized her wrist.

"Soul light," she whispered.

"Soul light?"

"I know the fellow you play chess with likes to think of blue things to calm himself. Soul light is blue."

• • •

The doctor seemed agitated. He did not offer her a seat in the usual manner but paced about the room. "Your continued defiance concerns me," he began. "It is natural to be mistrusting, at first, of a different view besides your own —"

"You tortured me with freezing water, to the point of unconsciousness!" Iris cried. "Should I be grateful?"

"Stop saying that word! It was not torture!" He sat down in his chair and pressed his fingertips to his head. When he let his hands drop his expression had calmed. "Why are you standing?" he asked in a quieter tone. "Sit. Sit."

She obeyed. The light was still muted outside the window, as were the cries of gulls. And the sky, a slate blue devoid of clouds.

He opened a file on his desk and began to read. "You absconded with your husband's property, which led to a loss of many thousand dollars' worth of —"

"People."

"Slaves."

"They — we — did not belong to him."

He took off his glasses and began to clean them. "It is not my position or responsibility to judge the laws of a society. I am against slavery personally, but that has no bearing here. Let me ask you something. If you were so against slavery, did you not think of more appropriate venues to have your voice heard?"

"I am a woman, Doctor. I do not have a voice."

He scrubbed at something on his glasses. Some spot that seemed to vex him. "Do you know the definition of insanity?" He started to put on his glasses, then rested them on the desk. He really did look weary. Exhausted, in fact. "It is a state of mind in which an excess of feeling — a hysteria if you will — causes a man or woman to fall out of step with their roles, their purpose, because without that purpose all of us are diminished. Sanity is the degree by which you serve your society, your community, and your household. I am of the opinion that with the right medicines, structure, counsel, and guidance, one can arrive upon, eventually, a cure. And a cure, in every sense, both is proved by and results in a reintegration."

"You sought my punishment yesterday, not my cure."

"I did not! My reasons were entirely benign!" He seemed desperate to be believed. "What I do is based not upon my whims, but on my theory. A theory that has gained much attention and admiration in your country . . ." His expression suddenly brightened. "I'll show you!"

He removed a small key from the pocket of his vest and unlocked the middle drawer of his desk. He withdrew a measure of parchment paper, covered with print and held together by a metal clasp. "This is the paper I wrote on the relationship between female hysteria and the rise of the suffrage movement. There is a direct correlation between areas in the country of outspoken feminine resistance to social norms and the incidence of institutionalization." He held up the manuscript. "This is my only copy, and I have never, ever allowed a patient to even glimpse it before. But I am entrusting it to you and all I ask is that you read it with an open mind." He handed it to her. "I know there will be some words and phrases with which you will not be familiar and I will be glad to — "

She leaped from her chair and threw the paper out of the window. Like a white bird with dirty wings, it spiraled toward the courtyard as the doctor let out a sharp cry and rushed from the room.

He never touched the rail. He took the stairs two at a time and hurtled through the heavy doors of the asylum, whipping his head from right to left.

"Where is it?" he shouted.

"Where is what?" asked a nearby patient, an old man with a bent back and powder-blue eyes.

"My paper!"

"My paper!" shouted the old man. "My paper my paper my paper my paper!"

"Hush! It's important!"

"HUSH! IT'S IMPORTANT!"

Just then the doctor saw his paper, his prize, his life. It had fallen into the small hands of Lydia Helms Truman, who was already nibbling delicately at a corner.

"No!" said the doctor, running toward her, his arms outstretched. "NO NO NO!"

Two days later there came a hard rain. It blew in from the east in the afternoon and blanketed the island with marble-size water drops, pelting the sand, filling up the shells that had washed face-up toward the sun, driving the birds to the cover of the trees and the patients into the shelter of the asylum, bending the shrubs in the courtyard, and soaking a row of sheets on a line. A nervous cleaning woman ran out to get them, mumbling in fear as lightning creased the sky. She jerked the sheets down fast and ran back into the building, her shoes squishing in the wet sand. The thunder sounded like the bark of a thousand night herons. The rain pinged upon the slate roof; the wind tore through the leaves of the sabal palms, flattened the sea oats, and tangled up the vines of the morning glories.

By dusk the storm had passed, and the sun set orange and red in the peaceful sky. As night fell, frogs began to sing from every corner of the island. Not the least gust of wind could be found anywhere, and the moon's edges were crisp and hot.

Iris's windowsill remained wet. Water from the storm had run down the walls and pooled upon the marble floor, and the light from the half-moon followed down the walls to the pool of water and turned it silver on the top. Through the bars could be heard the far-off singing frogs and a closer, hushing sound. The ocean waves lapping at the shore. The storm had left the perfect tableau for a dream. Shiny and damp and wet with color. Iris slept on her cottage bed, on her side, her hands taking a prayer position, fingers twining, knees drawn up, the sheet pulled up to reveal her bare feet, dreaming of a white hen sitting in the middle of a pasture. It was a lazy creature, groggy in dream-light. Its lack of ambition felt peaceful to Iris and lulled her farther into sleep. She turned on the bed, scratching her bare leg with one bare toe.

A scraping sound interrupted the dream. The hen opened one eye, annoyed, and so did Iris. Another sound, and Iris's other eye came open.

Wendell stood at the window, drawing a stick back and forth across the bars. Iris threw off her covers and fumbled for her robe. She rubbed her eyes sleepily as she approached the bars.

"Stop that."

"Sorry."

"Don't you sleep?"

He shrugged.

"I was having a perfectly ordinary dream and now those annoying frogs will keep me awake all night."

He let the stick fall from his hand. "I heard something today. Something one nurse said to another, about the reason you are here."

"I'm sure those nurses gossip all day about us."

"Well, is it true?"

"Is what true?"

He put his face against the bars and lowered his voice as though someone might hear. A passing nurse, a calling frog.

"That you ran away with the slaves."

The frogs were deafening now, as though the boy's question had left them agitated. The bars were pressed so hard against his face they must, at this very moment, be leaving impressions in his skin. He stood motionless, waiting, as Iris considered her answer. This boy who seemed claimed by no one, and in this sense could be anyone's son, perhaps had a mind clear enough to listen to her without judgment. He knew the asylum and, no doubt, the woods beyond it. Knew when the guards fell asleep on the job. Knew where the keys were kept.

"Yes. It's true."

"But why?"

"I'll tell you the whole story. Not tonight, but soon, when I feel stronger. Are you sure you want to hear it?"

Wendell looked somber. His gaze went off somewhere, found something or someone. His fingers tightened on the bars. Slowly, he nodded.

19

THE LAMB TOTTERED down the gangplank one day in early June, led by a rope. Halfway to the dock he planted his hooves and stood blinking in the morning light. From his fishing place by Wendell, the chef turned and let out a low whistle.

"They did it," he murmured, his face reverent. "They got the lamb. Little fellow's come all the way from Naples. Not Naples, Italy. Naples, Florida."

Wendell studied the little creature. "What's it for?"

"What do you mean, what's it for?" the chef snorted. "It's for lamb stew. Although that's not much lamb to go around, is it?"

"It's just a baby," said Wendell.

"Ah, yes," said the chef. "Just a baby."

The lamb was imprisoned in an empty pigpen in the back, by the gardens, while the rumors of lamb stew swept the asylum. Later in the afternoon, Wendell went out to visit him. He was all alone, sleeping on the ground, which still stank of the excrement of pigs. Wendell crouched low, hooking his fingers on the wire of the fence and staring at the doomed creature. He whistled softly and the lamb woke up. Wendell continued whistling until he rose to his little feet and wobbled over to him. His eyes were dark brown, eyebrows expressive, white lashes longer than any woman's. He had a slight, natural smile passed on from generations of pleasant-featured sheep. He was curious and trusting and had a lamblike ignorance of his impending fate. Wendell pressed his face to the mesh of the wire and the lamb touched his nose with his own.

Wendell felt a huff of his warm breath.

Meanwhile, in the kitchen, the chef had pulled down an old cookbook from the cabinet and had it open on the table. His eyes eagerly scanned the list of ingredients. It was all coming back to him now. He would make a salad too, using the soft inner leaves from the yucca plant. And didn't he have some dried basil somewhere? He went about gathering the ingredients, whistling a song he'd learned from one of the Cuban fishermen who traded at the docks. Midafternoon he found his ax and sharpened the blade against a block of limestone, still whistling. He tested the blade along his thumb until he winced and then smiled. A crease in his thumb filled up with a hairline sliver of blood. He put on an apron and went out to the lamb's pen with his ax.

He stopped. No. It could not be. The sweet saliva teasing his mouth all day suddenly evaporated.

The gate to the pen hung open.

The lamb was gone.

He stood there, mouth agape, the ax hanging useless by his side. This could not be. Pride. Joy. Anticipation. The chef had perfectly seasoned himself for dinner that night and he would not be denied. He ran back, sounding the alarm, and a hasty search party was convened, the chef and some of the kitchen staff and the gardeners and a few of the orderlies. They stampeded through the asylum grounds and into the forest, beating at the undergrowth with sticks, slapping at bugs, wary of crocodiles and snakes. Some of them called the lamb as if he were a dog, their voices high and desperate.

"Go with them," Mary told the doctor.

"No, I'm not going to go stomping around in those woods and

getting bites all over me. I'm a doctor. I have patients waiting for me."

"I want that lamb!"

"They'll find the lamb, Mary!"

Word spread around the asylum that the lamb was missing, and those who could understand the news did, and felt sorrow over the loss of the special dinner that would have made this night different from the others. Some of them had laid out their best clothes for dinner. Clothes they'd worn back in Charleston, or Boston, or Maine. Back when they were a husband or a father or a wife or a daughter or a dentist or a hunter or whatever they were before they were lunatics. The presence of the lamb had awakened their names. Now that the lamb was gone, that part of them was gone too. They went to their windows, stared at the sea. Felt themselves diminish back into what they had become.

Iris took her good dress and put it back in her trunk. It was trimmed with ribbon, too special to wear just any night in an insane asylum, but fairly appropriate for this night of lamb stew, and now because the lamb was missing, Ambrose would not be able to see her in that dress. She had wanted so badly to watch him look at her.

Ambrose himself had carefully shaved, or rather had begged an orderly to shave him, for he was still not allowed to handle a razor himself. Later he had asked the patient next door, a bit of a dandy, to borrow some bay rum to put in his hair. He had planned to wear his best shirt to dinner that night because the lamb had given him permission to look his very best for Iris. Now he rubbed his face and smelled the cool odor of bay rum filling up the room. The light was fading.

Lydia Helms Truman felt her eyes moistening. She had been looking forward to the lamb stew and was not planning to swallow it in the way she did buttons and marbles and pebbles and rings and coins, with a quick gulp and an arch of her throat. No, she had planned on savoring that lamb meat, hoarding it with the tongue before finally surrendering it to the gullet. Closing her eyes, taking her time. Spoonful by spoonful. Remembering lamb dinners around the table with her husband and children. Back when she belonged in that house. There, with her family. The taste of lamb had inextricably linked itself to her place at the table. Now, both were lost. She sighed, dabbed at her eyes delicately with a handkerchief, and looked around for something smooth and small.

The old woman whose husband was clear as day to her but invisible to others broke the news to him, taking his warm hand and explaining that though they would not have lamb for dinner that night, they still had each other. And though disappointed at first, he had nodded in agreement. They still had each other, and wasn't their companionship as savory and spicy as the lamb would have been? And wasn't their love a perpetual lamb that blinked itself awake each day? She had laughed and said, "You have a way with words, my love," and had kissed his cheek and then gave him a lingering kiss on the lips. His hand moved up her back.

Eleanor Beacon, who felt too much, had heard of neither the lamb's arrival nor its escape. All talk of living creatures and their fates and their place at the dinner table had been kept from her, and, as she did every day, she had taken her meals in her room, bread and cheese and fruit, foods that would not cause her grief. And so the news of the lamb's escape went down the hallways and courtyards and into day rooms and offices and even down to the pier, but the news skipped over Eleanor's room, and she passed the afternoon kneeling before the window, watching an ant take bread crumbs one by one into a crack in the wall. She imagined the ant's back aching from the strain, its ant children calling for the food from their little nests, all the expectations upon the creature, so tiny, so hard outside, so soft inside, so vulnerable to birds and footsteps.

She stared at it. Moved close so that her words huffed against it and slightly altered its course. *I love you. I love you, I love you, I love you.*

Doctor Cowell had won the battle with his wife and was not out in the woods. He was in his office, listening to the man who'd blown out his eyes with a Colt .45. The man was immaculately dressed, as always. His face perfectly shaven. Hair perfectly combed. He had been a successful attorney in his former life. Were this woman he had loved never born, he would still be practicing law and appreciating sunsets, and his sense of smell would be no better than that of any other man. But now he had his head turned to the open window. His nostrils flared slightly.

"I don't smell lamb cooking," he said.

"The lamb escaped," said the doctor, preparing himself because he knew the subject of lamb and its aroma would lead his patient back to the subject that consumed his every waking thought: that of the woman he loved and lost, and her lavender cologne. He was correct.

"They say the smell of a magnolia tree blossom can carry for fifty miles," the man said. "But I could go to Spain, or the Arctic circle, and still smell that cologne. I smell it now. It's wafting through the room as though she had just passed by the open window."

The doctor wished the lamb had never been brought to the island. He hadn't missed it, not until it came and went. Now every other meat was going to taste like not-lamb before it tasted like chicken or pig or beef or fish.

• • •

Out in the woods, past the deserted Calusa village and its midden piles and the remains of open-air shelters, Wendell put the finishing touches on a fence he'd made from white mangrove saplings and rope. He'd sneaked into his mother's keepsake chest and stolen his old feeding bottle and filled it with milk. Now he held the bottle out and turned the tip down. Milk dribbled out. The lamb lapped at it greedily. The wind carried over the faint shouts of the search crew. They would not come this far. There was a line, invisibly yet implacably drawn, that designated how far men would go to recover the prospect of lamb stew. It stretched far into mangrove and bush, past alligator holes and the nests of ospreys and rabbit burrows, but it did not reach the line that designated how far a boy would carry that lamb to safety.

Within a few days, the lamb had learned a trick. He would rear up and put his hooves against Wendell's thighs as he greedily drank the milk. Wendell's journey to this secret place had not been easy on this day. Bernard, the burly, evil-tempered dock guard, had denied him the use of the chef's canoe.

"But I have permission," Wendell protested.

"Where's your note?"

"What note? I don't have a note."

"No note, no canoe."

They had argued for a few minutes before Bernard finally relented. "Just take it, then. You're the son of the superintendent. I suppose you think you can do anything you want." He untied the canoe, making Wendell wait as he took his time undoing the half-hitch that could have come undone in seconds. When the knot came loose, he pushed the canoe out to sea so that Wendell had to wade in for it, soaking his pants all the way up to the waist.

Now he tipped the bottle as the lamb drank the last of the milk and lay down contentedly in the wild grass.

"Get enough?" Wendell asked.

The lamb stared at him with his dark eyes.

"I'm crazy," he told the lamb. "Everyone thinks I'm a normal boy, but I have done terrible things in the forest."

The lamb rested his head against a woolly leg and closed his eyes, lulled to sleep by the monotone of confession. Wendell knelt down next to him and stroked his head, thinking now of Penelope.

He could still feel her soft, warm fingers around his throat and remember the joy that had flooded him as hc bcgan to lose consciousness. That was the last time he'd ever spoken to the girl, terrified to approach her lest the chef act upon his threats and report her to his father. He had tried to get a note to her explaining his mysterious actions, but a nurse had intercepted it, and he dared not write another one. She must have felt abandoned. Betrayed. He didn't know. He only knew that despite the pleasant scent of nearby honeysuckle and the lamb's pastoral breathing, he felt the familiar heaviness in his stomach he always associated with guilt.

He said goodbye to the sleeping creature, tiptoed out of his pen, and made his way through the mangrove forest back to the canoe. He paddled it out of the estuary into the open water and headed for home. The guilt was still with him, but so was the love, burning. He remembered an old legend from England. When a beekeeper died, someone had to go out to the hives and break the news to the bees. No one had informed the hive inside himself that his girl was dead and never coming back. Perhaps that was why she was still so immediate to him, her lips, unkissed, so rosy and soft, those long eyelashes and her crystal-blue eyes . . .

With a small sigh of defeat he turned back toward the shore, climbed out of the canoe, and performed the wretched deed again, ankle-deep in shallow water, turtle grass around his feet, in the shadows of the red mangrove trees, as two anhingas quarreled above his head.

The chapel was so small it barely qualified as a building. Wendell stood in the doorway, half in shadows, half in light. The chef, who had finally come out of his terrible mood brought on by the lamb incident, had explained the protocol to him.

"You cross your heart like this," the chef said, demonstrating on himself. "You say, 'Bless me Father, for I have sinned.' You tell him how long it's been since your last confession."

"I've never been to confession."

The chef was slicing potatoes in the kitchen and glancing into an old recipe book. "Leeks?" he said. "I don't have leeks."

"I said, I've never been to confession."

"Then you tell him that. Then you confess your sins." The chef looked at him sideways. "But what sins could you have? Have you wet the bed lately?"

"I don't wet the bed!" Wendell said hotly, and the chef burst into baritone laughter.

Now he trembled in the confession box. A drop of sweat ran down his face. No cooling breeze in the stagnant heat. The confession box door slid open and Wendell half jumped.

Father Byrnes didn't seem surprised to see him. He had the same neutral expression he'd always had. Wendell wasn't sure he could say the dreadful crime out loud, so he had written it on a piece of butcher paper, which he had folded and now held in his sweaty hand. He used his other hand to awkwardly cross his heart. "Forgive me Father," he began, his voice shaky, "for I have sinned."

The priest started to speak, but Wendell interrupted him, afraid he would lose momentum if he didn't rush forward. He had made the chef tell him the exact words he needed and he was determined to see them through. "You know all things, Lord, You know that I love You it's been never since my last confession and I don't know if I believe in God so if I am still crazy after this then perhaps there either is not a God or there is a God and He doesn't love me for you see I have done terrible things in the privacy of the woods and I was not crazy when I came to this island I was just a normal boy minding my own business—" His words broke off with a short cry and he bolted from the confession box and ran into the sunlight, realizing, with a terrible pang, that the folded piece of paper was no longer in his hand. He turned and ran back into the sanctuary, where the priest was just opening the piece of paper. Wendell tore it from his startled hands and ran. He did not stop running until he was beyond the pier on a flat expanse of beach, and he tore his confession into shreds and gave it to the wind. He stood watching the confetti bob on the waves as brown pelicans dive-bombed it, consigning the unspeakable act to the secrecy of their gullets.

20

THE SOLDIER WAS looking at him, but tapping on his knee, and something about his posture and the look in his eyes suggested to the doctor that he was really somewhere else.

"Mr. Weller?"

He straightened. "Yes?"

"You seem distracted."

"No, I'm listening."

The doctor frowned. His favorite patient had been slipping away in recent weeks. No longer hanging on his every word. This left him feeling hurt and wistful, like the sight of his son fishing next to the chef. Hadn't he brought the soldier peace and healing? Didn't he deserve at least the respect of attention? Whenever the doctor looked down and saw him at the checkers table in the courtyard, he looked anything but distracted. He was ramrod straight, riveted on the woman at the table with him.

"Mr. Weller, I've noticed in recent weeks you seem less assiduous about your mental exercises. You ask fewer questions. Have you stopped caring about your cure, and the hope you can someday leave this island a whole man?"

He looked surprised. "I still do my exercises, Doctor. I still care about my cure. In fact, I think I'm making great progress in my recovery. I haven't had a fit in some time."

"While that is true, I don't want you to become careless. You know as well as I do that these episodes have a way of returning suddenly."

The soldier was quiet. He folded his hands and looked out the window. The doctor felt very far away from him.

"Mr. Weller," he said. "Did you hear me?"

He looked at him again. "I heard you."

The doctor detected something in his tone, something so subtle as to perhaps be his imagination. But nonetheless, there it was. Resentment? Defiance? Hard to say. A subject hovered in the room, waiting to be invoked, like the righteous scream in a rooster's throat waits for breaking light.

"Iris Dunleavy." His voice had done a strange thing. Gone down low and soft. He watched the effect the name had on the soldier. How it brought a guarded look to his face, as though that name had to have permission to be spoken, and the soldier was in charge of applications.

"She is a friend," Ambrose said. "You said I could keep her company."

"I'm just concerned that you have forgotten why you are here, Mr. Weller. You are here because you are ill, and you need to recover."

"I know that," Ambrose said, and surprised the doctor by rising and pacing the room. "But I am feeling better, and I enjoy the times when I can just be a person again, without so much constant thought turned inward. You know what, Doctor? This morning I looked at the sky and thought, What a beautiful color. That's what I want, Doctor. For blue to just be blue."

21

THE LONG DAYS of summer stretched time, made it sleepy and companionable. Profusions of lizards hung in the trees and jumped from the roofs. Mosquitoes came in droves, clogging up drains and darkening windows. Screens were put over the bars on the rooms and then covered in turpentine. Smudge pots were passed around. And the sound of slapping was heard all day. One lunatic slapped a mosquito that was full of his blood, and when he lifted his hand, he saw a patch of blood where the mosquito had been. The lunatic thought he could commit suicide fairly painlessly by slapping the blood out of himself and went into a self-slapping frenzy with such sustained alacrity that he was put in restraints.

The mosquitoes feasted ravenously on some people and left others alone. Doctor Cowell could not step outside in his summer suit for ten seconds without a cloud of them descending on him, sending him scurrying back into the asylum and the comfort of his office. And yet mosquitoes never touched his son, and Ambrose and Iris were still able to play checkers relatively undisturbed. Or, as it was, pretend to play checkers. They hadn't moved a chip in weeks. Instead they had left the orchard of their childhoods and spoken of everything under the sun. They had even revealed a bit of the histories that had taken them to the asylum, but what was left unspoken was vast and deep. Iris had spoken of the plantation, of the husband who did not love her and the slaves she grew to respect and admire; he had spoken of battles, the privation of the march to Fredericksburg, the snow-ball fight in winter quarters, his increasing disenchantment with the war. So much blood, and for what? He believed in states' rights, but not slavery. And he could not fight for one without fighting for the other. This paradox haunted him. If he could only fight for states' rights with his right arm and slavery with his left, he'd march into battle with the left arm raised in surrender. There was a slave one of the lieutenants kept at camp. Ambrose used to rankle the other men by refusing to let the slave — whose name was William — pour his coffee.

They released these stories to each other with caution and even fear, as though releasing wild birds back into the wild after mending their broken wings. But the darkest birds stayed in the coop. They were not ready yet, and perhaps would never be.

Ambrose watched her now. "What's the matter?"

"Nothing."

"You seem somewhere far away."

"It's your imagination. I'm right here. Everything is the same." That lie was easy to tell. Everything was not the same. She was leaving soon.

Iris and Wendell searched for shells on the beach. The sun was low and their shadows skulked out behind them, crouching when they crouched, reaching when they reached, collecting the shadows of the shells they collected. She'd told her story slowly and carefully, in a way she'd never been given the opportunity to tell it before. Not by the judge, or certainly the doctor. She had arrived, over this measure of days, to the beginning of the end of her marriage.

The Civil War was destroying everything in its path, every-thing but sky and stone. The plantation was suffering. Supplies cost much more, and because Robert Dunleavy, in his zeal to increase his tobacco output, had never cycled the growing season with crops like cotton and rice, the ground was suffering. Too much had been expected of it. The steady, patient overseer was fired one day, and a new one took his place. Clyde Sender, who had nothing but contempt for slaves and women.

"Why the new overseer?" she dared to ask her husband. "The slaves were happy with the last one."

"The slaves are getting lazy. They need to do more work. This new man will keep them in line."

She dropped the matter, but then Robert cut the slaves' rations of meat and clothing and refused to provide even smock shirts for the children under seven, and so they ran around naked.

"It just doesn't seem right to me, Robert," she said, "that those children have no clothes."

Robert was writing figures down in neat print on a ledger. He looked up. "Many, many other plantation masters never give clothes to young children. They stay warm indoors in the winter and play outside in the summertime. They don't need clothes. I provided these as a kindness, and now I can't afford such gestures. So I'll thank you to stay out of my business."

That was the end of the discussion. He didn't speak to her again for three days, which she imagined cleaved to some standard of punishment for uppity wives. She didn't feel married anymore. She kept her letters home cheerful, so as not to alarm or disappoint her parents, and they wrote letters back full of the same love they'd always had for her. Constant, steady love that made her weep as she read her father's handwriting — the strict but loving cursive of a preacher — or opened one of her mother's letters and dried violet petals fell out. The Union army was occupying Winchester once again, streets filled with the colors of the Zouaves, Yankee music playing all hours of the night. They made the people of Winchester take in the sick Union soldiers. Privations were great. Thank goodness their daughter was living the good life of a plantation mistress. The thought of her living in happiness sustained them in these bleak times.

What the war didn't ravage, the tobacco worms did. Light green, a beautiful color wasted on the ugliest creature in the world. Long as a finger. They could strip a field in a matter of weeks. They multiplied so fast that the slaves couldn't keep up with them. Every morning, a flock of turkeys were driven into the field, where they ate tobacco worms all day, and were driven out at night bulging with their feasts. Almon, a teenage slave, was in charge of keeping the turkeys in the field and preventing them from escaping into the woods. But Almon was distracted by a teenage slave named Rose, with braided hair and a heart-shaped face, who helped around the house.

One morning in April, when Robert was away buying a new horse, Almon's mother pounded on the door.

"You gotta come!" she screamed. "You gotta come now!"

Iris would never forget the wet tearing sound, as though a giant man were eating a giant apple . . . followed by a piercing scream. Another, then another as she ran across the property, her heavy keys jangling, past the icehouse and the stables and the beginning of the tobacco fields, to a group of slaves gathered around a sycamore tree, sorrowful, helpless, women on their knees, men with their hats on their chests. Almon was tied to the tree and his bare back had three bloody streaks on it. Before Iris could cry out, Clyde Sender swung the whip again. Almon's flesh parted, and he screamed as blood ran down his back.

"Stop it!" Iris cried. "Stop it!"

Clyde, who was panting and sweating for his efforts, looked around at her. "You get out of here, ma'am. This ain't your affair. Not at all."

"But what could he have done to deserve this?"

"He let all them turkeys run off into the woods while he was over at the clothesline, talking to his little gal." Iris glanced into the crowd and saw Rose shaking her head slowly back and forth, the only act of protest she had in the world.

"We don't beat our slaves," she told Clyde.

"That ain't what I heard." He wiped his brow and went back to work, planting one foot behind him and pulling his arm back for the next lash.

Iris lost that span of time, the two or three seconds it took her to rush to the tree and stand facing the overseer, her body pressed against Almon's back, his blood leaking through her shirtwaist dress.

Clyde Sender lowered the whip. He looked shocked.

"You can't whip him anymore," she said. "I won't allow it."

He raised the whip and the assembled slaves murmured. Iris was paralyzed with fear but stood her ground, and time moved so slowly that Iris could feel the beating of Almon's heart and see a butterfly take its time landing ever so slowly on a milkweed near her feet.

Clyde put down his whip, defeated. "We'll see what Mr. Dunleavy says about this," he muttered. The slaves ran over to attend to Almon, and Iris returned to the big house, the back of her dress sticky with blood. An hour later, after the water had turned pink in the porcelain tub in which the dress was soaking, Robert came through the door and seized Iris's arms, shaking her.

"How dare you? How dare you undermine the authority of my overseer? You ignorant fool." His voice was flat and measured, and not a single muscle moved in his face, but his hands were wild as anything unbranded; they shook her and they shook her.

That night, she went to her bedroom and locked the door behind her, giving him no recourse but to sleep in the guest room from then on. And they were divorced in spirit because that was the neatest and quietest divorce, a fissure taking place under the skin, away from human eyes. Her body had the chill of the spinster but not the freedom. She had no say in the house or the farm anymore, and she stopped receiving seeds for the flower garden she cultivated in the back of the house. A week later, Robert sold Almon to a rice farmer from North Carolina. He was led away with a rope around his neck by his new owner, who rode beside him on a palomino. Almon's mother screamed and clung to his legs, wailing to the skies and begging the man not to take him. Rose said nothing, did nothing, because she was not free to pursue either avenue of expression. She had only the recourse of any other slave — a chiseled account of the crime etched perfectly into a piece of slate somewhere inside herself where a soft spot used to be. This darkness showed on her face. She hung the sheets, but they didn't stay put. Some kind of latent energy tore them off the line, and the sight of them, airborne over the tobacco fields on breezy days, always recalled the story of Almon and the grief of that loss.

By the time Iris had finished that part of her story, she and Wendell were sitting on the cool beach, near the tide line, and Wendell had dug a baseball-size hole in the ground with the edge of a scalloped shell. After her voice faded, he kept digging for a while.

"How many slaves did you have on the plantation?"

"About fifty."

"Couldn't fifty slaves beat up one overseer?"

"Not an overseer with a whip and a gun."

"Isn't that against the law, to treat someone like that?"

"There are two laws in this country. One for black people and one for white people."

"That doesn't seem very fair." The next wave washed up close to the hole he'd dug in the sand. Another few minutes and the hole would be filled. "My father says slavery is primitive."

"Your father runs his own plantation," she said without thinking, immediately regretting her words when she saw the look on his face, half hurt and half puzzled. "I'm sorry, Wendell." She touched his arm.

Dr. Cowell watched them from his office window. They sat, legs akimbo, leaning toward each other. He had rubbed his wife's rose oil on his exposed skin in the hope he could take a walk on the beach at sunset without attracting midges and mosquitoes, but after seeing the woman with his son, he had lost his appetite for the encroaching tide and declining sun. Now he would smell like a woman for nothing.

Since the day Iris Dunleavy had thrown his paper out of the window, they had engaged in what could not be called treatment or even discussion, but open combat, the two of them a microcosm of the great war raging in the far distance: one side that desired autonomy, and the other that took independence as a sign of madness.

"There's a woman in this asylum, Doctor," she said one day, "who never says a word. Who merely claps in delight at anything spoken to her. And I suspect that if I merely clapped at everything you said, I could clap my way to freedom."

The statement made his face flush with anger, and this reaction, in turn, made him angry with himself, that the woman could vex him so. It had been the doctor's custom to make sure each patient was out of his office not one minute after the hour elapsed, as he was a stickler for time, but he found himself so invigorated by the arguments that the sessions began running over. Sometimes he stood up to make a point. Sometimes he raised his voice. Threw words at her he was absolutely sure she didn't understand. But even in these moments he felt somehow returned to his youth, as though if he had turned to a mirror in mid-rant he'd see a man with a smooth, young face and a black beard with no hint of gray.

When inevitably the hour had passed, the nurse's knock would jolt him out of the moment and he would feel the most profound irritation. "Not now!" he would snap, but five minutes later, the knock would return, and Iris would have to leave, and other patients take her place, and the day would progress, taking her away from him, farther and farther. He fought to remain detached, to focus on her treatment and the promise he had made to Robert Dunleavy — to send back to him the wife he'd once known. But he found himself increasingly less aware of the form and substance of their sessions and more of her expressions, the way her hands moved, the angles of her face and the way her dress color affected the tendency of her hazel eyes to fall to green or blue. He tried his best to shake away those thoughts. The woman was mad. And yet, her words were so well chosen and her eyes were as sharp as anyone's walking the free streets of the mainland.

During their last session, things had taken a sudden turn that had left him delighted and strangely disarmed. The incident had reverberated in him, and he found himself going back to it time and time again, analyzing it, reliving it.

They were in the middle of a heated argument about women's rights, or lack thereof, when Iris suddenly offered up a story from her youth. "My grandmother's name was Beatrice, and she used to tell my grandfather every morning upon rising how lucky he was to have tricked her into marriage. She told him she was a great treasure on a ship bound for Spain, and he was the pirate that stole her. She told him he should wear an eye patch, and a parrot on his shoulder. When she died, my grandfather put a flagpole on her grave and refused to lower the flag, even in the rain."

Dr. Cowell responded, to his own surprise, not with analysis but his own story. "My grandfather refused to bathe. He disliked the feel of water, and this drove my grandmother to distraction. He wore the same pair of trousers every day except Sunday, when he would concede to putting on his Sunday suit. One Sunday my grandmother told him she felt ill and could not go to church with him. When he returned from church he found his favorite pair of trousers in flames in the front yard. She told him unless he started bathing, he would be next."

"And did he bathe?"

"Yes, once a month. My grandmother accepted the compromise."

Iris pondered this. And suddenly began to laugh. He was startled by the musical quality of the sound. Like the experiments he'd performed as a boy, tapping glasses of different volumes of water with a spoon. And he himself was laughing. His own laughter startled him. There was no more contribution to the medical canons to be had here, no more treatment, no more progress. Just the joy of accomplishing nothing, the mind abandoning its duties and surrendering. A nurse pounded on the door, startling him, saddening him, angering him.

"Not now!" he shouted, and the sternness in his voice made him laugh some more.

And now the sight of her taking such an intimate posture with his own son filled him with a longing envy. The windowpane was warm against the palm of his hand. The other hand shielded his eyes from the sun as he continued to watch Wendell and Iris. Suddenly she reached out and touched his boy on the arm. He drew his breath in when he saw the gesture. A hard knot formed inside of him. The sun sank lower in the sky. He stared at it, closed his eyes, and saw five suns, all of them blinding green.

That night at dinner he broached the subject with Wendell. "What did you do today?" he asked.

Wendell shrugged.

Mary let out a high, ringing laugh. "Surely you must have done something!" She was in a gay mood, some combination of laudanum and the arrival of an order of ribbon that had come in on the boat, and which she now wore in her hair. The doctor knew that tone in her voice promised something for him later, and this he accepted with a weary, tacit gratitude.

"I saw you on the beach," the doctor said to Wendell. "You were talking to Mrs. Dunleavy, I believe."

"Iris Dunleavy?" asked Mary. "Is she the plantation wife? She dresses so well for a lunatic. She had the most colorful flounces on her skirt the other night."

"We were collecting shells," Wendell said. "We found three alphabet cones and a king's crown and a Scotch bonnet."

"You weren't collecting shells. You were sitting on the beach, facing each other. She reached out and touched your arm."

"Oh, Wendell," said his mother, losing her gay voice. "Don't ever let a lunatic touch you. You don't know what kind of diseases they are carrying. And there are certain mental illnesses that can be contagious." She looked at her husband. "Am I correct, darling?"

He didn't answer her. That hard knot had formed again.

Later that night, he and his wife made love upon their walnut bed, oil lamps turned down by half, listening to the uppity bark of a night heron flying over the roof, the bedsprings creaking, some winged insect hurling itself over and over at the window-pane above their heads. His wife gulped air, her sign of approval. He pressed his hands against the mattress, raising himself so he could look down at her face in the bare light of the lamp. That face, so much younger in the gloom. That girlish expression, open and curious, her eyes and her mouth, it was like going back in time, back in the days he rehearsed what to say to her, back when her beauty moved him so, it was not possible to imagine a future in which he did not worship her completely. That was the folly of youth, to believe someday they would grow old but still love with their younger hearts.

But the way she was looking at him now, the way she said his name twice, *Henry, Henry,* moved him, shook him, cracked him open, so that the moment of climax was a split-second opportunity to visit himself at an earlier age, when he was not alone. He said her name back in a rush of breath as his body relaxed against hers.

The expression left her face, replaced by a look of familiar concern that caused him to get up and find a handkerchief to put over the wet area of the mattress. In mid-step as he tiptoed back through the dead air of the broken spell he realized why the sight of a man's white handkerchief always left him unaccountably depressed.

Mary, lover of chocolate and silk brocade, believer in the restorative powers of Peruvian bark, jalap, and laudanum, couldn't sleep that night. Moonlight came in ribbons through the decorative holes in the curtains and streamed onto the sheet that covered her body and that of her husband, who slept beside her. Such a pretty color, that moonlight, somewhere between daffodil and cloud. An owl hooted outside the window. Its call seemed particularly urgent or sad tonight, but like the keening of the lunatics, its meaning was forever a mystery.

Her husband's face was turned toward the wall. She placed her hand against his back so she could feel the expansion and contraction of his rib cage. Early in their marriage, they would both stir awake for mere moments before falling back into their dreams, and his hand would find hers under the covers and clasp it briefly. It had been years since he had held her hand during the night — or the day for that matter. Earlier, when they had made love, she had recaptured him for a second or two. He had probably mistaken her cry for orgasm, when it was more true to say that the sound came from the pleasure of the look he gave her. That sliver of the same unbridled fondness that used to follow her around in the early years. The sight of it there on his face was like the taste of laudanum. No, it was better. But like the laudanum, it wore off and left her craving more.

22

IRIS SHADED HERSELF with her parasol as she and Ambrose walked parallel to the tide line, darting away when the surf frothed in too close to their feet and then returning to their path when it retreated. An invisible line existed somewhere ahead of them in the sand. If they were to cross that line, guards would materialize and they would be returned to the asylum. Still, they had learned to walk with the air of enfranchised civilians. Iris had been talking fondly of her father, and his prayers, so beautiful and earnest.

"My father is the wisest man I ever met," she said. "It grieves me that he has no idea where I am, or what's become of me. The doctor says that I can write him, but only if my letters are 'rational.' In other words, only if I take full blame for my predicament. I cannot do that. My father hates a lie."

"Your father sounds like a man of character," Ambrose remarked.

"Have you had contact with your family?" Iris asked, and immediately felt the tension of broaching a subject for the first time. He had spoken of his boyhood as a series of images and sensations with no mention of human contact. It was as though he'd been raised by a vortex of experiences instead of human beings. She found this quality of narrative a warning against intrusion and had thus far respected it.

"I have two older brothers. They both went to war before me. I do not know their whereabouts. And my mother died in childbirth. My father never spoke of it, but my aunt told me I came out of the womb in an unnatural position, and she succumbed from blood loss. I was told, again by my aunt, that she nursed me as she died. My brothers remembered her somewhat. They'd tell me little stories and I'd treasure them. She sat for one formal portrait with my father. I look quite a bit like her."

"Did it make you sad," she asked, "growing up without a mother?"

He stopped walking and considered this as saltwater froth ran up and covered the tips of his shoes. "I was more puzzled about it. And I felt a vague guilt, that it was my awkward birth that killed her." He put his hands in his pockets. "But, you know, there was work to be done. We had to help our father run the farm. He didn't believe in sadness. He believed in getting on with things. When my dog was kicked by a mule and died, he made me bury him, forbidding tears. 'Don't say goodbye,' he said. 'You will only look ridiculous, speaking to a carcass.' That's how he was." Ambrose stared out at the water. "My father has never written me. He believes the correct way to return home from the war is in a coffin, on crutches, or in a victory parade. I came back ranting and raving, tied to a buckboard. I was put in the local hospital with the other veterans, but my screams kept them awake. So I was put in a jail cell. Handcuffed to the bars. Fed like a dog."

The surf came crawling up. Ambrose didn't move and neither did Iris. The warm water covered their shoes. A gust of wind made Iris hold on tight to the trembling staff of her parasol.

"Your father sent you here?" Iris asked.

Ambrose nodded. "He was not a rich man, but my great-grandfather made a fortune in steel in Canada, and my father used his inheritance to send me here. I suppose I should be thankful he provided me with the best care in the country. And I am. I just can't wait for the day, Iris, when I walk back into town restored. My own man with my own mind. Everything in the past where it needs to be. Quiet like a dog in a grave. I'll come back and I'll look my father in the eye and I'll shake his hand and I'll say, 'I'm home.'"

Iris had accustomed herself to the odd way Lydia Helms Truman ate a grapefruit, taking the precut sections, tossing them in her mouth, and throwing her head back. It reminded her a bit of a swan gulping a series of tiny pink frogs. And yet, she seemed to accomplish the action with a certain daintiness. Lydia had gone through exactly seven sections of grapefruit this way when she said out of nowhere, "You love him."

Iris blinked at her, startled.

"Love who?"

Lydia dabbed at her lips with a white napkin and took a sip of her coffee. "The crazy soldier," she said.

"He's not crazy."

Lydia smiled. "Look at your posture as you defend him. You straightened up indignantly. Your eyes narrowed. You're already willing to go to war over an adjective. That's love, my dear."

"That's ludicrous," Iris said. "I'm married."

Lydia could not quite set down her coffee in time to beat her laughter. It spilled on the tablecloth and spread out to the size of two quarters as Lydia's peals of laughter continued. Her eyes watered. Her shoulders shook. "Yes, married," she said. "So am I. Isn't married life grand?"

Iris tapped at a boiled egg with the side of her spoon, hitting it too hard, leaving a savage gash in the shell, out of which the yolk protruded. She was not sure why Lydia was irritating her so. It was perhaps that *love,* spoken so boldly, was such a dangerous word. Hot enough to melt the key to freedom she'd been stealthily crafting. She set the egg down. "I do not love him. I simply find his companionship comforting, given my situation."

Lydia gained control of the frantic hummingbird inside her that was her laughter. She dabbed at the corners of her eye with a napkin. "I see the way you look at him, and he looks at you. Don't question love, Iris. It may have come to you in an inconvenient form, one that society finds scandalous, but it's a gift from God. A reminder that this institution can't interfere with natural processes, like laughter, prayer, a dream that comes to you in sleep. Or love. Do with it what you want, but know that it means God still sees you not as a lunatic but as His child."

Iris later took a walk down the beach, as far as the guards would tolerate and then back again. *Love.* The word came out of nowhere, rattling her. She had never thought of her feelings for Ambrose as love. The desire to be with him, the lying in bed at night thinking of him, and even the occasional daydream of kissing him, or lying in his arms . . . she had simply let these feelings exist without naming them. And so that word *love* had flown at her out of nowhere, like an osprey come to steal an eagle's fish.

23

A WEEK LATER, after a night punctuated by intermittent rain and loggerhead turtles dragging themselves up the beach to lay their eggs, Mrs. Lydia Helms Truman was found dead in her room, half of a silk handkerchief hanging out of her mouth and the other half lodged so firmly down her throat it had to be extracted with a Nelaton probe. As the details of her passing raced around the asylum, Dr. Cowell unleashed a scathing rebuke upon the matron, who in turn reacted by instituting a reign of terror, screaming at nurses and patients alike.

Iris wept when she heard of the fate of the small, cheery, neatly coiffed woman, a unique individual ready to bite someone for justice or swallow a pebble for no reason at all. Sweet Lydia, forever denied the chance to return to the world from which she'd been taken.

"What did they do with Mrs. Truman?" she asked Wendell later that day, as they collected shells on the beach.

"They buried her out back. They've got a graveyard for the patients."

"What if one of the staff died? Would they bury them there, too?"

Wendell toed a spot in the sand where the bubbles gave away the presence of a sand dollar. He dug for the sand dollar and held it up to the light before gently placing it down. "I suppose they would have to make another graveyard. Crazy people and regular people don't get buried together."

"The idea being that crazy people aren't good enough to be buried with the sane?"

Wendell looked uneasy. "I don't know. I don't make the rules." He caught her look of annoyance and added, "But I would be buried in the same graveyard as you. That would be fine with me."

Iris brushed the sand off the beaded periwinkle she had just discovered. "At the plantation where I used to live, the Dunleavy family graveyard was at one edge of the property, and the grave-yard for slaves and pets was at the other end. If you were a Dunleavy, you were laid to rest among holly and gardenia bushes, with a pink granite tombstone. If you were a slave, you'd get a wooden cross and be laid to rest next to an Irish setter." She stopped talking then, because those two graveyards were tied up with the story she couldn't tell the boy, the part she'd had to skip because, as desperate for escape as she was, she didn't want that story in his mind.

Over the past weeks she had released the details of her history to the boy a little at a time, earning his trust in the narrative. She felt she was making good progress. He liked her. She could tell that. And he was lonely. That was obvious, too. And though she did feel a certain guilt about luring this lonely boy whose accent belonged to no country in particular to be her coconspirator in her escape, she saw no other way.

She sat across the checkers table from Ambrose. She was thinking about Lydia again. She was pinioned in death, labeled mad for eternity. But Lydia had been so much more than that. Mad, perhaps. But more.

"What are you thinking about?" Ambrose asked.

"Lydia."

"Oh," said Ambrose. "I'm sorry." He looked at her intently.

She wasn't sure what was going through his mind, but she liked the way he stared at her.

"Lydia Helms Truman told me last week I loved you," she said, surprising herself. Immediately her cheeks burned. She had started something. She knew it. With great intention and in memory of Lydia, she had defiantly said the word, not to banish it but to offer it. It was reckless. She was married. But there was no ring on her finger. She'd removed it long ago, had flung it into an eternity of tobacco plants. It was plowed under now, part of the soil.

Ambrose leaned over and kissed her on the mouth. The kiss insisted upon itself, made the biggest shadow, called the loudest call. Held itself as king, according to natural law. He did not pull away, but kept kissing her until suddenly she felt a strong hand on her shoulder, wrenching her away from Ambrose.

"What do you two think you're doing?" the guard shouted. "There is no kissing allowed between patients!"

He took Ambrose by the arm, pulled him from the checkers table, and led him away toward the doors of the asylum.

Ambrose looked back at Iris with steady eyes. No regret, no embarrassment. Nothing but the desire to do it again.

24

IT WAS IN HIM now, the kiss. He was too thrilled by it, too changed by it, to let it go. But could he have the kiss and the peace too? All during the war, his greatest terror had been to lose his faculties and end up like those wrecked creatures for whom things remained: birthmarks, the colors of their eyes, the way peaches altered their breath, a grimace or grin that recalled the way they used to be. The rest was the mush of pure stranger. Once, at a temporary hospital set up at an abandoned school for girls, he had volunteered to help the surgeons and had witnessed one of them pull a flattened bullet from a soldier's head. The soldier lived, but he no longer knew what side of the war he was on, or how to button his shirt. His mother rode all the way from Asheville in a one-horse cart. No one had told her about the condition of her son, only that he was alive. She came into the room and saw him, froze for a moment, and then sat down on the edge of his bed, kissed his forehead, talked to him. She found the part of him that was still hers, adopted the rest, got him back into his clothes, and took him home. Ambrose was haunted by the memory, terrified of being that man who was never the same.

The doctor would surely tell him that the kiss was a threat to his sanity, that it would leave him vulnerable to the terrible visions that always threatened to overwhelm him at any given time, but for now he felt strangely free of the doctor's judgment. In fact, he felt exhilarated, so much so that, as the guard led him down the hall, he welcomed the prospect of going to his room where he could be alone with the kiss and the memory of the woman who had welcomed it.

But the guard suddenly turned into the day room.

"Wait," said Ambrose. "I don't want to go in there. I want to go in my room."

"Dr. Cowell thinks you need to spend some time around other men. And from what I just witnessed, I imagine he is right."

Ambrose had little to say to the other men. He crossed his arms and stood with his back toward the window, watching two madmen play a game of billiards. One kissed the cue ball every time he took a shot, and the ritual seemed to be working. His opponent, an excitable Greek man, accused him of using magic and began kissing the cue ball as well. The game grew more heated, and the Greek man continued to lose. When it was his turn again, he kissed the cue ball, gave it a stern, warning look, and hit it so hard it leaped off the table. From that particular height, in the acoustics of that particular room, the sound a clay-fired billiard ball made against a marble floor sounded exactly like a rifle shot. Ambrose, who had been daydreaming about the kiss, was caught by surprise. The sound of the shot entered his consciousness, yanked him away from Iris, and gave him back to the South.

He saw himself in a field in Pennsylvania, the stock of the gun still warm against his cheek, Seth's body not so much falling as slumping, and it was too late for blue, blue was as ineffective and sad as brandy forced between the lips of a corpse, and Seth's knees took a terrible angle as he slumped but did not fall, forever slumping, never falling, this was eternity, this was hell, and Ambrose tried to scream those legs into straightening but it was too late. He screamed and screamed, strong hands holding him down. A spoon was forced into his mouth and the warm hot liquid within it burned his tongue and then his throat, and Ambrose's horror turned soft and sweet and sad. He wanted to kiss the boy goodbye but he was dissolving himself, into the white nothing that was better than the sky.

When he awoke, the room was dark, and Dr. Cowell sat in a Windsor chair next to his bed, his arms crossed, sleeping, a single tallow candle casting the doctor's shadow on the wall. Ambrose tried to shift on the bed but found that his arms were bound to the bedposts, and he could move only his feet, which he employed to kick off his hot blankets.

The doctor awoke and rubbed his eyes.

"Mr. Weller," he said, in a voice both anguished and relieved. "How are you feeling?"

Ambrose squinted, trying to pick out a word from a long line of them that drifted by in his mind, one most appropriate. But so many seemed to fit.

"Tired."

"I suppose you are."

"What time is it?"

The doctor read his pocket watch by candlelight. "Nearly midnight. You've been screaming for hours. What happened to you?"

He tried to gather his thoughts. "I had another fit," he said slowly. "I thought perhaps I was done with them. I'm very surprised."

"I'm not surprised. I'm not surprised at all."

Ambrose caught the disapproving tone in his voice. The straps that held him to the bedposts were biting into his wrists, and his arms ached from the strange position. "What do you mean?" he asked.

"You kissed her!" He practically spat out the words. "In open defiance of everything I taught you! Did you not listen to a word I've been trying to say? You aren't well. This kiss has caused a terrible regression in your treatment."

"That is not true!" Ambrose said, surprising himself with the anger in his voice. "I was in the day room. They were playing billiards —"

"That means nothing! What matters is that you kissed her and less than ten minutes later you went raving mad again. She will destroy you, all your progress. Do you want that?" Ambrose caught a look of something in his eyes. No, it couldn't be.

The doctor moved the chair close to the bed and sat down in it. "Mr. Weller," he said. "Do you remember how you used to tell me I saved your life?"

"I remember."

"And do you still believe that?"

"Yes," he said, relaxing a bit so that the straps were kinder to his wrists.

"And do you trust me?"

"Yes."

"And do you want to leave this island a whole man, one who can make your father proud?"

He stiffened. It wasn't fair, evoking his father.

"Don't undo all your progress, Mr. Weller. Don't sacrifice your healing mind. Give this woman a wide berth."

The way he said "woman" confirmed Ambrose's suspicions. It was an uncertainty. A stutter. A weakness and a pain.

"Doctor," he said, feeling a sudden glee at the consternation he knew he was about to cause, as though the doctor's calm demeanor was a sleeping cat and the words were a shoe coming down on the tail. "Perhaps you should take your own advice."

25

AS DOCTOR AND patient argued, a gentler conversation took place in another part of the asylum. Pacing her room, in the sweet, calming odor put off by the smoke in the smudge pot, Iris told Wendell the rest of her story. She felt guilty about the parts she'd left out, and also somewhat anxious, as the story of the baby and the two graves — one new, one open and filled with water — would explain the inevitability of flight. At the same time, the boy was young, and very sensitive. So Iris finished the story as best she could, with no mention of the baby at all. This hurt her; everyone else who had loved the baby was dead, and she was the only witness to the fact that indeed he had been born and had breathed and had fed at his mother's breast. She ached to say his name. But not now. Not to the boy.

She spoke rapidly, rushing the ending of the story along. Now that Ambrose had kissed her, she was fighting against time. The kiss was in danger of softening her resolve. Taking away her determination to leave this island. Since that kiss she had steeled herself, trying to make the kiss smaller in her mind. As it was, it had spilled across her plans like the contents of an inkwell, spreading a stain in the shape of his face. All day long she had tried to scrub it clean. She was losing the battle. What future could she have on this island with this madman? Her father was waiting for her, with his prayers and his wisdom, and her mother waited by his side with more practical offerings: tea and something to put in her hair to make it soft again. She could not let herself fall in love with Ambrose. But she was falling. As she fell, she finished the story as fast as she could.

Rose had an old tabby cat she loved, named Sirus, who often wandered back in the slave quarters to visit her. She was helping her mother cut out the patterns for a jersey shirt when Iris, passing by, heard her say: "But who will take care of Sirus?" And her mother said, "Shhh. Sirus will be fine." Having led mostly an invisible life, Iris was used to sneaking around a burgeoning story's outer edges, listening for scraps of conversation and too-loud prayers, and even for the messages hidden in songs, and it wasn't long before her suspicions were confirmed: Some of the slaves were planning an escape. Iris took off her apron one night, put on her shawl, and walked right in among them in the middle of their meeting in the stables, seven of them hovering in an empty stall: Rose, her mother, Verna, her father, John. Mattie, the old woman with the creaky knees who worked in the big house. Nate, young and wiry, the best field hand on the plantation. Thomas, who carried a Bible with him everywhere, and Jackson, the blacksmith.

They all stepped back when she walked in. She was the mistress, perhaps their enemy, perhaps their friend; they had seen white people turn on a dime.

Iris said: "What are your plans?"

Thomas never lied, so it was up to Jackson to say, "What plans, ma'am?"

"Your plans for escaping," Iris said, as calmly as though she were describing a butterfly's plan to rob a milkweed.

The slaves looked at each other.

"What is your destination?" she asked.

No one said anything. Then Nate said, "North," and was quickly shushed by the others.

"North?" she asked. "Just north? It's far too dangerous. You will be captured long before you pass the river. We'll travel east. There's a Quaker village about fifty miles from here. They'll protect us."

Verna looked straight at her. "We?"

"I am going with you."

"No!" said Rose's father, John. "Please, ma'am, a white woman don't have any business running with the slaves. They'll think we kidnapped you."

"She's not going!" Nate shouted. "I will not travel with her!" The slaves began to argue among themselves, agitated, their voices growing loud and then someone letting out a warning "Shhhh." The argument would fall into whispers, then build again. Iris left the secret meeting with no resolution.

Later, she appealed to Mattie. "Please," she told her. "I can't stay here. If my husband suspects I knew, there is no telling how he'll react. You see how he treats me. I've become a slave too."

Mattie looked at her balefully. "With all respect, ma'am," she said, "you ain't no slave, and never will be." But Mattie finally consented to speaking to the others, and shortly thereafter came the word of the reluctant decision: She would go with them.

They left two nights later, in the pouring rain, moving into the forest surrounding the plantation as lightning crackled through the sky. The rain was a blessing. It would wash away their scent. They took old cart paths through the woods, hid among the trees in the daytime, and traveled after dark, seven dark shapes and one pale one by the light of the moon. They crisscrossed rivers and broken ground to throw the dogs off their tracks. Stole chickens and eggs from farms. They drank from the wells and broke into smokehouses. Once they found a barrel full of molasses and licked it from their fingers until they spooked and ran away.

They reached a field that stretched endlessly, the middle of nowhere that people talk about, nothing but goldenrod and sheep sorrel. Grasshoppers jumped away from the sound of footsteps. Here they camped for the night. No fire. Dark clouds were bunched up in the sky, as if thrown there by someone done with them. Iris sat apart from the rest. On principle, she was not accepted. Dirty and tired and hungry though she was, she would never be dirty and tired and hungry enough to be one of them. And there had been grumblings about her insistence upon going east, not north.

"We'd be fine now," Nate said that night, "if everyone had just listened to me."

"I'm sorry," Iris said. She felt helpless and miserable and unwanted. "I'm sure the village is just a little further."

"Sure it is." He took out his .45 and began to clean it. He'd stolen it from the big house before they left. John watched him, making a face. Nate noticed him.

"What are you looking at?" Nate said.

"Crazy boy like you shouldn't have a gun. That's all I'm saying."

"What you gonna do, old man? Take it away from me?"

They'd had the same argument for days.

"What's the matter?" Wendell asked from the other side of the bars. It was harder to see his face through the screen they'd put up for the mosquitoes. "Why did you stop the story?"

Iris wasn't sure how long she'd been quiet. She'd been lost in the memory. She backed away from the window, but not far. There was nowhere to go.

His voice was quiet, respectful. "People start dying now, don't they?"

She lay apart from the others as she always did, using as her bedding a sheet she'd stolen from a clothesline, full of ordinary scents: spring air and bluing and the clean sharp smell of nothing in particular. In the near distance, gaunt cattle stood huddled together. The war had started chewing on the cities and was now moving into pastoral scenes. It couldn't stop the flowers, or the grass, and the trees looked the same. But a steer that could have fed ten families now could feed only half that. Strange how she could hate slavery but hate the Yankees, too.

She fell into a stretch of sleep, flat, gray sleep meant only to rest the body. She awoke to Verna's scream. Horses were coming down the dirt road that ran along the side of the pasture. Iris jumped to her feet, confused, horrified. A man in a slouch hat on a palomino was ahead of the rest of them and was closing in fast. A loud shot went off next to her head and the lead man fell. Iris turned and saw Nate pointing his weapon. He fired twice more as they ran into the cypress forest.

A confusion of voices. Labored breathing. Biting cool of swamp water. Dawn came and shots rang in her ears and then they were all bunched up and dying in that cypress cove. She was on the ground, water soaking the back of her dress.

Rose, John, Verna, Mattie, Nate, Jackson, Thomas. When she came to her senses she was tied to the back of a horse, riding toward Fort Lane, where a judge would say the word that brought her here.

Lunatic.

She knew boys did not like crying women, and so she had held in her tears while she finished the story. Wendell looked at her steadily. She moved closer to the window.

"Do you think I'm a lunatic, Wendell?"

He shook his head.

"Then let me go."

"Let you go?"

"Help me leave this place and go back to Winchester. You are my only chance for salvation. Please don't abandon me. I'll die here, don't you see?"

26

PENELOPE WAS STILL ALIVE.

The last of the baby loggerheads had broken out of their eggs and crawled toward the horizon line. The rest of the country had cooled down for winter, but on the island, a profusion of bougainvillea continued to bloom on the courtyard wall.

Banned by the chef from any contact with the girl, Wendell had to content himself with glimpses from afar. The pain equaled, then eclipsed the pleasure, but still he could not help himself. She seemed so solitary, wandering the grounds, clutching her doll and stopping every so often, and peering around her, so that Wendell had to duck behind whatever wall or bush he was using as his Penelope-watching fortress. Did she miss him? Did she feel abandoned? The marks on his throat had turned into faint, petal-shaped bruises, and he longed for a potion that would keep that color there forever. He stroked the marks idly as he watched Penelope collecting small, round stones, washing them in the waves and then piling them on the beach just beyond the vegetation line, the same perimeter in which the loggerhead turtles had deposited their eggs in the summer months.

Wendell squatted next to the pile of stones by moonlight, chin in hand, staring at it. It seemed to beg for decoding. But he could not figure it out. Perhaps Penelope was building a shrine to her own isolation, or simply counting out some quantity that existed in her head. He longed so badly to talk to her, to be near her. Not even by night could he have her company. By some aberration of

architecture and, beyond that, fate, Penelope had the only room
without a barred window through which they could have held
clandestine meetings. The thought of his beloved, her blue eyes
filled with tears, her flame-colored hair matted and wet, her red
mouth ovoid with an endless scream as cold water pounded on
her head, was too much for him to bear. And so he stayed away
from her as his throat turned back to an everyday, uninspired
flesh color and her pile of stones grew in the shape of a pyramid.

One morning Wendell found a stone in the fork of a gumbo
limbo tree next to a Calusa burial mound. He plucked it from
its place and held it to the light. It was smooth, pinkish in tint,
and shot through with blue veins — much like Penelope's skin.
He decided to add it to her mound of stones as a secret gift, but
when he returned to the beach he found them missing. Nothing
there, just an empty nest of broken sand. He knelt, running his
hand over the place, mystified.

He tried to catch a glimpse of her in the courtyard. Failing
that, he searched the halls and the day room. Her blank stare and
dreamy smile were nowhere to be found. A sense of foreboding
came over him, and he ran down to the beach, taunted by the
cries of willets and gulls, his shoes heavy in the sand, calling her
name to the wind. Near the pass he saw something washed up
on the shore. It was Penelope's doll, its dress quite wet but its
springy red hair unaffected. Wendell turned and ran back to the
asylum, shouting for the guards.

For three days the staff and even the fishermen searched for
her. Wendell looked as well, with a desperate obsession, in all
his favorite hideaways, wild places no one else had discovered.
Middens, abandoned villages, mangrove forests, alligator haunts.
At night he soaked a cattail head in kerosene and kept looking
for her by the light of that torch as the forest around him spoke.
Buzzings, rattlings, chirpings, the hoot of an owl, and the call of a

night bird so close it seemed to come from the crook of his arm. As he searched he prayed to the indistinct God in that forest, a neutral essence among the odor of sulfur and animal droppings and rotted berries and decaying fish.

He searched everywhere but the most obvious place, a place that could be found at the end of a short and hateful common-sense equation. The place her body was found, three days later. She had slipped away from the others and walked into the sea, her pockets heavy with the missing stones.

Wendell edged through the group of people surrounding her and looked down at her face. Her skin was loose and ghostly blue. Her eyes and lips had been eaten by crabs. He turned and bolted back toward the asylum, making it only a few yards before collapsing on all fours to throw up in the sand. Instantly he sprang back to his feet and kept going. He jumped the low wall of the courtyard and took the shortcut to his family's cottage around back, bursting through the door and dashing past his shocked mother to the dining room table, which had been set for dinner with silverware and glasses and a vase full of mauve flowers.

"Darling! What's the matter?" she cried, but he paid her no mind. He seized the tablecloth, which was edged in rose-patterned lace, and yanked it hard, sending the contents atop it cascading down to the stone floor. He ran back out of the house as glass shattered and his mother shrieked his name.

The chef saw him coming, dragging the tablecloth, and tried to intercept him, but Wendell's rage at the sight of the man who had kept him from his beloved gave him the sudden strength to butt the large man in the stomach like a goat, causing him to stagger back in surprise, and Wendell broke through the crowd around Penelope and laid the tablecloth over her body. No one stopped him, not even Dr. Cowell, who had been kneeling near her shoulder and now watched his son gently tuck the tablecloth around her body. The birds circled, shrieking. The waves went in and out. The chef straightened, grimacing, his hand over his solar plexus. The crabs, unaccountably, had left Penelope's nose alone so that beneath the cloth, her face still had the contours of a normal girl.

His mother's breast was wedged against Wendell's ear as he wept in her arms. He was not usually a crier, but there were not enough tears in the world for proper expression; his grief was unbounded, unknowable, unfathomable.

"Oh, Wendell," his mother whispered, stroking his hair. He felt three of her tears in rapid succession drop into the part in his hair, sympathy tears that were a comfortable temperature.

His bedroom door creaked open. Wendell heard slow, heavy footsteps approach and peered up out of his mother's bosomy nest to see his father standing there, his posture awkward, his expression confused. He seemed utterly lost, just as lost as Penelope had seemed these past weeks when gazed upon from afar. The doctor scratched his beard, rocked on his heels. Started to say something, stopped himself.

Wendell felt his mother stiffen.

"Go," she said. "There's nothing you can do."

"But—"

"Go."

Wendell put his head back down. His father cleared his throat. A short silence followed. His footsteps faded from the room.

For weeks Wendell sat on the beach, gazing out to sea, near the place where the blue body had rested. He was sure that if there was a God who sees all things, criminals and thieves and wretches and private-fondlers, then this God had taken Penelope from him to punish him, and if this was so, he was not a boy at all, but a moving target for a bully who lived in the heavens, and he wanted so badly to ask for answers from the priest, who either did or did not have a melted crucifix in his chest that would offer definitive proof of miracles and mercy from above.

Penelope tormented him in his sleep, swimming underwater toward him, her long red hair flowing behind her, trailing along the ocean floor, brushing over stonefish and coral reefs, tickling barracudas into reverie, tangling in the flowers of anemones and then pulling loose. When he awoke he'd find his sheets wet, and he realized, with horror, that his private-fondling now entered his unconscious hours. The madness did not even end when he closed his eyes.

He and the chef were no longer friends. After all, if the chef had not banned him from seeing the girl, she would still be alive.

It was mullet season. They passed by in groups with their peculiar roar, a sound like thunder. Instead of fishing together, Wendell and the chef fished far apart, using bread dough as bait, tossing a light hook into the place where the mullets roared.

Wendell began to miss the chef. The stories of his days as a slave, his get-rich schemes, his rapid-fire philosophy, the gospel tunes that came humming out of his oversize nostrils, his rough humor, the way he punched Wendell in the arm and then, laughing his baritone laugh, held him at arm's length so the boy couldn't punch him back.

As the days cooled slightly, Wendell and the chef fished a few feet closer together, until one morning, without any acknowledgment of the miracle, they were fishing side by side.

The moon was high overhead. Wendell stood over Penelope's grave, which was covered with shells. Those he found on the beach, plus the ones from the shadow box in his room, had become offerings to her memory. In the center of the grave was a bare circle, the size of a Mason jar lid. The dirt in that circle had lightened over the past months, while Lydia Helms Truman's grave, set up nearby, still looked fresh. Wendell had thrown away the perfunctory wooden cross someone had nailed together for Penelope and made his own for her out of balsa wood and sinew, fitting the pieces together and then painting her name on it. The first time he misjudged and the last two letters — the *P* and the *E* — ended up crowded together, so he had started over.

Wendell knelt by the grave, pulling a weed that was peeking up through the shells and then remaining in a kneeling position. The woman, Iris Dunleavy, had deeply troubled him with her request, and he had not given her an answer. How could he? Did she really expect him to go against his father's authority and help her escape from the island? The story she told him had made perfect, tragic sense. He would have run away with the slaves as well, to escape such a horrible man. She seemed perfectly sane to him. But surely she must be mad. His father believed so, and he was the smartest man Wendell knew.

And yet, the words she had spoken to him had given him a pain in his heart that felt so familiar. He put his hand on his chest. The blue painted letters of Penelope's name looked black under moonlight. The shells glittered on her grave.

He remembered Iris Dunleavy staring at him through the mosquito mesh on the bars of her window.

Please don't abandon me. I'll die here, don't you see?

27

THE DOCTOR HAD stormed from the room, leaving Ambrose tied to the bedposts. Punishment for his impudence, no doubt. He had dozed off and awakened again just as the dawn light was coming through the bars. The bonds were digging into his wrists again, and his full bladder ached. He started to cry out, then changed his mind. He didn't need the damn doctor. Perhaps he could free himself. He looked up to his right hand and studied the knot. He shifted on the bed and began angling for position, trying to reach the knot with his fingers. His brothers used to tie him up as a boy and he'd get loose more times than they had figured on. He never told his father on them. Just sought his revenge. Now he went back to that knowledge of slipping one's bonds. It was sweaty, lonely work. And only for the resolute. He worked patiently, his fingers aching, his bladder feeling as though it would burst. And as the sun grew bright between the bars, he went backward. Straight into the war, past the truly horrific moments and into a time of medium horror. Like eating steak with the blood cooked out, it was a more benign way to sample memory. His fingers ached. The leather binds stretched. The bedposts creaked.

The surprising thing was not that Ambrose had gone crazy during the war. It was that everyone else, every single soldier at arms, had not gone crazy too. That war, still under way somewhere past the line of palms and the mangrove forests and the willet colonies at the edge of the water, was made up of crazy. Crazy politicians, crazy preachers, crazy motivations, crazy ghosts, and crazy gods. Just a sea of delusion, blue at high tide, gray at low.

He was in a long line of Confederates trudging back up the Valley Turnpike, the sun so hot that they could not imagine ever being cold. Rumors of a Rebel offensive into Pennsylvania moved down the ranks. Enterprising old Negroes sold lemonade from carts. It was watery and undersugared and warm, but by now Ambrose had learned to supplement mediocre treats with his imagination, and as he tilted back his head and drank out of a metal cup, a beautiful girl stood by with an icy pitcher, rows and rows of girls stretching out across the fields and collecting tickseed on their stockings.

Seth drank deeply and then said, "I don't like the idea of invading Pennsylvania. We should stay here in Virginia and let the Yankees come to us."

"We don't get to make the plans." Ambrose took another gulp of lemonade. He couldn't taste it at all; it was simply water with a price attached.

"I have a bad feeling about leaving Virginia," Seth said.

The drums sounded again and the march resumed. Jokes and songs moved up and down the ranks, but the voices had thinned. The best tenor in the brigade had died at Fredericksburg, and the keeper of a thousand punch lines had died in winter camp. The brigade crossed the Potomac at Shepherdstown and then headed for Antietam Creek. A deep gloom settled over the soldiers. Sharpsburg reminded them of terrible things. They still carried wounds from that battle, and visions of dying men. One soldier simply stopped and would not go any farther.

"I'll shoot you," the sergeant warned.

"The devil wouldn't make me go back there," the soldier responded. "Half my company fell in the cornfield and I'd just as soon die right here than smell that place again."

By dusk, the brigade had reached a familiar road that led to the Piper Farm and the Dunker Church. The corpses that once hung on the fence were gone, along with the bloated horses and the angry bees. But the ground was still torn up with graves. Many of the farmers had fled. Their threshing machines were rusting in the fields. Wrens called from empty barns. And the flowers of broken ground — yarrow, goldenrod, and thistle — had taken over the fields. Just past the Dunker Church sat the West Woods, where Ambrose had killed his first soldier.

The brigade made camp near the church as dusk fell. Flames rose quickly. Fireflies were out and so were locusts, whose abandoned shells were attached to the trees by hollow appendages. No one sang or played cards. They either drank themselves into a stupor, took lanterns to visit the graves of friends, or both. Half a dozen men passed out in the sunken road, which had once been filled with so many bodies that someone could walk a good distance without touching the ground. A dog from F Company found the place his master fell, lay down upon it, and would not get up.

Ambrose fried some hardtack in bacon grease and then sat looking at it. The clouds blew away and the stars came out, white as the church had once been. Someone was crying in the direction of the Miller Farm. The cornfield razed in the battle had grown back, and the wailing seemed to come from the center of the moving stalks. They passed around the bottle as the hour grew late. A hickory branch was jutting out of the fire and Ambrose pushed it back with the tip of his shoe, sending out a sheet of sparks that rivaled the fireflies.

"It's not right," Ambrose said. "The living shouldn't have to make camp on top of the dead."

Ambrose and Seth shared a tent. They lay awake, listening to the sounds of the night. This new clearing where they were camped smelled clean, just pine trees and undercurrents of sage and something musky and sweet. Here the crickets sounded innocent, and so did the locusts, and the shadows crossing their tent were made of branches or low-flying birds, but nothing restless or dead.

Their brigade had run into a group of Federal prisoners being escorted by Jubal Early's troops, and the Confederates had made the prisoners stop and give them all their shoes.

"I got a blister from those shoes," Seth said in the dark. "They're too big."

"You should have kept your old shoes. They were worn, but at least they were the right size."

"I'll just walk barefoot."

"No, don't do that. You'll get used to them."

They were quiet again.

"Ambrose?" Seth whispered. He always sounded younger at night, his true age instead of the one he pretended to be.

"Yeah?"

"I have to tell you something."

"Tell me."

"All these fights?"

"Yeah?"

"I ain't never shot anyone."

Ambrose thought he hadn't heard right. "What?"

"I've never fired my gun. I can't, Ambrose, I can't."

"Why'd you join up, then?"

Seth was quiet for a moment. "Same reason everyone else did, I guess. But I didn't think war would be like this. It's worse than anything I ever imagined."

"Well, you're not doing the South much good if you're not killing any Yankees." He felt a sudden anger for this boy whose hands weren't bloody. "What do you think would happen if none of us pulled the trigger?"

The tent was quiet.

"Ambrose?"

"What?"

"I'm gonna run. I can't take this no more. I'll go hide out in a smokehouse. Sleep in hickory ashes."

"They're shooting deserters now. You know that."

"I know."

Ambrose watched the orange glow of a campfire through the fabric of the tent. A hickory log sputtered in the fire, briefly scalding the song of nearby crickets. A soldier muttered something in his sleep. A dog padded by on three legs, from the sound of it.

"Never figured you for yellow," Ambrose whispered, bitter.

"If that makes me yellow, fine. I'll be yellow as a pound cake, yellow as lemonade. Yellow as a field of daisies. Let the cows graze on me. I don't care."

They were keeping watch the night Seth ran. Ambrose knew he was leaving. He could tell by the look in the younger man's eyes.

Fifty yards behind them, the camp slept.

"Stay off the roads," Ambrose said. "And travel at night."

"I know."

Ambrose thought he was going to feel jealousy at this moment. Raging jealousy, because he just didn't have it in him to run. Instead he felt only love. And that was the miracle. The surge in hatred since the war began had created more love around it. It was indomitable, mad, and everlasting, scattered through the rich and the poor, deep and calm in the Quakers, hot and fierce in the mothers, faithful in the warriors, wistful in the pets, seeping its way into mercy and atrocity, destroying things, rebuilding them.

He let Seth go, out of love. Seth leaned his rifle against a tree and walked away into the dark.

Just as Seth freed himself, Ambrose broke free as well. The knot on the leather strap of his right hand finally came loose, and he wasted no time untying the left hand and leaping from the bed. His bladder was going to burst. He walked over to the window. Outside was a clump of pampas grass, two circling butterflies, and then bare sand moving into dunes and then finally finishing at the surf. Ambrose unbuttoned his pants and urinated through the bars, a high arcing stream, yellow as the butterflies. Ambrose smiled. Because, because, because.

28

IRIS STIRRED HER oatmeal but could not eat it. The kiss had taken her appetite, and her ability to sleep. She could feel her plan for escape unraveling. Her desire to leave had been compromised by her feelings for the soldier. But what right did she have to feel anything for another man? She was, after all, a married woman in the eyes of the law. Once she was safely back home in Winchester, she told herself, Ambrose and everyone else on this island would fade away, leaving her to the sanctuary of her old bedroom in her old home. Why couldn't the boy, Wendell, have given her an answer last night? Why did he say he needed time to think? What was there to think about?

She detected a disturbance in the dining room and looked up to see Dr. Cowell stride into the room directly toward her, ignoring the curious glances of the nurses, the attendants, and the other patients. "Papa!" one of them shouted, but he paid no attention. He came right over to her table and sat down directly across from her.

"Do you know what you've done?" he asked by way of greeting.

"Done?"

"Don't pretend innocence. Mr. Weller had a terrible fit. His worst so far."

She felt twin stabs in her stomach, one at the mention of Ambrose's name and the next at the mention of his torment.

"Oh, no," she whispered. "Is he speaking?"

"Yes, he is speaking. But it is how he speaks to me that gives me concern. He is sullen and disrespectful. I fear he is relapsing into madness. All because of you and your influence upon him. How could you kiss that man? Never mind you are married. He is seriously ill!"

She nodded. "I'm sorry."

His eyebrows rose. "You are?"

"Yes. I don't know what came over me. I was in a vulnerable state and I allowed the kiss. But I was immediately regretful."

"Well," he said, his authoritative voice creeping back, "you are not to see him anymore, or talk to him again."

"I think that's for the best. Believe it or not, he is proving just as unhealthy for me as I have been for him." She smiled at the doctor, feeling sad but grateful that he had removed the torment of Ambrose's company for her. She was almost fond of the man sitting in front of her with the cravat tied crookedly and his expression of rage slowly dissolving into confusion. He studied her a moment, looking utterly lost. He rose from the table and left the room.

Wendell knew what dinner would be. Sheepshead. He'd helped the chef catch it earlier in the day. He stared at his plate with a measure of pride.

He hadn't slept well the night before. Shocked by Iris's story and scandalized by her demand, he'd paced his room. He glanced at his father. Judging by the older man's mood, Wendell sensed he shouldn't engage him tonight. He did it anyway, because he was a boy.

"Father? How do you know when someone's crazy?"

The doctor sighed. "That's a very complicated question. There's no simple answer. Now, can we stop talking about madness while I eat my supper in peace?"

"He was just asking a question, Henry," Mary said.

"I *know*."

Wendell had heard that tone before in his father's voice. Like a red buoy, it warned a boy to swim no further. And yet he did.

"Father. About the woman, Mrs. Dunleavy."

The name seemed to make the doctor's fork-holding mechanism go haywire. The utensil clattered to the plate. He picked it up again.

"Are you sure she's crazy?" Wendell asked.

"Of course she is. She was judged insane in a court of law. A judge signed the order. A deputy escorted her to this asylum. And I myself evaluated her."

"But, is she crazy because she ran away with the slaves?" Wendell asked.

"She ran away with the slaves?" Mary asked, fascinated.

The doctor glared at his son. "How did you know that? You're not supposed to know that!"

"I heard it from a nurse!" Wendell sensed he had gone too far but the red buoy was bobbing behind him now; he was in free ocean space and he paddled madly, kicking his legs hard. "And she told me herself! But she had her reasons! Good reasons. Has she told you the reasons?"

His father had turned quite red. "You are not to be talking to that woman, do you understand?"

"Lower your voice. You're frightening him," Mary said.

"Hush, woman!"

Mary looked shocked.

Wendell stopped kicking. He was so far out to sea he couldn't see the shore. "I'm sorry, Father. We just collect shells. It's . . . it's . . ." He searched for the grand word he'd heard his father use. "It's therapeutic!"

His father threw down his napkin and rose from his chair. He pointed his finger at Wendell. "I am telling you right now, that if I see you speaking to that patient again — that lunatic, that demented woman — you will be confined to the hospital grounds. Do you understand?"

Wendell glanced at his mother, hoping for a bit of support, but she, too, seemed stricken by her husband's behavior. She just sat there, blinking, as the members of the family stared at each other in the aura of cooling fish and dying candlelight.

"I understand, Father," Wendell said at last.

"Good. Because I am the head of this asylum and I am the head of this family and I will be respected!"

The door slammed behind him. Wendell turned to his mother, bewildered.

"Why does he hate Mrs. Dunleavy?"

She stared at the door, her head cocked. "Oh, no, son," she murmured. Her voice was soft and measured. "He doesn't hate her at all."

The doctor took the walkway of broken shells around the building and out the courtyard to the sea, slogging forward in the sand. Ghost crabs skittered away from his feet. A startled cormorant on a dune took flight, scolding him with its call. Overhead glowed a waxing moon and the same sky full of stars that had seemed so fascinating his first night on the island, when his dream of sanctuary still held so much promise.

A great, lumbering shape moved in the darkness. He froze, squinted, and recognized a giant loggerhead turtle crawling toward the dunes to lay her eggs. She dragged herself through the sand with her great fins, moving as though already tired from the journey yet keeping steady progress. He'd heard stories that loggerheads cry when they lay their eggs, great tears by moonlight. But he was not in the mood for another crying female.

The sea rolled back as he stomped toward it and he kept going, down the wet slope, marching purposefully toward the receding waves. Finally he stopped, shoes sinking in sand, as the water roiled back, covering him up to the ankles.

Another patient had applied at the same time as Iris Dunleavy, a woman from Cleveland with terrible waking dreams, but he'd gone over the two applications and chosen the Dunleavy woman, admittedly because hers was the more intriguing story.

So far she had caused nothing but trouble. So far she had refused to listen to him, assaulted the matron, called him terrible names, and driven his favorite patient into outright defiance. Now she was causing his own son to question his authority. She who could not fit into her own society was now destroying his little island colony, breaking the rules that had served as its bedrock. She had searched the recesses of her mad brain devising the schemes of his undoing.

This morning, when he had marched into the dining hall prepared to confront her over her rash and psyche-unraveling kiss, she had completely taken him off guard by meekly acquiescing, agreeing with him for the very first time. Indeed, he had even glimpsed the same look of genuine gratitude in her eyes as once lived in Ambrose Weller's. Her voice had been so gentle, so reasonable.

He gave in. Crouched down, placed his hand over his heart, bowed his head. And surrendered to it. That fantasy he had pushed out of his head so many times. He let it come now. Tears in his eyes, he felt her, naked beneath him. She stared into his eyes and that fire in them wasn't madness or the quest for independence. It was lust, ferocious adoration, worship. For him, for him. He put his nose into the nape of her neck and smelled her, the scent of wild and sweet, like an animal thrashing inside a nest of honeysuckle. The syrup, the musk. *Henry,* she said in his ear, breaking the final boundary between doctor and patient. He shut his eyes tighter, horrified and ecstatic.

A strong wave rode up the shore and soaked his shoes, ending his daydream. He opened his eyes and stood. The water swirled around his feet. His socks were cold and heavy. A mullet jumped a short distance away in the water, animated over something in a fish's world. He sighed and started back home, sand clinging to his wet shoes, his steps heavy. The loggerhead was coming back the other way, retracing her path through sand she had broken on the journey to her nesting place. Somewhere above the high-tide line, her sticky eggs clung together beneath the surface of the sand. In a few weeks, the young turtles inside would begin to crawl out and make their way toward the horizon lights as predators from the air and ground rushed forth to eat them.

The doctor and the turtle approached each other, his shoes shuffling, her massive flippers churning the sand. They stopped and exchanged a long stare, man and beast under tropical moonlight, each with their own burdens. He put his head down and kept walking. A mosquito buzzed and he slapped at his neck.

You cannot do it, can you, Henry? The voice in his mind was utterly defeated. *You cannot let her go.*

29

CLAD IN HER housedress and fox fur slippers, Mary picked her way around the back of the asylum toward the women's wing. She bumped into yucca plants, gasped at the furtive movement of ghost crabs and rodents. Birds called suddenly over her head. The island turned alien at night. A series of bumps and tweets and flutters and slithers that left her breathless with anxiety. Her slippers sank into the sand.

She had extracted directions to Iris Dunleavy's room from her reluctant and bewildered son.

"I'm not going to hurt her, my darling. I'm not even going to talk to her. I just want to see her up close."

And in fact, that was what she did want. To study this beautiful woman she had only seen from afar. The one powerful enough to send her husband into a fit of rage. Mary stumbled on a rock, nearly fell, and then righted herself. It wasn't fair at all. It was hard work keeping herself groomed and sweet-swelling in the middle of an embargo. Every morning she dressed herself with such care and did the very best she could to please her husband, and he'd returned the favor by falling for an especially comely lunatic.

Iris stood at the window. She had removed the mosquito netting and now held the bars, staring out into the night. She'd successfully banished thoughts of Ambrose, at least for the time being, but now her anxiety centered on the boy. A day had passed since she'd asked him to help her escape. Surely he would come and give his answer that night. Had she made her story convincing enough? Every word had been the truth. Did he know that? And even if he did, was she asking too much of him? Perhaps she was. But what else could she do? Without the boy, escape seemed impossible. All hope lost. She closed her eyes and offered a brief prayer to the God she believed in only in hours of need. When she opened her eyes again, she was staring into the face of Mary Cowell, the doctor's wife.

Iris gasped.

Mary Cowell screamed and vanished.

30

THE PRESSURE ON Wendell felt unbearable. He could see Iris Dunleavy's eyes following him. She wanted an answer and this he could not give, so torn was he between his father's authority and his innate sense of justice. The pressure had kept him from sleeping yet another night and invited in that insidious demon — the urge to find relief in private-fondling. This he fought off most of the morning, but by noon he could bear it no longer and he sadly acquiesced to the calling, setting off, heavy-hearted, for the docks. He tried not to look at the maniacs he passed in the courtyard — his brothers and sisters in lunacy.

Bernard was in an especially evil-tempered mood and would not let him take the canoe.

"Why do you do this every time?" Wendell asked.

"Because I am the dock guard and I have the responsibility to watch the boats. And you are not the owner of this boat!"

"The chef gave me permission. Like he does every single day!"

"You don't have a note!"

"I had a note yesterday! The chef will not write me a note every single day!" Wendell's groin ached maddeningly. Reason deserted him. "Let me at that goddamn canoe or I swear I'll punch you! I'm a madman, can't you see?"

Bernard looked shocked. He recovered, placed one great paw on Wendell's chest, and pushed him down in the sand. "You think you can swear at me, do you, because your father's the superintendent? You little bastard."

Wendell picked himself up, his face quite hot, on the verge of just giving up and punching Bernard because he didn't want to live anymore. Wendell cocked a trembling fist. The canoe bobbed tauntingly in the distance. Bernard crossed his arms and waited.

Wendell lowered his fist. Almost tearful with frustration and shame, he turned around and trudged off to find the chef. He spotted him in the surf, up to his knees in water, fishing. And what a day he was having. His pole was bent double from the weight of some invisible beast struggling under the sea. He was covered with sweat, knees buckling from the effort. Wendell waded out in the water to help him, splashing to the scene of battle and reaching down into the water. He felt something tug at his right hand and then break loose. Odd, he thought, staring down, why the water was turning red. He pulled his hand out of the water. All his fingers were missing on his right hand, leaving bloody nubs in their place that shot out fountains of blood. Only his thumb remained, sole survivor, pale in the sunlight.

Wendell had never heard the chef scream. It was a sound both girlish and shrill, and Wendell would have laughed had he not been staring down at the bloody water, where two of his fingers circled in the froth of an eddy. The chef grabbed him and hauled him to the beach, screaming at the top of his lungs. Wendell's head spun and great patches of darkness swirled in front of his eyes. He fell down in a dead faint in the hot sand as the chef's screams died in his ears, and he plunged into a sweet, brief darkness that smelled of Penelope.

When he came to, his father and the useless priest were on each side of him, leaning over close. He tried to say it didn't hurt, not at all, but his eyelids were growing heavy again, and the sun was going down prematurely, but even though he had lost a lot of blood, it had not washed out the last of his curiosity. With Father

Byrnes so near, Wendell couldn't help but solve a mystery with his last strength. Just before he slid into another warm darkness, he reached up and pressed his good hand against the priest's chest.

Wendell drew in his breath. His jaw fell open.

Under his hand he felt the outline of the melted cross. Evidence of miracles. Evidence of God. Half of his right was missing but his left was so much more enlightened. Wendell smiled and let the sun go down.

They carried the boy into the infirmary, where he regained consciousness just long enough to call weakly for the chef and to whisper the secret of the lamb in his ear. "He needs his milk," Wendell said, and passed out again.

The chef went back to the kitchen, his stomach hurting, but was soothed by thoughts of the lamb. The chef, who had spent his own boyhood on a rice plantation in southern Georgia, had been taught that a rich meal equals happiness, no matter what the circumstances. And he remembered all those meals. The slaughtered hog in the wintertime just when his ribs were showing. The rabbit he'd managed to kill with a rock and then eaten raw in secret, without sharing any of it. The joy and the shame. For nothing seemed so bad to him when the gullet was full. Cakes, pies, vittles, fried chicken, broiled squirrel, found mushrooms, ripe berries. Sweet potatoes. Dandelion leaves stuffed dirty into the mouth. Bread with weevils in it. It all meant life was bearable. And now the lamb was recoverable after all.

He sharpened the ax against a block of limestone, his mood gradually improving despite the shock his system had taken. He opened the cookbook to the chapter on lamb stew and busied himself in the cupboards, taking down spices. Finally he took the ax and went to the boat dock, where Bernard kindly asked about the condition of the boy.

"He'll live, I suppose," said the chef, and put the ax in the canoe and set off through the pass and into the sound on the other side, rowing toward the red mangroves, where the boy had directed him.

The fence was right where he said it would be, between two midden mounds. The chef straddled the fence and stepped inside the enclosure, looking with astonishment on the careful craftsmanship of the structure, how delicately the saplings fit together. The lamb, who had been fast asleep in the grass, rose and tottered over to the chef, reared up, and placed his hooves on his thighs, gazing up at him. The chef stared down at him. The lamb blinked his dark eyes and nosed at the chef's pockets, looking for his bottle.

That night, the dining hall filled slowly with the patients, some walking with purpose and others being led, some with bright eyes, some with vacant eyes, and yet they shared a common hunger with the sane. They took their seats and ate an offering of summer watermelon as an appetizer. Then the main dish was served. And though it was garnished with parsley and seasoned with the perfect blend of spices, and even was accompanied by fresh bread and some sea grape jelly the chef had plundered from the back of the cupboard, the men and women sighed collectively.

Chicken again.

31

WENDELL AWOKE IN the infirmary in a laudanum haze, the sun streaking in. His mother had cried herself to sleep with her head on his chest and now snored peacefully in the morning light. The laudanum had put him in a happy place, and his mother's head felt like the weight of a tabby cat, not ideal but tolerable. He stroked her hair with his good hand. He looked out the window, saw a palm tree moving, and this tree, such an ordinary sight, filled him with appreciation at its exotic wonder, for everything was exotic and everything was new.

He, Wendell, the former lunatic, had been cured by God of his affliction — harshly, that was true, with the severing of his private-fondling fingers — but this same God had, a few moments later, offered proof of His existence and power in the form of the crucifix melted into the chest of the priest. No prayer, no sacrament Father Byrnes had uttered, no blessing he gave, no bread he dispensed, could ever mean so much as the simple fact that the legend was true. Wendell had felt it for himself and now, like his mother's head, the weight of God's authority was tangible and easily borne.

Now he knew what to do for Iris Dunleavy, for, as a new man, risen sane from the bloody sand of an ordinary afternoon, he realized that he needn't follow any rule or law except what he thought might be pleasing to God, and what was pleasing to God was justice, whether it was a lamb spared, or a sane woman freed. Yes, he believed her story. Believed in her sanity, even though that belief came in direct opposition to his father's diagnosis. Wendell's confirmation of God's existence had given him the strength to suppose, for the first time in his life, his father might be wrong.

Mary shifted, groaned. He patted her head, not too hard, because although waking her up would cause her to move her head from his chest, it would also release, in the morning light, a new flood of tears and lamentations.

The vile sea monster could have his hand. He had recovered his soul.

32

AT FIRST IRIS held to her resolve not to let Ambrose interfere with her plans to leave the island. But the kiss was a bee in the house that eluded the swatter, and she could do nothing about it. Although she now only glimpsed Ambrose from afar, it didn't matter. The kiss made the life that she imagined as a free woman sad and empty without him. This was her true suitor, not the plantation owner but the madman, pure of heart and strong and kind. The one who made her feel completely a woman and not an ounce a prisoner or a patient or a lunatic. It was settled in her mind. He would go with her because it was impossible for him not to. One morning in the dining hall she had her chance, quickly darting over to him and whispering the thought into his ear before she was hustled away. His shoulders straightened and he shot her a look of unbridled assent. Now it was only left to tell the boy.

After a few days, when he had healed enough from his terrible accident to finally come to her window and whistle softly to wake her from sleep, she groggily rose, found her robe, and lit the tallow candle on the windowsill so that his features sprang into life. She was surprised to discover in his face a sudden maturity, as though whatever had taken his hand had left wisdom in its place.

"I'm so sorry about your hand," she said.

He nodded. "It feels fine. I'll get along."

She nodded. "You are being very brave about it."

"Not at all. It was God's will."

She looked at him curiously. He'd never mentioned God before. "Does it hurt much?"

"Sometimes, but I am given a spoonful of laudanum and everything is fine again." He looked directly at her. "I've come to a decision. I'm setting you free. Because I think you are sane, that somehow there has been a mistake, somewhere. My father is a wise man, but he doesn't know you like I do."

"Thank you, Wendell, I am truly so grateful. But there is someone I want to bring with me to freedom."

"Who?"

"Ambrose."

"Ambrose!" He sucked in his breath. "You're not serious. That man is crazy!"

"Don't call him that!" she snapped before she could stop herself. "He's had a recent setback, but he was doing very well before that, and I'm confident it won't happen again. He just needs a woman's affections, a woman's understanding. I can take care of him."

Wendell shook his head slowly. "No, no, no. I have seen four strong men unable to hold him down. That man could hurt you. He could hurt himself. He belongs here."

"He does not! He belongs with me. Now either it's the two of us or nothing."

Wendell lifted his bandaged hand and touched his head. Winced when it made contact. Lowered it again. "I'm sorry. I can't do that. He is crazy, and if you think you can cure him, then you are crazy too."

"You insolent boy! You are just like your father!"

She picked up the tallow candle and threw it at the wall. It went out and rolled to the floor, leaving the argument lit only by the stars and the moon. Wendell's eyes went dark. His breathing slow and steady.

"I'm sorry," he said, and was gone.

33

THE DOCTOR OPENED his eyes at some hour of night when the deepest sleep occurs. Those who wake at this hour feel a lonely separation from everyone but night birds and ghost crabs, never imagining the legion of kindred souls scattered in the darkness, who stare at ceilings and pace floors and look out windows and covet and worry and mourn. For a few minutes he simply lay there, his hands clasped over his chest, while Mary remained asleep. He slid out of bed and crept down the dark hallway. Wendell's door was open a crack. The doctor pushed on it gently. His son was still asleep, on his back, his hands — or what was left of his hands — crossed upon his chest. After the accident, Mary had screamed at him that he had been to blame.

"If you only paid attention to him more, maybe he wouldn't always be keeping company with the chef! He wouldn't have been out there at all!"

She'd said other things, strange and terrible things.

"And maybe God was punishing you through your son!"

"Punishing me? For what?"

"You know what!"

"I don't know what!"

"Liar!"

He had finally had to silence her with a spoonful of laudanum, and her accusations had grown slower and sleepier until finally she had sprawled out on the bed, fast asleep, arms and legs akimbo. What Mary didn't know was that the doctor felt truly, achingly guilty for Wendell's injury. That night on the beach, meant to be his single indulgence of the imagined company of Iris Dunleavy — the woman, not the patient — had manifested itself over and over, each time more real, more passionate, more hopeless to the tormented doctor. In fact, at the very moment the sea monster had swum up to take Wendell's hand, Dr. Cowell had been staring out the window of his office into a scenery that did not involve sky or sea or cormorants or unguarded son, but lunatic and bed sheets and candlelight and flesh and mouth and breasts beneath his hands. And when the chef's high girlish scream had roused him from his fantasy, he looked down and saw the horrific scene unfolding: the blood, the crowd, Wendell's head thrown back.

Now, in the boy's room, the doctor reached out and tentatively stroked his face, content as a doctor to find it warm but not hot, wistful as a father just to touch it. He crept back out of the room, but instead of returning to his sleeping wife, he put on his clothes and set off for his office. Once there, he lit the oil lamp, retrieved Iris's file, opened it, and began to read the transcripts of her trial. What if, he asked himself now, the woman was telling the truth? What if these terrible things had occurred? And what if these words before him were not proof of a plantation wife's madness, but of a plantation master's crimes?

What if?

Could such a horror be true? He imagined Iris sitting shackled, testifying to a courtroom full of men. Imagined her straight shoulders and her steady gaze. Those hazel, angry eyes. The pale hands, clenched.

What if they were all wrong? Every man in this story?

And what if he, Henry Cowell, had also been wrong? Wrong

about her, about women, about madness, about everything? All his life he had lived in fear of being wrong. And now the wrongness felt strangely liberating.

If he was wrong, he could love her.

He put up her file and retrieved his thesis from the middle drawer. Put the thesis on top of her file. The paper that had brought him fame and wealth and respect. An idea entered his head, so wrong, so destructive, so insane that it grew immediately, breathed into itself, nursed itself, raised itself from a cub to a beast in the blink of an eye. And Dr. Henry Cowell felt, for the first time in many years, the joy of madness, not of the seized and the broken and the haunted, but of a boy, that demented voice that tells him to jump in a river or build a fort out of sticks or attempt to follow a bear to its cave. That madness — extinguished by learning and time and responsibility and a shrill voice in his ear night after night — had returned.

He knelt in the sand, shaking with excitement. The breeze was so quiet that the papers of his thesis, which lay in front of him, didn't flutter. Next to the doctor was an empty Mason jar he'd pilfered from the kitchen.

The waves pounded before him. Fish jumped in the distance. A rustle in the sedge behind him turned out to be a raccoon darting out of sight. This was the hour of furtive creatures. When rules slept and even gravity loosened its hold.

He took out a match, struck it, and held it to the corner of the thesis. The dry parchment had made for an excellent career but now made even better tinder — the flames spread across it, a perfect yellow, a sun whose path could not be shaken.

34

DR. COWELL LOOKED in the mirror and straightened his cravat. His eyes were red from lack of sleep and the smoke from the fire. He combed his wiry hair, which was less manageable than usual today. He frowned, went to a small cabinet, and hunted through his wife's toiletry items until he found her macassar dressing. He scooped out a small amount and applied it to his hair. He ran the comb through it and studied himself in the mirror. His hair looked a bit greasy, but at least it seemed smoother.

Mary was slumped in the recliner, drinking some tea, and he gave her a kiss on the cheek before walking out the door. Next to the cottage was a small dagger plant. From behind this dagger plant he drew out the Mason jar, which was filled with the ashes of his thesis, and a little sand. Had Eleanor Beacon been nearby, she would have noted that his sacrifice did not just involve himself but that innumerable microscopic things had died in the inferno. He shook his head. Why was he thinking like a crazy person? He held the jar up to the light and admired the contents. What a perfect gift for Iris. So eloquent, so sacrificial. So elemental. Sand, ashes, passion. The very basic gear in the kit bag of the universe.

Iris was his second-to-last appointment of the day. As the hour of the fateful conference drew near, time began to crawl. Finally came the hour of their meeting, and he opened the office door and ushered in Mrs. Dunleavy, who looked drawn and pale. He gestured to her chair, took his own, and began to speak, halt-ingly, as she stared past him. He had, perhaps, not listened to her closely enough, or approached her with an open mind. He was stammering, not making any sense, when out of nowhere she burst into tears.

He stopped, astonished. His heart began to pound; he was thrown into confusion. He knew better than to think his words had caused her sorrow. He was simply in the room, drawing the same air that she drew upon to fuel her wracking sobs.

"Wait, now," he said. "Whatever is the matter?"

She lifted her head, gathered herself for a moment, and shot him a look of pure hatred. "I'm trapped here. I thought I could leave but I cannot!"

"But wait, what makes you say that?"

"You wouldn't understand." She wiped her eyes.

"Yes, I would. You would be surprised, Mrs. Dunleavy, at how well I understand you."

He reached down next to his feet toward the Mason jar filled with ashes, but she began to cry again, burying her face in her hands, compelling him to leave his desk and kneel by her chair.

"Mrs. Dunleavy . . . Iris . . . ," he said, touching her shoulder.

Her hand shot out and pushed him away. The tears in her eyes had turned them bright green. "Leave me alone!" she cried. She jumped from her chair and rushed from the room, slamming the door behind her.

He stared after her, wounded. He was not sure whether it was his touch or the invocation of her first name that had caused her violent reaction. Numbly he picked up the jar full of ashes, but it slipped from his hand and broke on the floor. Ashes and sand scattered. He tried to pick up the broken glass but he punc-tured his finger and it began to bleed. He found a sheet of paper, gathered the catastrophe — paper, ashes, sand, and blood — and deposited it in the bottom drawer of his desk, overcome with grief.

That paper had been his life. Somehow, he'd thought it made him important, as though God could pick him out of a crowd. Now he had no paper anymore. He had nothing. He was nothing. And he was collapsing into something very tiny, some creature Eleanor Beacon would pity. The loneliness. The joylessness of his life, of his routine. Iris Dunleavy thought she was trapped. He was trapped. And it had been quite tolerable before she'd come along, but now everything seemed so much worse in the light of knowing her and not knowing her. Things that had merely caused him unrest now tormented him outright. What he had never been, what he could never become.

By the time his last appointment of the day came in, he was struggling not to weep.

The blind man fumbled for his chair. Dr. Cowell dabbed at his eyes and grasped at the threads that defined himself. He steadied his voice and asked the man how he was, which was usually all it took to get him to talk about the woman who haunted him, whose scent could still be found everywhere, even among the blooming marlberry of the island, breaking through salt spray and summer watermelon and the rotting carcasses of fish left after a storm or the bracing freshness of lemon juice.

As the man launched into the latest variation of his lovelorn tale, the doctor was astonished to find himself not just listening to his words, but moved by them. He could feel the man's pain so exquisitely that his hand rose to his own heart, and he almost had to tell the man to stop, he could not bear it anymore, this tale that circled in on itself, that had no ending but another sad beginning every dark morning when the sun streamed in his window and warmed the blind man's face, and he awoke to the odor of his solitude. The doctor bit his lip. He was coming apart, this man moved him so, and if he didn't stop himself he would go through this building, room by room, in his mind, and feel the things all of the people within them felt. These doomed souls, these trapped men and women.

When the appointment was over, the doctor staggered out of the building, drained and broken. All the patients were back in their rooms, preparing for dinner, and but for a few wanderers here — asylum staff, or fishermen, or the tanned old man who lingered by the pier with no discernible business at all — the beach was largely empty. The sun low in the sky. A breeze against his face. He stepped out in the sand, felt its peculiar gravity as he slogged toward the dock, his shadow out behind him. Looking back, he found his shadow was impossibly thin and tall, the legs high as palm trees. He felt so very strange. His feet were too heavy. He thought Sunday was a wolf. He was a mote in a dusty universe. He wanted to swallow smooth, tiny objects like mourning rings and stones. And what about pigeons? What if each pigeon actually had a name and no one ever said it?

He shook his head, trying to will himself back into the man he'd been last week.

He trudged to the end of the dock and sat down. There, his feet dangling over the water, he began to weep. His aching over the woman was attached to the pain of other things, things too large and vague and smoky to even be described. Through his tearstained eyes, he saw the sun, larger and rounder and more golden than it had ever been, sitting just a few feet above the horizon line of the sea, throwing down a white gleaming path all the way to his feet. So narrow and defined was that sparkling path, made of shadows and water and dying light, that he felt he could walk upon it, all the way to something yellow and hot enough to burn away his misery.

Stop it, you fool, he told himself, not like a command but in the same broken voice he'd heard so often, from so many.

When Dr. Cowell did not arrive at the supper table, Wendell was dispatched to look for him. He found the door of his office unlocked but the room empty. Looking out the window and scanning the beach, he saw, to his surprise, someone the approximate size and shape of his father sitting alone at the end of the dock.

He went out to the sand to investigate, taking off his shoes to make his chore more pleasurable by the inclusion of cool sand against his feet. He dropped the shoes and left them behind, spreading the fingers of his good hand to the breeze. He still felt the fingers of his right hand too, and if he did not lift his bandaged hand and see the stump for himself, he would have believed those phantom digits were still whole and unhurt and capable of grabbing a cookie or a starfish.

He stepped onto the dock and began the long walk out to his father, stretching his good hand out to admire its shadow, its long reach onto the calm, flat water. Ever since the accident he had felt giddy with the presence of God and had reveled in his restored sanity. The terrible curse removed in the harshest and yet the fairest way, a way for which only God could be forgiven. As he approached his father, he realized with shock that the older man was weeping.

He had never seen his father in such a state before. He stopped behind him, his right knee hovering close to his father's left shoulder, wondering what to do. The answer came to him in a tingle that rushed down his body like the light across the water. He had been carrying the secret within him since that miraculous day he had thrust up his hand and felt the gold of a melted cross in the chest of the priest.

Wendell knelt down next to his weeping father and whispered the precious story into his ear.

The doctor said nothing, his shoulders steadying as he listened. Wendell felt exhilarated at the thought that his story had dried his father's tears. But then the doctor turned his red eyes to his son.

"Wendell," he said, his voice hard and even, "that's just a silly legend. You were delirious. Of course you thought you felt a cross."

Wendell stared at his father. All the good feeling drained from him. His missing fingers ached again. He turned and ran back down the dock, up the beach, past his shoes, as the sun slid into the sea.

35

ALL WAS LOST. Iris knew she couldn't leave Ambrose here on this island. Thus, she would be trapped here indefinitely with the man she loved, barred from speaking to him. Their orchard had burned to the ground. The apples were scorched and the trees blackened.

In the afternoon she forced herself to indulge in a few minutes of swimming, so sick was she of crying in her room. She had just waded into the warm water with the others, in her bathing gown, shuffling her feet so as to warn the stingrays, when she heard a splash behind her. Such an indelicate entry into the water could only come from a boy or a colt. She turned around. Wendell's pants were soaked to the knees. His eyes were cold and his mouth was set.

"I will help you escape," he said. "Both of you."

36

SHE DIDN'T KNOW what had happened to change the boy's mind, nor did she want to know. The answer had been given. And now it was late at night and he stood before the bars of her window as they talked about the plan in whispers.

"We don't have any money," she said.

"I don't have any money either."

"Can you steal us a bag of sugar? That's worth at least forty dollars, now that the embargo is on."

"Sugar is very precious to the chef. But I'll try." He paused. "I could also try to steal a bottle of laudanum."

"Why would we need that?"

"For Ambrose. In case he has a spell."

"He doesn't need laudanum anymore," she said, noticing the hard tone in her voice and correcting it. "I'll take care of him."

Wendell looked uncertain but nodded.

"Are you going to steal the keys to our room?" she asked.

He shook his head. "That would be impossible. Only two people have copies of those keys. The matron and the head guard. They keep them on their person at all times. There's only one way for you to escape." His voice had a confidence she found reassuring. "They have room check every night at eleven o'clock. And there are guards at all hours in both wings. The only possible way of escape is to steal away after dinner, instead of going back to the rooms."

"But where would we go?"

"To my father's office."

She raised her eyebrows. "I don't understand."

"I have a key. Father gave me one because he's forever sending me to the office to fetch things for him. I will tell the nurse on the women's wing that Father has called you to his office after dinner."

"What for?"

"It has been quite a while, but he will go through periods when he schedules sessions at night. Usually when my mother is being especially difficult."

"I see."

"And I will find a guard in the men's wing and pretend that my father has called Ambrose. You will both go to his office and wait there. When the time is right you can make your escape."

"I'm afraid of the forest. The alligators and the snakes."

"You won't be going that way. You'll go by sea. They won't think to look by sea until it's too late."

"By sea? How?"

"You'll take the chef's canoe. He'll be angry, but I'll help him build a new one. My father always said we were going to build a canoe together, but we never did."

"Isn't there a guard at the dock all night long?"

"Bernard. He's a very mean man, but I know he has one weakness."

"And what is that?"

Wendell smiled for a moment, then the smile faded, replaced by his characteristic intensity.

"Never mind. I'll take care of him."

She sensed his anxiety but dared not investigate. She herself was shivering in fear and anticipation. She was escaping an island the way she'd entered into marriage — completely bewildered, unsure of the way.

Iris felt suddenly sorry to be leaving him. "You're the only friend I made here, besides Ambrose." She reached through the bars and touched his hand. "I'll write you from Virginia."

He didn't answer for a moment. "Do they have boys there?" he asked.

"Yes. Many boys."

"I wonder if I'm ever going to get off this island."

"You will," she said, her heart breaking for him.

She remembered something. "Wendell, can you bring me a pen and a piece of paper?" she asked.

Wendell crept through the courtyard, carefully holding the folded note Iris had written to her lover in his good hand. To-morrow night the moon would be full. Full moons meant very low tides, and good shelling. His grandmother, who died when he was seven, believed there was a phase of the moon for just about anything: birthing a baby, curing a drunk, digging a grave, planting a garden. Perhaps there was even a phase of the moon for helping lunatics escape. If so, he imagined a night with no moon would be optimal. Of course, the woman wouldn't wait. He could see that on her face. He'd agreed to help the soldier es-cape, out of anger toward his father, but now that he had commit-ted to the plot, he felt an ominous dread that had grown athletic, flip-flopping in his stomach, pounding in his head, and making his phantom fingers throb all at the same time.

In this gloomy state, he turned off the path back to the cottage and took another path instead, one that wound around behind the citrus grove and ended at the tiny cemetery. He entered and stood over Penelope's grave. The shells looked especially pretty in the moonlight. A single weed grew out of the bare circle at the center of the grave. He pulled the weed and smoothed the dirt. He could pretend that what Iris thought was true — that love could conquer all, and lunatics could be healed simply by the fact that someone wished it so. But he had seen too much and had lived too long to believe it in his heart.

He should just tell her no. But the plan was very big now. He was sinking into it, drowning, as though his pockets were full of stones.

37

HE MISSED THE woman, missed her more than blue could cover. He longed for the contours of her face among the shadows of palms. He imagined the girl she used to be. How he loved that girl. Once she had found a speckled egg in the woods and believed she could hatch it with the warmth of her body. Believed there was life inside. Believed, night after night, cradling it under her arm, that a creature was sleeping inside, growing, yellow eyes half-open. And when the egg burst one night and spilled its sour soup, it did not spoil her heart for other eggs waiting out there in the woods.

The story reminded him of his own boyhood. Knotted shoe-laces and love of snakes and candy. Lemonade on a Saturday. Block letters, pulled-off scabs, bitten-off honeysuckle tubers. Straight pew in a small church, the boredom of mid-sermon. Cow manure, bee pollen, acrobatics of blown dandelion seeds, underside of toadstools, knuckle blood, frog eyes blinking. The only war he knew then was the one he waged against bees, throwing rocks at their hives just to feel the ecstasy of adrenaline as he ran away through Johnson grass, chilly with sweet terror. Tolerable grief. A lizard kept in a jar that died of his fumbling boy-care. Love so elementary it could be drawn on a tablet with the blunt edge of a pencil.

Ambrose didn't see the boy coming toward him. When he finally looked up, there he was, in a pair of tow-cloth pants that were dirty at the knees, blond hair uncombed, right hand bandaged, left hand clutching a folded piece of paper, which he handed over silently. Ambrose had never seen what his name looked like as she wrote it, and he lingered over the pleasure of the sight. One of the legs of the *A* was longer than the other, hobbled like a veteran, but the letters that came behind it were perfect and full. His eyes traveled over the rest of the letter, forgetting their shape now as he was pulled headfirst into their meaning. He drew in his breath. The plan was insane, and yet so tempting his hands shook, and in this state of weakness the memory saw its moment and attacked him full on.

Seth was tied to the post. Hair damp with sweat. The sun straight up overhead. Grave dug in the near distance.

Ambrose shook his head. *No.*

Yes, said the sergeant. *You're the one who let him leave.*

No, sir, I can't. I can't.

Time slowing down, warping, wandering. Seth shivered against the post. A body born from a winter march, pants loose on the waist, vocal cords standing out in his throat. Someone tied a handkerchief over his eyes.

Wooden coffin. Smell of smoke. Blue, blue, blue. Sunlight moved in waves. Snort of a mule. Shadow of the handkerchief, fluttering like a bird. First thump of a red drum.

The provost marshal read the charges. Hot sun, baked ground. Bored dog yawning in the shade. Camp pastor, who always smelled of spring water, holding a Bible and murmuring into Seth's ear what Ambrose imagined was a tale of God's forgiveness and loss, that deserters were not yellow in heaven but blue, color of divine and eternal circling, and do you, Seth Holden, have anything to confess?

Handkerchief slipping a bit when he cocked his head, uniform hanging on him like a sack. Ambrose could only stare at him in the space of time allotted, could feel his love for the shy boy, crafted and real and wild, the texture of a nest. That's all he had left from this war. No nerves to calm his shaking hands. No fire left in his belly. No God to hear his prayers. Take away the love and he would have been translucent, a ghost.

Seth's body straightened as the pastor stepped away. A gesture made toward bravery that only looked like it was: a boy trying to act the man. How old could he be? Sixteen? Seventeen?

The sergeant's voice was in his ear. *Shoot him.*

I can't, sir.

Yes, you can.

He put the gun to his shoulder.

He's my friend, sir.

The sergeant lifted his own gun, placed it just behind Ambrose's ear.

Shoot him, or I'll shoot you.

The sergeant cocked the trigger. Seth's head weaved back and forth as though following the flight of a feather.

Ambrose had to calm his mind. Calm it. Blue of the sky, blue of an angel's wings on a cold day in heaven, blue of a streak down the Roman nose of a Sioux Indian. War-paint blue, ceramic blue, Zouave blue, rainbow blue. Blue as a fishing hole, blue as a smile in December, blue as a bruise, as a robin's egg as an Easter ribbon as the center of heaven as a voice in the dark as eternal reckoning—*NO!* Ambrose screamed as the gun went off.

Iris's note fell out of his hand. The wind took it in the direction of the sea.

Wendell looked stunned. "No?"

"No! No no no no no!"

38

AFTER A SERIES of whispered messages brought back and forth by the boy, Iris and Ambrose met in the only place they could — on the shore, under open sunlight. They would have perhaps a few minutes before a guard came over to separate them, for they were under doctor's orders not to speak.

"You can't say no."

"I can't go with you, Iris. I'm not well. I can't sleep. I can't forget."

"I can take care of you. I can heal you." Out of the corner of her eye, Iris saw a guard making his way toward them, lazily walking in the sun.

"I'll go mad," Ambrose said.

"No, you won't. I won't let you."

She could not sleep that night. She wouldn't allow herself to think about what she was going to do with Ambrose, or where the two of them could possibly find a life together. And so she simply concentrated on the plan. The hour of stealth and escape. The matron had sprung another surprise inspection earlier that night, had taunted her and torn her bed sheets off and made her turn the framed still life just so, and just so again, so it was in its original position, no straighter for all the trouble.

Iris didn't care. The matron was just a character in a story that would have its ending tomorrow night, together with the guards and the lunatics and the birds and the hermit crabs. The only people she would remember from this time would be Ambrose and the boy. Everything else would wash away.

"Why are you smiling?" the matron demanded. She took the pillow from her bed and threw it on the floor. "Fluff that pillow. You're a swine. You have no manners. You are worse than a dog."

Wendell came by later that night. He was subdued and seemed troubled, but she dared not ask him about it, afraid she would tilt some delicate balance inside him and cause him to change his mind. She wondered what would happen to him when his father realized he was part of the plot but didn't allow herself to dwell upon it. She'd had no choice but to use the boy. And it was all for good, wasn't it? She and Ambrose didn't belong here. They belonged in Virginia, among whatever sane lovers were left in that land.

"My father has a clock in his office," Wendell said. "Leave the office at exactly ten o'clock. Make sure no one sees you. By then, the doors to both the wings will be locked for the night, but the front door will be unlocked. Keep near the shadows. Make your way to the dock."

"I understand."

"Good luck." He looked somber. The moon swelled behind his left ear. His shirt pocket bulged with something. Probably a shell.

"You don't have to sound as though you were at a funeral," she said. "We won't be caught." As she said these words, she tried to believe them herself.

He lowered his eyes. "That's not what I'm worried about."

Wendell trudged away from Iris's window. The air was calm and clear, his parents were fast asleep, and the night was his alone. He could hunt for shells along the beach by the light of the full and glowing moon. Build a sand castle right at the edge of the water so he could watch the waves destroy it. Play among the citrus orchards. But he felt no desire to play tonight, and a midnight swim was out of the question. He had not dared to go back into the water since the day he'd lost his fingers.

The heaviness in his chest precluded any kind of activity but worry and regret. Tomorrow night the lovers would flee, and he would help them. The path was set and the woman's will indomitable. He held his hand up to the pouring moonlight and wondered what the stump would look like when the bandages came off. He decided he would like to wear a hook, like a pirate. He debated, briefly, if this hook could be worn to bed at night, but the reverie vanished as his dark thoughts intruded again, and he set off for the cottage because there was nowhere else to go.

Because the hour was so late and he was certain his parents were asleep, he did not crawl through the window of the bedroom as was his custom but quietly turned the key in the lock of the front door and let it swing open soundlessly, closing it just as quietly behind him.

He tiptoed in the direction of his room, rounded a corner, and found his father slumped in his favorite yellow chair, staring off into space, lost in some climate of his own. Wendell froze, but the spell was broken; his father had seen his shadow and heard his breathing and looked up at him with the vaguely embarrassed look on his face that people have when they are intruded upon in the midst of deep thought, as though the images in their mind might be floating around the room in plain sight.

Father and son watched each other in the shared space of the living room. Something had to be said, even some pleasantry, in order for the son to pass. He had barely spoken a word to his father since he'd rejected his miracle on the dock, and even now, even with the older man looking so uncertain and awkward, he could not find it in himself to forgive him. Anger hurt his heart and made his missing fingers throb.

"What were you doing outside at this hour of the night?" his father asked.

"Looking for shells." Wendell still felt too resentful to bother coming up with an energetic lie.

"Ah. It's a full moon tonight. That's good for shelling, isn't it?"

"At low tide."

Wendell began to walk in the direction of his room.

"Wendell?"

He stopped. "Yes?"

"Perhaps you and I could look for shells tomorrow."

Wendell's face flushed and his heart raced with anger. How many times had he asked his father to go shelling? *No, Father,* he wanted to say. *Tomorrow I am helping two of your lunatics escape the island.* Instead he let his voice go flat. "I have enough shells, Father. Good night." He squared his shoulders and stalked to his bedroom, closing the door behind him. Felt the tears coming. Tried to wipe them away with fingers that were no longer there.

The doctor watched his son leave the room. *Good job, Henry,* said a voice in his head that was usually kinder. *You've done it again. He was trying to make you feel better, out there on the dock, and you reacted from your own bitterness and rejection. You killed his miracle because your own didn't come to pass.*

Why didn't you apologize, then, just now? How difficult could it be?

He felt so foolish trying to talk to Wendell, stammering around, afraid that by being too direct he would somehow earn his scorn. Boys liked a certain amount of things to go unsaid. Or so he remembered.

He felt alone. Mary wasn't talking to him either. Evidently he'd offended her as well.

"What is it?" he'd asked her, finally. "What did I do?"

"Nothing, Henry. You never do anything. You are perfect and I am just your old, fat wife."

She was already asleep in the other room. He'd given her a spoonful of laudanum as a peace offering. He had no idea what to offer his son. His chair creaked when he stood up, and the sound depressed him. He had a flash of Iris, and that depressed him. He blew out the tallow candles by his chair, and the new darkness depressed him. Slowly, sadly, he made his way to his room.

39

DAWN BROKE SOFT and clean on that island of shell and marl and current. It was a day like any other, one more day in a season when marking the days was difficult, since the balminess was resolute and the birds were attuned to the tides, the tides to the moon, and the moon to the lunatics, under their crazy spell, waxing and waning in accordance with the fluctuations of their madness and the depth of their passions. A group of terns had gathered at the edge of a calm sea, and a single raccoon, caught after daylight, skittered out of the dune vegetation and into the forest, leaving behind a loggerhead nest full of ruined eggs, shells broken and half-formed turtles spilling out in the sand. Morning glories opened on the dunes. A fisherman tossed out his line. A wet anhinga sat on the beach, drying out its wings. In the mangrove swamps, an alligator surfaced, a lizard jumped for a branch and missed, and a lamb woke up crying for his mother.

The blind man could not see his room fill with light, but the rising heat released the odors of the island, even the ones that existed only in his mind. The smell of the woman who haunted him came through the bars of his windows. The bullet had damaged one of his tear ducts, so that it leaked at inopportune moments, and evidently it had cried in his sleep, cried over an unremarkable dream, and now his face was sticky to the touch.

Morning arrived as it always did for the old woman who refused to be a widow. She turned on the bed and kissed her husband on the cheek, then smoothed back his white hair. He mumbled something. A few more kisses would bring him to life. Her imagination was so perfect that the form his body made under the sheet was a faithful replication, and she kept the rose from the top of his coffin and threw the rest of his funeral away.

Dr. Cowell awoke next to Mary. He did not want to get up. Doctor, father, husband, dreamer. He had failed at everything. For the first time in many years, he was not sure how to begin the day. Where he belonged in it. He was heartbroken and destroyed. His boy wasn't talking to him and neither was his wife.

Iris had slept fitfully, a rhythm that recalled the haystack and meadow sleep of her nights as a fugitive, when something as simple as a drop of dew forming on the face or a star going out in the back of the universe could trigger a sudden waking. By the time the light came in she'd been up for hours, pacing her room. What if something terrible happened? What if they were caught, or lost at sea?

She chose the same dress she'd worn when she arrived on the island. She had washed it in her basin several times, so that it had lost the scent of doomed cattle. She would worry about other clothes later. The bag of sugar would fetch money for food and shelter. She would have time for vanity when other needs were filled.

Ambrose was running out of blue. Blue tears, blue windmill in a Dutch painting, blue teacup, old blue horse in an open field. He grabbed the bars and soaked in the blue sky, all of it, drinking in the blue like his last drink, he gulped and gulped and gulped. He did not know if he would make it, but he knew his victory or failure started from within, and he could not think of Seth anymore, could not think of what he'd done to his friend; he had to go forward, forget, forget, the sky hurt his eyes, he shut them tight, face pressed to the bars, *I love you I love you I love you.*

The doctor's last patient came in at midafternoon. The man had terrible fears that his penis would fall off in his sleep; that all his math schooling had been off by one digit and everything was subsequently wrong, including the time of day; that he had accidentally buried his mother when she was not quite dead; that the staff urinated in his cucumber soup. He was afraid of certain sounds. He was afraid of wading in the ocean, sure that the seaweed would come alive. He was afraid that all the spiders he had killed in his life had joined forces and were waiting for him behind a tree. He knew these fears were delusional, and yet the feeling was so real and so insistent. His feelings were stronger than his thoughts. That was the problem . . . The man looked over at something on the doctor's desk and gasped. "Where did you get that?" He pointed at a spiral shell with brown checkered marks.

"I found it on the beach. It's odd, isn't it?"

"Don't you know what that is? That's a junonia! A rarity! I've only seen one in my life!" The man's eyes filled with light, and all the insanity went away for an instant, leaving him with the face of a boy.

"It's special?" the doctor asked.

"Indeed!"

After the man had left, Dr. Cowell studied the prize. Now he had a gift for his son that no one else could offer him. He took out his handkerchief, breathed on the shell, polished it, and held it to the light.

40

IRIS FOLLOWED THE matron out of the dining area and down the hall. Time had passed so slowly, but at last the day was done, and she'd been summoned to the doctor's office. She watched the broad back of the matron, her severe gray curls held back by a hairnet. She would never have to follow the matron again, or listen to her hateful voice, or look at her cross expression. In the coming years, her stout body would be ground up by the hours and days and years, into the gruel of forgetfulness.

The matron sighed deeply at the bottom of the spiral staircase, shooting back a hateful look at Iris, as if it were her fault that the doctor worked on the second floor. With a deep breath she began the slow ascent, gripping the handrail. When she was near the top, Wendell came out of the office and breezed by them down the stairs, saying coolly to the matron: "Father says send her on in."

With that the matron stopped in her tracks and turned around. She breathed heavily from her labor.

"You know the way," she told Iris gruffly.

Ambrose was standing just inside the office, wearing cotton pants, brogans, and a long-sleeved shirt and vest. He'd taken off his jacket and put it across the back of his chair. He held his slouch hat in his hands. His hair was neatly parted and his cheeks were smooth, the angles and shadows of his face so strikingly handsome that she stopped for a moment, shy, admiring. She closed the door behind her.

"Perhaps you should lock it," he said.

She turned the lock in the door and they were safe. They stood a foot apart from each other, unsure what lovers do in a situation like this. Do they kiss, do they touch? Are there whispered things to be said? Neither had any idea, so finally each just took a seat across from the other, their knees nearly touching. Outside the window the sun went down, dragging all manner of shadows down the beach, bending the shadow of a palm tree to intersect with that of a wading crane. They sat in the empty office and watched the sun's trek into the sea's horizon, halving itself, then leaving only its orange tip arranged like a cap over the water, turning from yellow to orange to red.

They lit the oil lamp in the doctor's office so that anyone approaching could see a light inside and assume a session was ongoing. They didn't speak. The diplomas on the walls had gone dark, as had the blueprints of his building.

She remembered something. "Wendell said he would leave the bag of sugar under the desk."

Ambrose crouched down to search for it. "Here it is," he announced. He lifted the sugar onto the desk, bent down again, and picked up a brown bottle.

"What is that?" she asked.

He held the lamp to the bottle so she could read the label by its light.

LAUDANUM.

A pang in her chest, instantly. "I told him we didn't need that!"

Ambrose hesitated. "Maybe we should take it. Just in case."

"You don't need it. You have me. I promise you, I will keep you well and safe."

He set the bottle on the desk and shrugged. "The doctor will probably need it when he discovers we are gone."

Her smile was wasted. It was outside of the penumbra of lamplight and couldn't be seen in the dark.

Wendell kept his eyes downward at the dinner table, afraid his plans would be revealed in his eyes.

"Stop eating so fast, Wendell," Mary said. "A little girl who went to my school when I was a child strangled on a Christmas ham. Her mother had urged her, countless times, to eat more delicately."

His father said nothing. A small object wrapped in a white handkerchief sat next to his glass of water. On any other night, Wendell's curiosity would have been aroused. Now he merely glanced at it before he stood up.

"Where are you going?" Mary asked.

"I have to work some math problems for class tomorrow." Wendell headed to his room. He closed the door and waited, pacing in the fading light. After the sun went down, Wendell opened his window and slid out of it, his bare feet coming down in the sand. He knelt and began to dig with his good hand. His fingertips touched the neck of a bottle and he pulled it out of the ground and knocked the sand off the label. It was the chef's good brandy. He'd stolen it from the kitchen that morning and prayed the chef would not notice. He had tried it once, out of curiosity, and found it terrible. He had no idea why the chef was so enamored of it, but since it played an important role in the plan for the evening, he carried it carefully as he crept down the beach, the liquor turning amber under the moon. Mullet jumped out on a still ocean, dark shapes in the light.

He stopped halfway to the dock and stood there in the tension between carrying out the plan and stopping it, let it pull at him until it hurt too much. He enjoyed this in a grim way, pretending he still had a choice when he had already given the choice away.

He kept walking. The brandy sloshed in the bottle. He could see the dock up ahead, Bernard slouched in a wooden chair, arms folded. How many nights on this island had been just like the others, divided only by a falling star or whether a raccoon darted left or right or which breed of bird started off a quarrel about a fish?

Bernard scowled as Wendell approached him, and the scowl was suddenly familiar, almost comforting. This man had scowled every day of his life and would scowl into eternity, like the sun rising in the east. A boy who does not have the right or the means or the parents to enjoy a constant smile must make do with other constancies.

"What do you want?" Bernard demanded.

"Nothing."

"You can't take the canoe."

"I don't want the canoe." Wendell kept his voice calm. He'd rehearsed this moment and was thrilled, listening to himself, at how dignified and manly he sounded. He'd swear his voice had dropped a half-octave.

"It's my birthday today," Wendell lied.

Bernard crossed his arms. Nothing was interesting about a boy under full moonlight. A pirate? Yes. A woman? Yes. A boy? Bernard stared out at the sea.

"The chef gave me this." Wendell held up the bottle. The light picked up a yellow slant in the center. Bernard turned his head. His eyebrows rose. His nostrils flared slightly.

"Brandy," he whispered.

"It's Peruvian."

"You can't get brandy for your birthday. What are you, thirteen, fourteen? Brandy is a man's drink."

"That's why I came out here to drink it with you. I hear you know your brandy."

"Damn right." Bernard motioned to the ground next to him in the slightest gesture of invitation. "The chef didn't give me anything on my birthday. Here after all this time guarding his damn boat."

Wendell sat down in the sand and unscrewed the bottle cap. He took a deep sniff at it, making a face as its odor traveled up his nose and stung his sinuses, which, after a moment, swelled pleasantly.

"You're not gonna tell your father on me, are you?" Bernard asked.

"Why would I do that?"

Bernard motioned to him. "Go ahead, then. Take the first drink. It's your birthday." A note of friendliness had crept into his voice.

Wendell shrugged and tilted back his head. The brandy slid down his throat and hit his stomach in a golden bitter burst, as though a ship whose cargo was molten gold had just crashed on the rocks inside him. It was uncomfortable at first. But a feeling of wellness soon spread throughout his body. He actually felt the warming of his heart. He took another quick slosh and passed it to Bernard, watching the older man's vocal cords pulse three times as he drank. Bernard finished with gusto. Brandy ran from the corners of his mouth. He wiped his face with his shirtsleeve.

"Goddamn, that's good brandy. Too bad it can't be your birthday every day."

Wendell took the bottle and drank again, a longer, deeper drink. His turmoil at his situation was draining away, replaced by a dull serenity, one that inspired a short, watery laugh.

"What's so funny?" asked Bernard.

"Nothing." He handed the bottle back to him and they passed it back and forth in silence, listening to the birds argue and the mullet jump, comfortable in their silence. The brandy was talking for them, spreading companionship and greater understanding, and what a shame one could not take that bottle and empty it on top of the war, let blue run together with gray so the resulting muddy color would be the uniform of I don't give a damn, and each side would lay down their weapons because in the end, nothing was worth fighting for.

Presently, Bernard hoisted himself out of the chair and sat down heavily in the sand. "My back is going out. I'm getting old. I can still give a woman the what-for though, make no mistake."

"Me, too," said Wendell, who hadn't really been listening.

Bernard held on to the bottle and drank again. "I had a wife, you know. From Suffolk County."

"What happened to her?"

"Run off with another man, the sow."

Wendell nodded. "Sow," he said. He took another drink, held the bottle to the moonlight, and noted, with sadness, its declining contents.

"I was a good husband. She didn't think too much of me 'cause I wasn't a wealthy man. That's why she left me for a dentist. God knows how many healthy teeth he pulled on his way to his four hundred acres. He owned the damn lake. Wouldn't let anybody fish in it."

Something about a man owning a whole lake was funny to Wendell.

"What the hell are you laughing about?" asked Bernard.

"The lake," Wendell gasped. He was holding his stomach, he was laughing so hard. "He owned the lake."

"You know what?" Bernard grabbed the bottle and took another gulp before continuing. "I don't make much at my job, but I've been saving my money for ten years. In another ten I'll have enough for my own plantation. One of those rice plantations like they got in the Carolinas. I'm gonna have fifty slaves. I'm not talking about Negroes either. Frenchmen. I hate the damn French."

"Damn French," said Wendell, laughing again.

Bernard stared at him for a moment, then laughed too. He clapped Wendell on the back and drank some more brandy. He wiped his mouth, looking thoughtful. "Can I ask you something?"

"What?"

"What's it like to get your hand bit off?"

Wendell took the bottle back and drank so it would help him think. He squinted, looking out at the sea where the invisible beast still lived. "It just felt like a good hard tug." He held his bandaged hand up to his face. "I can still feel my fingers."

"Really?" Bernard's voice was full of wonder. "Can I see your hand?"

"What do you mean?" He turned his hand. "It's right here."

"Without the bandages."

Wendell hesitated. He'd been looking the other way when they changed his dressing.

"Please?"

"All right." Wendell began to unwrap the bandage. Bernard leaned forward, watching so intently he lost his balance and would have pitched forward into the sand if he hadn't thrown out his hands to save himself. "Oh, oh," he said, balancing again. "Damn sand is rolling tonight."

Wendell peeled off the last layer of cotton and the two of them stared at his hand, which abruptly ended just above the knuckles, the stumps bruised and swollen over a mass of black stitches. The thumb, though whole, was a sick grayish color.

"My God," Bernard breathed, passing his hand back and forth through the space where the fingers were supposed to be. "Took 'em clean off, didn't the bastard?"

"I don't think he meant any harm. He was just hungry." He started to wrap up his hand again and lost initiative, tossing the bandage aside and lying back in the sand, his eyes turned toward the shifting firmament. "I don't blame that fish or shark or whatever it was."

Bernard drank from the bottle and held it upside down. Two drops of brandy ran out and fell into the coarse fabric of his pants. "You know what you should do? Get an alligator to bite off your foot."

Wendell blinked. The stars moved in the sky like the pieces of a fast, crazy game of chess. The sand was soft as a pillow beneath his head. "Why would I want to do that?"

"So when people ask you how you lost your hand you can have a backup story. I mean, the hand's a good story but people are gonna get tired of it sooner or later."

Wendell considered this. "What do I do when people get tired of the alligator story?"

"Get a loggerhead turtle to bite you in the ass." They burst into laughter, rolling back and forth, thrashing the sand, the sea crawling up a little closer, frothing and retreating. They kept on laughing, but suddenly Wendell staggered to his feet.

"Where are you going?" Bernard asked.

"I've got to feed my lamb." Wendell took a step, lost his balance, and fell in a heap.

The doctor waited until Mary went to bed, then took the precious junonia shell, still wrapped in his handkerchief, to Wendell's room. He stood at the door and knocked twice with a tentative knuckle. His son had run off so fast after dinner that he hadn't had a chance to give him his peace offering, and now the anticipation was killing him. He rapped again, a bit harder.

Finally he turned the knob and opened the door a crack. "Wendell?" he whispered, pushing the door open wider to reveal a darkened room that smelled of dead sea creatures. He searched by moonlight for his matches and lit a tallow candle, moving it around the room, taking in all of Wendell's treasures: the shells and the turtle carapaces, sea anemones, crab claws, arrowheads, dried sedge, alligator teeth, butterfly wings, broken pieces of pottery. A small island's worth of entertainment. Wendell's bed was still perfectly made. The doctor tried the window. It was unlocked and slid open easily.

He stuck his head out the window and saw the footprints in the sand below. He sighed. Wendell had escaped, and he was so desperate for the boy's forgiveness he knew he couldn't sleep without it. He left the room, closing the door gently behind him. He had noticed a breeze when he looked out the window and prayed the midges were not so bad tonight. Just to make sure, he quickly applied a layer of rose oil to his hands and his face and the back of his neck before he stole out the door.

He could not find Wendell outside in the courtyard, nor on the beach — although, had he looked more closely in the direction of the dock, he would have noticed him sprawled face-up in the sand next to the dock guard, the froth of an incoming wave crawling up to his feet.

The doctor went trooping down the beach the other way, calling Wendell's name. How strange the name suddenly sounded when borne by the breeze. He was desperate to find him. He wanted to tell him how he felt when he saw him lying on the beach with blood everywhere, how pale he looked sleeping in the infirmary, his hand bandaged tightly, his fingers stolen by some warm water current. He wanted to tell him he'd gone back outside to the beach to the place where the blood had dried in the sand. He'd covered it up and smoothed it over while sweat and tears ran down his face. Most of all, he wanted to apologize for disparaging the miracle of the priest. *Wendell,* he wanted to say, *I just don't know. I don't know anything.*

He went to the cottage to get the kerosene lantern and set off for the gumbo limbo tree in which he was sure Wendell lurked, wounded and sullen under the full moon. He passed the citrus grove and the short expanse of sawgrass and cacti, moving into the forest of mangrove and buttonwood, down the old Indian trail.

So many things he'd forgotten to tell Wendell came back to him now — how his father took him bird hunting and made him shoot a goose, and how he'd shut his eyes and aimed away from it and pulled the trigger and shot a tree and his father shouted at him, *Shoot the goose! Shoot the goose!* But he never did shoot that goose; he was afraid of his father but dreaded killing something more, and he even secretly named that goose, in defiance. His father, that hard-boiled, scrappy Brit, never thought a whole lot of Henry, considered him whiny and weak and girlish, and had left him his shotgun when he died, as an insult.

He slogged through dried bracken, vines catching around his ankles, grasshoppers fluttering near his knees, a lizard crawling down his arm. He pulled it away by the tail.

When he arrived at the gumbo limbo tree on the old midden mound, he set the lantern down and peered up into the inky blackness of the branches.

"Wendell?" he called softly. "Are you there?"

He reached into his pocket, unwrapped the junonia, and held it up in the flat of his hand. "Look what I've got." He didn't know if Wendell was there. He couldn't tell. Would he have to go up after him? He stood still, as though any sudden movements would send his son skittering up further into the tree or whooshing out into the night like a startled owl.

"Wendell." On the day his boy was born, pink and wrinkly and writhing in the daylight, all twisty and upset, so new to the world, Mary wanted to name him James, after her own father. But he had won. Wendell was his grandfather's name, his gentle Quaker grandfather who had helped establish the York Asylum.

"Wendell." He held the precious shell up high in the air. "Look here, son. For you, Wendell." He kept saying the name out loud in the darkness. Proudly, fiercely. Not his father's son. Not his wife's son. His son.

Wendell. Wendell. Wendell.

41

AT THE APPOINTED hour, Iris and Ambrose left the office and descended the winding stairs, their movements cautious, as though the entire universe were booby-trapped to those stairs and the slightest provocation would set off a tree-bursting, magma-spewing, star-crumbling explosion. At the bottom of the stairs, they found the foyer deserted. Ambrose opened the door and waited for Iris to step outside first. They were still shy around each other, uncertain of the procedure of courtship under conditions such as these.

They moved quickly over the sand, shrinking from the moonlight that should delight all lovers, but they were on the run. Small dark shapes moved from the high-tide line to the ocean surf — tiny loggerhead turtles on their quest for the horizon. She and Ambrose stepped around them. Wendell had told her most of them would die, and that the area between the dunes and the waterline was treacherous and filled with predators. Now Iris was alert for predators herself.

As they approached the dock, they saw Wendell and the dock guard passed out in the sand, faces toward the twinkling sky, the empty bottle of brandy between them. The dock guard's arms and legs were akimbo. He mumbled something and turned his head, revealing a sand-covered cheek.

Iris knelt by the boy. "Wendell," Iris whispered, "are you ill?"

"He's drunk," said Ambrose, nodding at the empty bottle.

"Oh," Iris whispered. "He did it for us, didn't he?" She

stroked his face. Wendell slept with his bad hand over his good one. The light from the sky illuminated his mangled hand without its bandage, and Iris paused, leaning in close to study it, horrified by the way the fingers ended in stubs and stitches.

"We can't just leave him here," she said.

"There's nothing we can do," Ambrose answered. "Now let's go, before the guard wakes up."

"I wish we could take him with us."

"He belongs here."

"No one belongs here."

She picked up his bad hand and kissed it gently between the knuckles. "Good night, Wendell," she whispered, and arranged his hands the way she'd found them. She rose and brushed the sand from her dress. Ambrose untied the canoe and helped her in and pushed off, jumping in with a hollow sound that made the dock guard stir briefly, do a half-pushup, and then collapse again. The water was smooth and glassy, every bit of the night sky reproduced upon it in exquisite detail, creating two night skies, one of ether and one of saltwater. Ambrose paddled slowly as they drifted through the pass that separated Sanibel from its sister island. Iris looked back at the man and the boy and the courtyard and the asylum looming in the near distance. Soon the matron would discover her room. The cell of a crazy woman. Furniture rearranged, sheets pulled off the bed, clothes strewn about the room, ceramic pitcher broken on the floor, water spilled into a shrinking pool. Even the watercolor of a pear had been tilted on the wall so that the stem of the fruit pointed defiantly toward the window. She had left a beautiful wreck, and the picture of it she'd taken in her mind thoughtfully included the matron, framed in the doorway, hand over her mouth.

"We've done it," she said. "We've escaped."

Ambrose nodded.

Their canoe glided out of the pass and into the sound, into a newer, wilder world, the coast tangled with the prop roots of red mangroves. A wolf howled from the darkness of the thicket.

Ambrose kept paddling steadily. She lay back and watched the stars as the boat moved through the water. She decided that of all the moments of her life up until now, this was the perfect moment, perfect sky, perfect sea. This journey toward an unknown shore. She fell asleep and awoke to a hard rain. Ambrose quickly paddled into a copse of red mangroves, and they took shelter under the leaves, their bodies huddled over their bag of sugar, protecting it from the rain as though it were an infant child.

42

AT ELEVEN O'CLOCK that night, a nurse opened Iris's door for bed check. She squinted in the darkness, moving closer. The bed was empty, the sheets piled on the floor. She rushed to tell the matron, who lit a lantern and inspected the room herself, finding a wreckage of tipped-over chairs, rearranged furniture, and artwork defiantly atilt. The matron did not so much scream as bellow, a hybrid roar of buffalo and sea monster that brought the night nurses running. In the men's wing, a similar scene was playing out when Ambrose's bed was discovered empty, though his room was orderly and his bed neatly made.

A guard knocked on the door to Dr. Cowell's cottage five minutes later. His trip to the sulking tree had failed, and he was already in his nightclothes and dozing in his living room chair, the junonia shell still held in one hand. He answered the door sleepily, testily, but was shocked into wakefulness by the news. He threw on his clothes and rushed out into the light of the full moon.

The pieces of the puzzle fell together quickly, once the tale emerged that his own son, Wendell, had falsely told the male and female attendants that the escapees had night appointments at the office. Dr. Cowell listened with utter shock. Wendell. It could not be. He knew the boy was angry with him, but to betray him so utterly, so damningly . . . He pushed the thought out of his mind. He had lunatics to catch.

He charged out to the beach with a small battalion of guards and attendants. A storm was coming, and the air was still. They discovered Bernard passed out next to the dock, the canoe gone, and more puzzle pieces falling into place. Dr. Cowell leaned down and grabbed Bernard by the collar, shaking him as sand flew out of the drunk man's hair and clothes.

"Where are they? Where are they?" he demanded.

But Bernard was too brandy-soaked to offer any information of value. He opened his eyes a slit, mumbled something about enslaving the French, and passed out again.

Thunder rolled in the near distance and the first drops of rain of the coming storm fell on the doctor's face. By the time he made it back to the cottage, the rain was coming down in sheets and had already soaked his clothes. He went straight into Wendell's room. His son lay on his back, dead to the world. Dr. Cowell caught a whiff of brandy and frowned.

"Wendell!" He seized him firmly by the shoulders.

The boy did not move, and for a frozen moment the doctor thought he might be dead. He put his ear to Wendell's chest and heard his steady heartbeat. Relief washed over him.

The rain poured down harder. A bolt of lightning lit up the room, and the doctor noticed Wendell's hand was unwrapped and the stitches in his stumps were clotted with sand. He felt a bit sick. He hadn't seen the wounds since the day of the attack.

He went into the bedroom, where his wife was fast asleep, and retrieved a bottle of witch hazel. He poured the witch hazel into a porcelain bowl, found a cotton cloth, and returned to Wendell's room. He sat on the bed and began to wash the stumps of his injured hand, going slowly, with great tenderness. He was growing angrier by the moment — not at the boy, but at the woman who had made him a pawn and was now somewhere out there in the middle of a storm with his most fragile patient.

That conniving woman. That spiteful lunatic. She'd taken everything from him — his professionalism, his sanity, even the loyalty of his son. He would find her. He would bring her back and deny her all privileges and keep her locked in her room. No more checkers, or walking on the sand, or swimming in the calm, blue water. Then perhaps she would understand how pleasant island life had been, compared to the asylums he'd seen elsewhere.

He shook his head, hating her so much.

Wendell opened his eyes early the next morning to a pounding headache and the sight of his father sleeping upright in the chair beside him. His ghost fingers ached, and he was startled to find his hand unbandaged. Something terrible had happened the night before. Slowly, certain details came back to him. Brandy. Spinning stars. Sand beneath his head. Bernard's sow of a wife.

Ah, yes, that was it. He had helped two lunatics escape. Shame and guilt flooded him. He sat up, causing the bedsprings to creak and wake his father. The doctor rubbed his eyes and also seemed to require a few moments of orientation before a look crossed his face that meant he, too, remembered the night before.

"I'm not angry with you, Wendell. You're just a boy. And the soldier can't be held responsible for himself. I blame that woman. She played upon your mind. Took advantage of your trust."

Wendell crawled out of bed. Sand fell from his clothes and showered the floor. He went to the window and looked out at the morning. The storm had washed shells high on the beach.

"That's what happened, isn't it?"

Wendell sat by the window, his elbows resting on the sill, crying. After half an hour of his father's pleading, Wendell had finally broken down and given him the one piece of information he had on the whereabouts of the missing patients.

"North."

With that his father had dashed from the room. A short time later, the chef had knocked on his window and proceeded to yell at him through the glass. The chef was as angry as his father had been calm and wasted no time telling Wendell what a fool of a boy he was, letting two lunatics escape in his boat, and how dare he steal a bottle of brandy? Did the boy know what brandy cost? And did he know he got the dock guard fired? The chef's red, open mouth was a furnace stoked with pilfered brandy and the wood of a stolen canoe, and when he finally left, and Wendell's shoulders were slumping in relief, he suddenly appeared at the window again to lambaste him some more.

The chef was right. He was a fool. A one-handed fool. And what of Iris and Ambrose? Had they perished in the storm? Was there yet more death on his hands? Would two fresh graves be dug in the back of the property, in the tiny cemetery that held his beloved Penelope?

Wendell forgot and wiped the tears from his face with his bad hand, which made him shriek in pain and cry all the harder. His door opened and he heard his mother's footsteps, lighter and brisker than his father's, approach him.

"Mother." He turned his tearstained face to her. "I've done something terrible."

"Oh, no no no, son!" she cried, sinking to her knees and throwing her arms around him, crushing him in an embrace so tight it restricted his breathing. "I'm proud of you. I think you were very clever, helping that woman leave the island." She rocked him as, half comforted and half oxygen-starved, he blinked in confusion.

"You did fine, son," she murmured. "It was time for her to go."

43

THE DOCTOR COULD see so clearly now. He'd let a woman, a convicted lunatic, stand as his equal. He'd trusted her, even . . . loved her. And due to his brief flight of madness, he had nearly destroyed everything he'd built for himself and, in the process, let two inmates escape, one in dire need of care, and one who begged for comeuppance. The remains of sand and ashes on his office floor were an embarrassment to him now. He must leave orders that the entire area be scrubbed with ammonia water.

He threw his clothes into a valise as Mary watched him, arms folded, face the familiar color of an incipient breakdown. Out near the dock, a rickety, open-hulled fishing boat waited — the only craft available on such short notice.

"Why do you have to go after them?" Mary asked. "Why can't you just send the guards?"

"Because the guards are idiots. And they don't know how to approach lunatics. They only understand brute force. They'd probably beat the two of them to death in the process of capturing them."

He added a shirt to the valise.

"But you know that boats make you seasick. You vomited the entire way from Punta Gorda when we moved here."

"Thank you for reminding me."

He closed the valise and locked it.

"Whom do you want to bring back?" Mary asked. "The man, or the woman?"

"What in heaven is that supposed to mean? Both, of course. Both are my patients."

"But you only put macassar dressing in your hair for one of them."

The doctor stared at her, struck dumb.

"I noticed you had gouged some out of my jar. You used too much. Your hair was almost dripping with it. So I asked one of the nurses for your schedule of patients that day. You were seeing her. Iris Dunleavy. When is the last time you smoothed your hair for me?"

He picked the valise off the bed. "You are mad. Absolutely raving mad. I feel nothing for this woman but pity." He said the words so angrily that he believed them himself.

"You are a terrible man, to abandon your wife and child to chase after another woman." Her face was bright red now. He had never seen that color without the accompanying tears, and sure enough, here they came.

"A woman *and* a man, Mary! Lunatics!"

The open-hulled fishing boat awaited him at the end of the dock. Guards sat fore and aft, wooden paddles across their laps. The doctor looked doubtfully down into the craft. He was covered in rose oil in a desperate attempt to ward off insects and wore his widest-brimmed hat to protect his face from the beating sun. He handed down his valise to a guard and turned toward his silent goodbye committee, his wife and son. He leaned forward to give Mary a kiss on the cheek, one firm enough to leave a brief white patch on her scarlet face, but she seemed unmoved.

He looked at his son. Silently he reached inside his pocket, took out the junonia shell, and handed it to him. He watched, with a flush of pleasure, as the boy's weary eyes brightened and his mouth dropped open.

The doctor stepped down into the middle of the boat, and one of the guards released the knot that held it to its mooring. The current moved the boat swiftly away from the dock. Mary remained motionless, stone-faced, but Wendell stared at the junonia with a boy-size measure of joy that was still evident even in the advancing distance between them. The shell had effected its desired response, and the doctor felt briefly light and happy, until his stomach suddenly heaved, and he vomited over the side of the boat.

44

FORT MYERS COULD not be trusted. It was occupied by the Yankees. Ambrose and Iris saw the Union flag from the sea, and there was no telling what those men would do to a disheveled Southern couple washed up on their beach — whether they would be laughed at, thrown in jail, interrogated, or ignored. They kept north and as the sun went down on the second evening found a little town sitting up on a ridge. They beached their canoe and trudged up the slope. Ambrose slung his haversack over one shoulder while Iris carried the bag of sugar close to her breast. Lights glowed and the town was loud, full of voices and gunshots and music and laughter and high-pitched love spats between drunks.

They wandered down the dirt street, lost immediately in the bedlam. The chaos held them safe. The town swarmed with traders, freed Negroes, deserters, brigands, Indians, cowboys, cattle, and wounded veterans from both sides. No one cared who they were or what they wanted. It was a town for the lost. It had a trading post, a dry goods store, several saloons, a clapboard hotel, and endless carts set up, selling everything from cherry pies to cures for malaria.

The bag of sugar sold for thirty-seven dollars to a horse trader who waved his hands to dramatic effect when he bargained, and the two fugitives went to the single hotel in town to rent a room. Ambrose paid the clerk and put the remainder of his money in the pocket of his coat, and he and Iris ascended the creaky stairs to the third floor, where a simple room awaited them. They walked in and lit the kerosene lamp, revealing the furnishings: a bed, a chifforobe, a chair. Another room to the side, an indoor bathroom, contained a clawfoot tub, a washstand, and two large pitchers of water.

They moved around, touching things, saying very little, unsure with the proximity of each other in a closed space. This was married space, intimate space; they'd been herded here by circumstance, far too soon.

Ambrose went to the window and opened the curtains to reveal the dirt street and the milling people. Down in the street, an old Indian sat cross-legged in the path of a buggy. The man in the buggy shouted at the Indian, but he remained implacable, hands resting on his knees, as though the man in the buggy were a phantasm and so was the town. Ambrose turned away from the scene and paced slowly around the room, hands in his pockets. He took off his hat, set it on the chifforobe, and then reconsidered and put the hat back on his head.

"The bathroom smells like something rotten," Iris said.

"It's from the rain. And the heat."

He opened the window. Immediately the sound of a scream came into the room, followed by loud, crazy words that made no sense, evoking the asylum and its deranged inhabitants.

She sat down on the edge of the bed. "Isn't there peace left anywhere?"

He started to close the window.

"No. It's all right," she said. "At least the air is fresh."

He sat down in the straight-backed chair that was set against the wall without any desk or table to give it context. And so he sat, knitting his long fingers together, his legs slightly apart, resting his elbows on his thighs. He looked down at the floor and she watched him, his dark hair curling over his ears, the light from the lamp moving over the stubble on his cheeks. Darkened in all the brooding parts: hair and eyes, hollows of the face, lids, space made by the joining of his hands. Take away his shadows, and perhaps he'd lose his dimensionality and slip to the floor, flat as a piece of paper.

She was very tired, and her back hurt from sitting up in the canoe all those hours. She watched him as he stood, put his coat on top of the chifforobe, dropped the cash from his pocket on the bed, and silently began to count it.

"What will we do when it runs out?" she asked.

He shrugged. "Maybe there's some work I can do around town. I was handy around the farm before I went to war."

"I don't know if jobs exist here, beyond selling and trading."

He finished counting and rubbed his eyes. "Do we have to think about it tonight?"

"Of course not."

He gave her a smile of conciliation. "I'm sorry. I just have a bit of a headache from rocking in that canoe all those hours."

"I have a bit of one, too. I'm going to take a bath. I can feel the salt clinging to me." She went into the bathroom, shutting the door behind her. She put the stopper in the tub, poured in a measure of water, and climbed in, using the cake of soap she'd found on the washstand to lather her body, washing out the sweat and ocean salt from under her arms, her neck, her chest, her stomach. She was softening. Losing the grit of the hours at sea. When she finally felt clean she rinsed herself, dried with the threadbare towel, and found a thin cotton robe in the cupboard next to the washstand. She had managed to bring a comb with her, leaving all her other possessions behind in that asylum room, and now she faced the mirror, working the comb through the tangles.

She had no idea what to do with or say to Ambrose once she stepped back into the room. That part—what they would actually do, minute by minute, once they escaped — had gone unrehearsed. So intent was she on taking him with her, all her efforts had simply been focused on forcing her will upon him. Now that the escape was over, ordinary living left her without a rudder.

She opened the door and stepped back into the room. Ambrose slept on the bed, in the middle of the counted money. He must have collapsed from exhaustion while she bathed. She gathered the money from the bed, reaching under him for the last bills, and stuffed them in a drawer on the left side of the chifforobe.

The streets were quiet now. Nothing but wind came into the room. The shadows from the curtain were huge on the wall, fluttering in the light of the kerosene lamp. She sat down next to Ambrose, studying his face. Under his purple lids, his eyes began to roll as he slid further into sleep. Something about a man in repose left him looking pure, all essence and no façade, just breath and skin and shadow.

She took off his shoes and socks, found a washcloth, and wet it with the last of the water from the pitchers. He didn't stir as she bathed his feet. Perhaps he would not enjoy the sensation had he been awake; soldiers associated the bathing of feet by a woman with illness and death. His toenails were too long. She would clip them for him, she decided, glancing at the rest of his body to see what else was neglected. She longed to see him underneath his clothes, to be introduced to certain pockmarks and freckles and scars only nurses and lovers know.

She dried his feet, holding them in her hands, enjoying their warmth. She wanted to lie in bed with him, without clothing. Move her hand down the length of his chest. Let the lovemaking that followed reassert his manly position, no longer broken veteran but whole lover, in command, the natural way a man takes the upper hand. The shock of entry, the rocking and murmuring.

But for now, he slept like the dead. The ends of his trousers were wet from where she had bathed his feet. His shirt was untucked, the sleeves unbuttoned. Emboldened by the fact he didn't stir, she moved her fingers through his hair. Was it possible that their story could end well? During wartime, sad stories get sadder and even happy stories end in sorrow. But what if their love proved to be the exception?

She lay down on the bed in her robe, the hair covering her privates still damp. Outside was dead silence save for late-summer crickets and the far-off, barely heard baying of a dog. She blew out the lamp and the shadows died.

Ambrose woke up in the middle of the night. He blinked, eyes adjusting to the darkness as he tried to orient himself in time and space. He was not in the asylum. He knew that for certain. He turned to his left and found her next to him, sleeping without sound, just gentle, deep breaths, her hands folded over, her knees drawn up, her body on top of the bedspread, as was his. The light was so sparse in the room that he had to lean close to see her face. Her sanity intimidated him.

He heard a sound by the window and turned his head. A pair of legs stuck out from under the curtains. Jersey pants, army boots. Ambrose jerked up in bed and slid to the floor. His heart pounded and his body shook as his bare, newly washed feet crept across the wooden floor. He approached the window and eased back the curtain.

Seth stood shivering in the light of a waning moon, arms crossed, holding his shell jacket tightly around him. "It's not your fault, Ambrose," he said.

"I'm sorry," Ambrose whispered. "I'm so sorry."

"It's all right. I'm fine. It didn't even hurt." Seth opened his shell jacket and a swarm of flies poured out of it, hitting Ambrose in the face with their sticky bodies, others staying, crawling around the edges of the bloody hole in Seth's chest. Ambrose stumbled back, beating at the flies.

He woke up with a start, chest pounding, shivering, mouth frozen open in a scream. The curtains were empty. The room was quiet. He glanced sideways at Iris, who was still sleeping soundly, proof that he hadn't screamed out loud. He closed his eyes tightly, causing several tears to fall at once. God had tinkered in His cruel workshop a million hours making human recollection. How easy and cutting it was to recall Seth's eyes as the handkerchief was put over them, his final cry. The way the chest wound revealed itself, at first, as just a torn patch of cloth until the blood leaked through . . .

And now it was time to resurrect the color. Blue, his only friend. Blue his nurse. Blue his priest. Blue his doctor. Blue his mother. Blue blue blue blue blue . . .

He removed the bottle of laudanum from the inner pocket of his jacket. He sipped it once, twice, three times and stood straight to appreciate its effects. The medicine traveled down the length of his gut, down his arms, down his legs, weakening the memory until the edges of the open grave blurred and Seth blurred, too.

Ambrose got back into bed, next to the woman he loved. He moved his hand, found the fabric of her cotton robe, clutched it as she slept.

45

SHE AWOKE NEXT to him and suddenly it was real. She glanced at the sleeping man by her side, then stared at the ceiling. She'd been concentrating all this time simply upon their reckless plan. And now, what would they do? Where could they both go where they could live a normal life? She was, after all, both a married woman and an escaped lunatic. Her husband would never grant her a divorce. As soon as she was recognized, she was sure to be sent back to him, or back to the asylum. Would she and her lover have to live a secret life forever? Would she ever see her parents again? And what would her father, a Methodist minister, think of her right now, lying in bed with a man who was not her husband? Ambrose stirred awake, interrupting her thoughts, and he went downstairs to order breakfast. It was brought up on a tray, and they ate it in bed — biscuits smothered with gravy, bacon, and coffee. No bells announced the hour. No bars on the windows. No matron. No blue walls. No shrieking inmates or the monotony of the progress report. They ate together in contented silence as the quality of light sharpened in the window. She still had on her cotton robe. It was a luxury now, these decadent moments between the blowing on the coffee and the sipping. And so they sat blowing, sipping, listening to the noises outside, pleasant morning noises, when the world is too sleepy to fight.

"It's so strange," he said, "to wake up beside you. To share this bed."

She caught the tone in his voice. "Are you bothered by the fact that I am married?"

His blown breath made tiny ripples on the surface of his coffee. "Yes," he said at last.

"It bothers me as well. Don't imagine that it doesn't."

He looked uncomfortable. He swung his legs over the side of the bed, set his coffee cup down on the floor, and began putting on his socks and shoes.

She leaned back against the pillow. "It was a terrible mistake to marry that man."

He tied his shoes and said, "You must have been in love."

"I thought I was, at the time."

They went back to drinking their coffee. "I'd like to go to the trading post and try to buy another dress," she said. "Just something simple. And I'd like to explore the town."

"Someone could be looking for us. We need to be vigilant."

"Yes, of course."

She reached for her dress, laid out on the top of the chifforobe next to his coat, and brushed against the coat. It slid off and clanked as it hit the floor.

Instantly he was out of the bed. "Careful!" he said in a surprised, stern voice, seizing the coat. He withdrew the bottle of laudanum and held it to the light, checking for cracks. "It didn't break," he added with obvious relief.

"But you don't need this anymore," she said.

He put the bottle back in his jacket, saying nothing.

"Pour it out," she said.

He put the jacket on top of the chifforobe.

"Are you going to say anything?" she demanded.

"Let's talk about something else. Something nice."

"You're convinced you aren't well and will never get well because that's what the doctor put in your head. That and his silly palliative of blue this, blue that."

"Do you love me? Or do you just hate him?"

They stared each other down. A lovers' quarrel involving two people who had barely kissed. It was all upside down, like the little hamlet around them, like the war around that, like the world around that. She went into the bathroom and shut the door behind her, hard enough to throw a measured insult back at him. More pitchers of water had been brought up, and she washed her face and combed her hair and put on her dress.

When she came out he was sorry. He pulled her close to him, put his arms around her. Put his mouth to her ear and said her name.

In the afternoon they left the hotel and ambled down the dirt street, men leering from the tables set outside the saloons, an older man outside the trading post, gesturing and calling. Cattle ran freely, as did dogs. Ambrose took her hand as they walked together, past the saloons and the carts, past the abandoned fort that flew neither color, past some old A-frame houses with crape myrtle blooming in the yards. It was late in the summer, a time for the ripening of apples and grapes and the stretching of cornstalks toward the sky. Weeds broke through the street, and then the street simply ended in a meadow full of goldenrod, the sky above it so full of blue it could distract the madness of a billion men. They came to a low ridge and made their way through a gallery forest that bordered a twisting, turning creek, so clear and shallow she could see the minnows scatter in the water as a large sunfish approached. She took off her shoes and sat down at the edge of the creek as Ambrose stood watching her.

"Ah," she said. "Fresh water. We had a creek behind our house back home. A fisherman will say God made a creek for food. But a girl will say He made it for swimming."

"We bathed in streams when I was in the army. Up in the mountains, the water was so cold we'd turn blue. When winter came, we gave up bathing entirely. Just smoked our clothes over hickory fires to kill the lice."

Iris put her bare feet down in the cool water. She eased forward and the water crept up to her knees. Ambrose was still standing. A soldier forever on duty.

Iris pulled her feet out of the creek. She began to unbutton her dress.

"What are you doing?" Ambrose asked.

"I'm going to swim."

"But, what if . . . ?" He looked around.

"No one will see us. We're alone."

He retreated shyly to the edge of the trees as she pulled the dress over her head, then removed her petticoats and waded into the creek in her chemise and drawers. The water was chilly as it soaked through the fabrics, then grew tolerable again. A gentle current flowed, just enough to bear leaves and bits of straw along at a leisurely pace. A Sunday pace, although she was not sure what day it was. The water came to her navel. Her bare feet sank in the silt and she stretched out her arms, moving her hands flat on the cool surface of the water. She watched as a green frog swam languidly to the other shore, its legs pumping out to propel it along.

"I wonder if anyone's told this frog there's a war going on," she said. "He probably doesn't care. It doesn't affect him. He's caught the same number of flies since the war began. And the lily pads haven't changed their shape. That would be so beautiful, to live in that ignorance."

"I'm sure the frog has his worries," Ambrose said, but there was a catch in his voice. Something that had nothing to do with frogs and war. She was facing him now. Her chemise was soaked through and translucent. It was outrageous, to be seen this way in front of a man. But what was not outrageous? Slavery, war, madness, death? She didn't care anymore. She wanted to be cool and free of the dress and yes, she also wanted to see that look in Ambrose's eyes.

He looked away and then back at her again. Finally he put down his haversack and began to unbutton his shirt, his hands awkward with the buttons. He removed the shirt and pulled off his undershirt. He stood there bare-chested in the filtered light. Iris glanced at him and quickly looked away, her bravery fading a bit, shyness taking over. He removed his shoes and socks and waded in with just his trousers on, his face impassive. His trousers turned dark as the water soaked through, first to the knees and then to the thighs, and then he was fully inside the creek, moving toward her in the water, hands out to touch the surface. He stopped a foot away from her. This was the body she had longed to touch. Here was a freckle, near the right nipple of his chest. And here was a scar, tiny as a silverfish, near his throat. Here was a tuft of black fuzz on his sternum. This was no longer the man she'd argued with in the hotel room, the one whose voice was strangled with pain and anger. This was the man on the other side of the checkers table. His face full of shadows, a bit of light collected in the center of each eye. Here in this filter of sunlight and gloom, of green, of cool, of primary elements. His shoulders were still square from the endless drills, but the effect was softened by the flesh of his biceps and the fullness of his hands. The aureoles of his chest were as dark as his closed lids. He drank in the afternoon the way a soldier, hot and dusty from the march, would drink lemonade.

She touched his scar. It was puckered under her fingertip. Like a tiny sliver of a lemon rind. "Where did you get this?"

He kept his eyes closed. "I don't know. I took my shirt off to bathe and there it was. That was the funny thing about the heat of battle. Sometimes wounds opened painlessly. One time another soldier came up to me after a fight and told me about his favorite yellow dog. How the dog had a tooth that stuck out of his mouth and made his lip curl around it. He talked about that dog a good five minutes before he fell over dead. He'd had a minié ball in his back the entire conversation and never even noticed."

"It must have been terrible, to see your friends die."

He gave her a long look that seemed to come from an interior struggle, a parceling out of guarded memories from those less precious. The action seemed to pain him. He gave up on conversation altogether, took a breath, and slid under the surface, reemerging in a different place, his hair soaking wet, water pouring down his face. He dog-paddled toward her, into a renewal of sunlight, and submerged again. Iris swam toward him smooth as a fish. They met underwater, cheeks puffy with gathered breath. They stopped a few feet apart and lingered there, astonished by each other, the need for oxygen beginning as a tickle. Above them, intertwining branches and broad, flat leaves formed a canopy that held the sunlight out and provided the ambience of dusk.

They are still wet from the water. They have abandoned the creek and sloshed back to town, leaving dark footprints on the bank and then lighter ones farther away. Once they are back in the room, the wet clothes are not removed but assimilated into the act of love. Peeled back, pushed down. The bedspread is heaped on the floor, the wet back of the woman is pressed against the mattress; it makes a dark figure in the rough shape of her, like a child's shaded drawing on the sheet. They are together in a dark cave in the middle of nowhere, as the sun goes down and the room darkens and neither one rises to strike the Federal matches and light the lamp. Outside their hotel, in the warmth of twilight, stirs a motley gathering of people without homes or plans, but holding on and safe for the moment, great gouts of them milling around with the dogs and the beasts. Natural enemies on other days, in other lands. As dusk falls they coexist in this town that knows no point of view and cares for nothing but today.

They are not soldier and plantation wife. They are not lunatics. They are man and woman as they move together, natural in that motion, a small cry from Iris in the nape of his neck. In an empty house that volume of sound would wake a mother. On a battlefield or out in the cooling street it would be lost. Her fingertips press the flesh of his back and move down. The curtains flutter and at long last his wet trousers land on the floor in a tangle. The bedpost thumps the wall. The bedsprings creak. People in the room below or beside them might be cocking their heads toward the ceiling or the wall, but like another country's politics, it does not concern them.

There is not so much another cry from Iris as an inhalation, a quick lungful of something unspoken. She can't give words or voice to this feeling. The moment so pure and blank, time folded into a shape she has never seen before. She wants to tell him that she loves him; she wants to tell him she is sorry; she wants to tell him all her stories in one sentence but she has no breath left in her. They lie together in a tangle of sheets and clothes and perspiration, one-third dry and two-thirds wet — that fraction has shifted in the last several seconds. *Ambrose,* she thinks to herself. The orchard boy and the orchard girl have grown into a man and a woman. The branches bend under their weight.

And the time to say it was days ago, perhaps weeks ago, but it was never said. Like the fireflies she used to keep in Mason jars, the promise of its telling had glowed intermittently.

"I love you," he said. And now the fireflies shone with a constant light.

Neither knew what time of night it was. The darkness had neither deepened nor lightened but stayed true to itself, filling the room with a late-summer grayness, almost cool but not quite. Their wet clothes were off; their bodies had dried and a single sheet covered them. She lay with her back against his chest, naked under the sheet. All those days in the courtyard when they knew they could not touch, they had quieted their bodies before they yearned for this. But now, having been satisfied, the yearning reasserted all its memories of itself, all the untouched sensations of them aching for each other throughout that long summer when turtles pawed at the sand and the moonlight reflected on the water.

"I'm sorry," she said.

"About what?"

"The laudanum. I had no right."

"You meant well."

"Women can be foolish. A woman is never more proud than of the nurse in herself; a man might crow about his strength or his wealth or his prowess but a woman believes she can heal anything that limps."

He was quiet.

"I wanted my love to be enough for you," she said. "I wanted to be that important. If you need your laudanum, you should have it."

He moved his fingertips down the length of her spine, his fingers dividing, the index and middle finger trailing along one side of the bony ridge, the smaller fingers trailing along the other. He stopped where the ridge disappeared and rested his palm against the small of her back. "There was a tree back on Sanibel. They called it a strangler fig. It would wrap around a tree next to it and as it grew, it would wrap tighter and tighter until the other tree died. It scared me, to hear about that strangler fig, because it had no will of its own. It became a killer, just by following its natural course. I feel as though I am that strangler fig. I became a killer, just by living. Continuing to grow in a direction already chosen for me."

"You're not a killer."

"Yes, I am, Iris."

"You killed men in battle under orders. All soldiers do."

He straightened up in bed to a sitting position, putting the pillow behind his back and leaning against it. "I killed my best friend, Iris."

She drew in her breath. Sat up next to him and took his hand.

"He deserted. I was forced to shoot him. I had a gun pressed against my own head."

"What choice could you have made, then?"

"I could have made the choice to die. My father would have made that choice."

"You don't know that."

He said nothing.

"I didn't have your circumstances," Iris said, "but I feel responsible for the slaves who died in the massacre."

Ambrose nodded. She had told him the story in the canoe, under clearing skies. "But how could you feel guilty? You didn't kill them."

"I did, in a way. I insisted on running with them, and my husband chose to believe that they had kidnapped me. Were I not with them, they might not have been pursued so ferociously. And I told them to go east, Ambrose. I thought I knew the best route but I was too prideful to admit that I'd gotten us all lost. I keep thinking, Subtract me from the equation and where would they be right now? Mattie, Rose, and the others? Would they be sitting on a porch somewhere? Enjoying the stars? Living as free people? They're all dead, Ambrose."

"Forgive yourself."

They sat in silence, holding hands. "You're not a strangler fig," Iris said. "You're a coconut palm. A hurricane gale comes along and thinks it's knocked you down, but it's only bent you. Day by day you'll straighten toward the sky."

They could have said more, but they were exhausted. Their eyes grew heavy, and they slept.

Ambrose dreamed in prewar colors, quotidian light. The simplest dreams in the world. A dog and a stick. Grass falling under a swinging scythe. Mud prints across a floor. The dark pool made by a piece of chocolate melting on a windowsill. Boy dreams, motion and noise. Chintz curtains empty, demons at rest.

Merciful God. The demons at rest.

46

THE OLD INDIAN man sat there every day, outside the trading post, always in the same implacable position, usually in the way. People would move their horses around him as he sat crosslegged and silent, sometimes smoking a cigarillo but more often simply fixing everyone in his path with the same imperious stare. He might have been a Seminole, or a Cherokee, or even an Iroquois washed down from the North and deposited like sediment at the edge of the sea. It was impossible to ascertain his tribe by his manner of dress. Feathers and beads, yes, but also a white man's shirt and boots, and wire-rimmed spectacles sticking out of his pocket. A railroad watch and a straw boater. Iris liked seeing him every day, drawing some kind of comfort in the fact no one ever bothered with him. He lingered unmolested, nowhere to go, but content for now in this temperate patch of Florida coastline where no one was in charge and no one cared and no one knew what to do. This melting pot of the listless, the undecided, the weary.

The couple kept to themselves, on the lookout for pursuers, careful not to attract any attention. Lovemaking, conversation, and silence. A tolerable amount of memory. A larger, tentative amount of hope. One man, one woman. One mattress. One lamp. They never spoke of their time on the island. It seemed now like a dream, and the dream encouraged the dissolution of other memories. Perhaps the war had been a dream, and the plantation. Perhaps every heartache was nothing but a night sweat and a vision dissolved in morning light, while every joy, every moment of bliss, was as real as a blade of grass or a bar of soap or a leaf held in the hand. And they were real as well. Two beings who sometimes felt like specters were solid with each other. They took up mass and weight. Breathed in oxygen. Ate oranges. Kissed.

By day Ambrose seemed calm. But his sleep revealed a certain vulnerability. She would wake up in the night with his arms wrapped around her, holding her tightly, murmuring things that had no context in that room. Every few days she checked the laudanum bottle, saw the level of amber liquid going down. She tried not to think of it. She was in love.

They walked to a distant meadow one afternoon, removed their clothes, and embraced in high grass, the sun straight overhead, and the sky a place where sea birds and land birds circled each other. Grasshoppers jumped on their bare legs. Iris looked straight up. A white cloud covered the sun, allowing her a painless eyeful of sky and birds as Ambrose moved against her. She ran her hands down his bare back. His muscles moved when he did. In such a short amount of time, he had grown so vital. His broken parts were filling in. His sleep quieter. His love noisier. The patient in him was sliding away and the man was reaffirming himself, right here, away from the debilitating stare of his history.

By the morning of the fourth day, Ambrose's beard had grown rough against Iris's skin. He bought a straight razor and a bar of shaving soap at the trading post. She sat inside the dry tub and watched him prepare himself, pouring the water, wetting the soap, swirling the brush in the lather. This was not just the act of a man grooming himself. This was the lunatic who could finally be trusted to hold a razor to his neck without cutting open his jugular vein. She was quiet. Her bare feet pressed against the cool porcelain. The razor moved down his face. The lather from the shaving soap splattered in the sink. For a moment—just for a moment, after his face was smooth and he had lifted his head up and was scraping his pale throat—she was afraid. But the blade continued to move up, not sideways, and though his hand shook slightly, finally he finished, washed the blade, and wiped it off with a towel.

He lowered himself on top of her in the tub. His cheek against hers, smooth and smelling faintly of wintergreen. The claw feet of the tub scraped against the wooden floor. The bathtub moved slightly. If it could only break free of its plumbing, they could travel that way. Making love. The bathtub inching its way back home.

One morning by the trading post, she saw a young woman holding a baby and froze. Her stare went beyond that of a woman appreciating another's child. It went on so long that the woman herself turned away, and Ambrose put a hand on her arm and asked, "What is it?" She only shook her head, but he asked again later that night, as they were lying together in their room.

"What was the matter?" he asked. "Was something wrong with the baby?"

"No," she said. "He reminded me of another."

Ambrose said nothing, but she knew he was waiting. It was time to tell the baby's story. He had been quiet all this time, in his grave in Virginia soil, some of the only rich soil left on that plantation after the tobacco crops had ruined the land. That baby she'd held in her arms, his tiny hands opening and balling into fists. Pale blue eyes, a fuzzy patch of blond hair on his bald head. White as a ghost. She had never spoken of him to the doctor or even the boy. But even if that baby could rest without his story told, she could not. Babies died in that war; they died outside it for no reason at all. The guilty would never be punished, any more than she'd already punished them. The weak revenge of a woman, drawing no blood. But what else could she have done?

She could have killed them. Shot them both in their sleep with the same pistol Nate later stole. She'd thought about it, too. But her father had preached too many sermons. Thou shalt not kill. Vengeance is the Lord's. Shooting the men would startle the pheasants out of the soft reeds of Psalms. She'd left the pistol in the drawer. But now she held the story to the light. Ambrose lay on the bed next to her, eyes on her, listening.

From the moment her husband came home and saw her dress soaking in the porcelain tub, the water pink from the blood of the slave boy, he ceased to be her husband and slept in the guest room. She continued her duties as mistress — the overseeing of the making of the slave clothes, the maintaining of the garden, the keeping of the keys — but she was just a servant like the rest of them. They shared the same table for meals but he spoke to her rarely. Other things occupied his mind. The war was getting worse. The price of things still rising. The slaves uppity. The tobacco full of worms.

After the boy she loved had been sold, Rose, the wash girl, turned inside herself. Her silliness died and her eyes hardened. It was summer, then. Purple coneflowers blooming. The scent of bee balm strong in the meadow by the woods. The sheets Rose hung dried in no time at all. She was sixteen now, a beautiful girl whose heart was broken. The younger children splashed in the river. The older folks sat on Creole chairs at night and fanned themselves with corn husks. She was caught between, too young for most things, too old for others. A grudge born in the spring-time taking root in her chest. Her hair so thick she could barely braid it. It fell down her back and was tied with a strip of leather.

Too thick for a ribbon. Tawny, bare legs showed under her dress. Her breasts and lips were full. She was asking for trouble simply by existing, by growing up. No fault of her own. A strangler fig.

One afternoon, Iris looked out the window and saw Rose entering the coach house. Something was strange about her posture. A curving inward of normally straight shoulders. Iris waited for her to come out of the house but she did not. Instead, her husband, Robert, came striding up himself. He opened the door and disappeared inside. She watched that closed door. Her hands trembled on the windowpane. She leaned forward, the glass uncomfortably hot on her nose and the tip of her forehead. This could not be happening. She'd heard the tales of other plantation men, what they did with women of their choosing. But Robert was a deacon at church. The Bible was a book he quoted every day. The whisper of the New Testament, the growl of the Old. He'd even used it to justify the owning of slaves.

She could not look at him that night. She wanted to throw things at him, scream at him. But she had been silenced by then. She said nothing. She did nothing. She was afraid any trouble from her would mean Rose would be sold, just as Almon had been. She wrote her father and asked him to come and take her back to Winchester. But suddenly, all his letters back to her stopped, as well as letters from her mother. She could only conclude that Robert was keeping them from her. She stopped taking meals at the table, choosing to eat by herself on the steps. She no longer went to the other plantations, or spoke to the other wives. The parties had stopped, anyway. The war had put a layer of dust on the good china and the julep glasses.

The slaves on the plantation knew about the crime. It changed the tone of their singing, the splash of the children in the creek. Rose's father had the look of a man perpetually holding himself back from the act of murder. And Rose's eyes had turned blank.

Iris wondered if she blamed her. She was more slave than wife now, if shame could bind a people together whose skin was different colors. And yet, she was not one of them either. She was a ghost.

Late summer arrived, then the fall. Season of apples, pumpkins, and squash. Something else was growing. Rose's stomach began to swell. All through that fall and winter, what began as a whisper turned into a trumpet. She spent most of her time in the slave quarters. Her mother took over the laundry. She was hidden from view most of the time, but on those days when Iris glimpsed her making her way painfully across the yard, the baby in her large and heavy, she wanted to run to her. Beg her pardon. Tell her that if she could, she would take her and her family far away from here. Perhaps that was where the seed was planted.

This was survival. This was God's plan turned to rot. This was the dead of winter. The ice crackled outside. The bedroom was always cold. Iris piled up the blankets, but her feet still felt as though they'd turned to ice. She would lie awake at night, shivering, listening to the wind move through the bare branches of the sycamores. The bromeliads in the flower garden died in the frost. And the baby grew.

One day in March, nearly a year from the day Iris stopped Almon's whipping, she was summoned to the slave quarters by the old woman, Mattie. Rose was in labor. She'd been bucking and screaming for hours and needed a doctor. Iris saddled up the sorrel pony herself and went to find a doctor, knowing that Robert would object to the expense, but she was unwilling to let the girl suffer anymore. The doctor scolded Iris: "I have better things to do than deliver a slave baby," he said, but came reluctantly and used the forceps to finally make the delivery. Rose had stopped screaming and was quiet when the baby came out. Her blood soaked the sheets. Her head was thrown back and her lips were pale. Only the movement of her eyes and her jagged breathing proved she still was alive.

The doctor cut the umbilical cord and tied it off with twine. The baby screamed lustily. Covered with slime and annoyed by life. The doctor's lip curled. Iris could read his thoughts. A white baby born to a black slave. She wondered which parent he blamed. He packed his medical bag and left without a word.

Rose's mother cleaned the baby and put it on Rose's chest. Her father's face was a mask of confusion. Anger and pride and wonder. The tiny boy should have been Almon's baby, brown as cinnamon. And yet, he was still his first grandson. Rose's eyes focused on the baby. She studied it, smiled a little. The hours spent in the coach house belonged to the master, but the baby was hers. She stroked the wet hair. Kissed the pale cheek. Mumbled something into the nape of his neck known only to mother and child. Perhaps not even a word. A feeling.

Before she left the cabin, Iris asked to hold the baby. Rose looked at her mother for permission. She nodded and Rose handed him over. Iris hadn't held a baby in years, was surprised at his weight. He wrinkled his face as though to cry and then stopped, growing complacent as she rocked him. It had never occurred to her that the first white baby she held on this farm would not be hers. And yet, he was still so precious. The circumstances of his creation hadn't taken the miracle away. It clung to the baby, was part of him, and you couldn't remove it any more than you could scrape the yellow away from a fire. Rose had on a full smile now, made sleepy by the new fever the baby had brought.

"What was his name?" Ambrose now whispered as he lay in bed with her, in the darkness of the room.

She was silent a moment, let the name separate from the story that birthed it, let it gather on her tongue. It hurt her heart to say it, but it felt at home in the darkness of the room.

"Solomon."

"Solomon," he said, and she loved him for repeating it.

A few hours after the baby was born she heard a high-pitched scream from the direction of the slave quarters. She dropped a china plate and ran outside in her apron, following the sound of the scream to Rose's cabin.

Rose was hysterical, her mother trying to calm her. Her father was talking about killing someone; Jackson, the blacksmith, was attempting to reason with him. They turned their heads when Iris rushed through the door.

"What's happened?" she demanded.

Rose looked at her, eyes streaming. "They took my baby!"

Iris gasped. "Who took your baby?"

"The overseer! Mr. Sender!"

Iris ran back out the door without another word, straight to the overseer's house. She pounded on his door but he did not answer. She screamed his name, panic rising inside her. She rushed around the plantation, asking frantic questions of the workers she saw. Clyde Sender had taken the baby and ridden away with it under his arm. That's all anyone had seen.

When Robert came through the door later that afternoon, Iris hurled herself at him. "Where is the baby?" she screamed. "Where is the baby?"

Robert pushed her away, went to his room, and locked the door. Daylight faded and there was no word. The next morning, though, Robert and the overseer were gone again, and this time one of the young boys came to Iris's door and led her toward the slave cabins. He walked with a purpose, his head up as though fulfilling a manly duty. She asked him questions but he wouldn't answer her. He veered away when he approached the slave quarters and instead took a different path, one that led to the edge of the property. Up ahead, Iris saw the cemetery for pets and Negroes. A group of slaves had gathered inside the rail fence. As she approached, she saw one of the field hands digging up a new grave. Rose and her parents knelt beside it, watching. The crowd saw Iris and moved aside to let her pass.

She hovered near the grave, unable to speak, unable to move, filled with the horror of the possibility that was in the air but left unspoken. A few more shovelfuls of dirt and the shovel found the edge of a white sheet. The field hand threw the shovel aside and began digging in the dark, loose soil with his hands, pawing out the dirt, the others watching as though frozen.

He reached into the grave and pulled out a small bundle wrapped in a sheet and tied with hemp. He fumbled at the knots and then Rose's mother reached over and undid them with sure, narrow fingers. The crowd moved inward. Iris felt a small hand on her waist, someone's breath on her back.

The field hand unwrapped the sheet.

Rose fainted.

The boy was perfect and whole, more beautiful in morning light than in the candlelight of the cabin. His hands balled, eyes closed. Knees drawn up. Put the boy on his mother's breast, and you'd think he'd start to suckle. So nearly alive that way.

That was the story, told for the first time. Born whole, the cord still attached. "We ran away three days later," Iris said to Ambrose. "None of us could stand to stay there anymore."

She did perform one final act the last night before they fled. When darkness fell, she stole out to the slave cemetery with a spade and dug that baby up. Carried him over to the beautiful family cemetery of the Dunleavys and reburied him there.

The rain began an hour after the eight of them had run away. She imagined the empty grave the next morning, there in that patch of land that held the bodies of Negroes and dogs. A hole in the earth, filled with rainwater, reeking of quicklime and reflecting the clearing sky.

47

WENDELL HAD NO canoe, so he couldn't travel by water to feed his lamb. He had to take the long way through the jungle, wading in sloughs and struggling through briars. It was impractical, and even he could concede it was dangerous. He needed to bring the lamb home, and to do so, he had to win over his mother. Since his father had left the island, her mood had alternated between childish gaiety and great bouts of weeping.

"Am I pretty?" she would ask Wendell between sobs.

"Of course you are, Mother. Very pretty."

Wendell used his innate sense of timing, the exquisite natural rhythm a boy uses to predict the weather and the best time for catching frogs, to introduce his new pet during the high point of one of his mother's mood swings. Indeed, Mary was sipping tea on the living room sofa, and in good spirits, when Wendell came through the front door and, with some gentle pulling on the leash, beckoned the lamb into the house.

"It's a lamb," she whispered. She put down her china cup and clapped her hands together. "This is wonderful! Wendell, you are the best son in the world to bring this lamb to me. We can have lamb stew tonight!"

The creature blinked his long eyelashes at her, seemingly unmoved by the suggestion. He had the same vague smile he had always had. A lamb-smile that meant a certain languid acceptance of every turn in the road.

"No, Mother. This lamb is not for eating. This lamb is our friend."

Mary let out a laugh. "Oh, Wendell, don't be silly. Where I come from, lambs are for supper."

Wendell led the creature closer to the sofa. He took his mother's hand and guided it into the stiff wool, moving her hand back and forth.

"Not supper. *Friend,*" he said with the same gently instructive cadence the bookkeeper used when she taught him algebra.

"But it would taste so good!"

"No, Mother. Friend."

48

THE OLD INDIAN didn't blink when the rock landed in front of him. Another rock landed near his knee. Another rock, thrown a bit harder, hit him in the arm. He simply stared straight ahead.

Ambrose and Iris had been walking hand in hand on their way to the creek. Iris felt his hand stiffen in hers. He swiveled his head around, looking for the source of the stones. Three men loitered on the front porch of the trading post, dusty and hard-traveled. One of them drank from a bottle of whiskey and passed it to the others. They had the wicked laughter sometimes employed by the strong in the company of the helpless. One of them — long, red hair under his beaten hat and a thick red mustache — picked up another stone.

Ambrose let go of Iris's hand.

"No, Ambrose," she said, but he was already striding up to the man with the stone in his hand and Iris could do nothing but follow, watching the squaring of his shoulders and the deliberateness of his gait. She could not help but feel a flush of pride even though the prickle of fear made her dress moist under the arms.

"Ambrose," she said again, but Ambrose had reached the red-haired man.

"Stop it," Ambrose said.

He smiled. "Stop what?"

"He's a harmless old fellow and he's never done anything to you."

"Might be good for you to mind your own business."

Ambrose kept his voice even. "You throw one more rock at him and you'll be sorry."

The red-haired man turned to the others and said, "You hear that?"

They crowded in closer. Their laughter had died. They had guns in their belts.

Iris took her lover's arm.

"Let's go, Ambrose."

But Ambrose ignored her, staring his enemy down in the way that men do, judging strength and valor upon things just outside of a woman's awareness: a blink, a twitch, a jump in the pulse or a muscle in the jaw. Who has something more to lose in his eyes.

"Please, Ambrose." She tightened her grip enough to break some kind of spell, and Ambrose relented, allowing himself to be ushered down the street, but not before giving the man a steely look and saying, "You leave him alone."

"It's such a pleasant day, Ambrose," she said, angry at the bully but fearful of a confrontation in this wild and violent town. "Let's forget we saw such a thing."

They had been on their way to the creek to take advantage of the cool water, but the argument over the Indian had taken away their easy mood, and they shuffled to the edge of town and through the broken field of goldenrod in silence. They'd forgotten, in the bubble of their courtship, how easy war or its fragments could come and get them. The creek was clear and slow and inviting, but this time they stayed on the bank, a few feet apart, backs resting against two different trees. That new-lover spell, when the world must be right because their joy wills it so, was broken, replaced by the sullen realness of the day, when a creek was pretty without being magical, and birdsong was pleasant but not transcendent, and shadows and light make puzzles but not revelations.

Iris looked over at Ambrose. He leaned back against the tree, eyes closed, trousers dirty at the cuffs, his shirtsleeves unbuttoned. His shoes untied but not removed. It was time for them to leave this town. They were running out of money. You could get lost in this town. You could also get shot. You could rest and die. You could love and lose. And yet there was nowhere to go. She could not take him to her father. He could not take her to his.

She stayed in that position, thinking those thoughts, looking at Ambrose, until a knurl of bark had pressed against her back long enough to hurt. She shifted, rose. Crouched and took his cold hand, squeezing until his eyebrows moved, and he stirred and mumbled.

"We should go back to town," she said.

He opened his eyes and sighed. "Very well."

"Were you sleeping?"

He didn't answer. He rose, and they walked away together, hands at their sides.

The old Indian was dead. He lay on his back in the street, a bullet hole in his forehead, the same unfriendly look on his face, except the fire in his pupils had been replaced by milk. A cigarillo was still in his mouth, the ash burned down to his lips. Death had come too quickly for him to contemplate it at all. He had simply been an old man and then a dead body, stiffening in the sun. No one was gathered around him. People simply slowed down, side-stepping him, getting an eyeful, and then moving on. He was no one's business and in no one's care.

Iris did stop and knelt. She went to touch him but jerked her hand back. Lice were flowing off the old man's body, abandoning the cooling host. She leaped up and backed quickly away from the stream of vermin, open-mouthed in horror.

"Those bastards killed him," Ambrose said. "They just shot

him like he was nothing." He turned and looked toward the trading post. The men were gone. Lost somewhere in the forever of the town.

"The poor fellow," Ambrose murmured.

"Isn't someone going to bury him?"

"Who would? It's no one's job."

"It was no one's job to shoot him, either."

Ambrose glanced at the hotel. A man with one leg sat on the front steps, playing cards with a boy.

"Go to the room," he told Iris.

"But what are you — ?"

"Just go."

Iris obeyed, climbing the steps to the hotel, passing the boy and the man, who reeked of tobacco. She felt a lurch in her stomach and pinched her nose against the odor. She went upstairs to their room and moved the curtains aside so she could look up the street. The Indian was still lying there, and the second glimpse of him was nearly proof to her that he had always been dead, always a part of the scene like the milling cattle and the pie carts. A terrible feeling had started in the pit of her stomach and had grown the last few hours. Once, as a little girl, she had stopped by the side of the road and looked into the front yard of a green house. Under a blue sky, a perfectly yellow butterfly perched upon a red spider lily, and something about that scene, the crisp perfection of the colors and the simplicity of the action, seemed foreboding to her. She couldn't remember now if anything dire had happened, but something about the scene she saw through the window — the Indian's repose, a horse hitched to a post nearby, and the dust rising in the street — reminded her of that sight. They were saying the same thing, the spider lily and the dead man.

Ambrose approached the corpse, carrying a shovel and a white sheet. He spread the sheet out, took the old man by the arms, and tugged him onto it, as his straw hat came off and fell into the street. No one stopped to help. They glanced over at Ambrose and kept on walking. This wasn't their business. It wasn't even their town. Ambrose began to drag the dead Indian away. He moved him several feet and went back for the hat. He put the hat on the Indian's chest and dragged the sheet again, slowly and steadily, until Iris couldn't see him anymore. Iris sat down on the bed and waited. She wanted to help him but sensed he wanted to be alone. Find a good place where the earth was rich and loose, and do the job no one else was willing to do.

This was as good a place to bury a man as any. Ambrose's coat lay on the ground. He was out behind a saloon, in a plot of land filled with weeds. Claimed by no one. A one-legged chicken hopped nearby, pecking at something invisible. Its shadow darted with it.

Ambrose stuck the shovel in the ground and lifted a measure of dirt, weeds trailing off it, and dumped the earth to the side. He repeated the process, the earth filled with small pebbles, the shovel scraping against them. Grasshoppers bounced around him, pinging off his arms and hands. The sun a muted yellow, neither hot nor cold. Neutral, like Maryland once pretended to be. The hole grew deeper. His clothes were soaked with sweat. He braced his back and threw a shovel load of dirt into a patch of wild bergamot that grew by the split-rail fence. He eyed the Indian, estimated his height, and lengthened the grave. What a human bit of caprice to fear for a corpse's comfort.

A pang had started in his chest that wouldn't go away. An un-loosening. He knew better than to dig a grave, for the fact he had once been forced to dig another, Seth's grave, and the fangs in that event were coming back to bite him. So burying the Indian was a foolhardy mission, and he would pay for it later, he knew it, but no one else had stepped up for the task, and it was indecent to leave a dead man rotting in the street. He and his fellow soldiers had been forced to retreat from some of the battlefields, leaving their dead behind, but there was no excuse this time. He wasn't in a hurry, wasn't forced away, and no one was shooting over his head. The act was dangerous only inside himself.

A whippoorwill landed on the branch of a tree nearby and sent down its haunting song. No small tragedy of bird life could have made that song. God had placed leftover grief in its trembling body, all that unexpressed sorrow from the centuries past. Women who lost their children, men who lost their wars. Terrible reversals of fortune. Storms and famines and cruel twists of circumstance.

He finished the hole as the sun set. It was deep and wide enough. He'd seen bodies buried too shallow during the war. At night those hasty graves would glow with an eerie mist. Some kind of gas put off by the body, the camp surgeon said. Anyone who'd seen that glow would forever dig the deepest grave they could. The piles of loose dirt around Ambrose's feet had hardened into shapes. In the indistinct glow of dusk, the piles looked like grave-dwelling creatures crawling out to gather food. He threw down the shovel and banged his hands together to knock the dirt away. The Indian was smiling now. A slight, wry grin, uninspired by any amusement. Just things drying inside. That hateful insouciance of nature taking its course. Nothing was sacred.

Ambrose knelt, staring down at the Indian, at the crusts of blood around the hole in his forehead. The old man's hair was braided and stunk of animal grease. Had he opened the filthy shirt, some thready trading-post castaway, he no doubt would have found tattoos and scars and marks. They had all meant something. Now their stories had abandoned them. Ambrose pressed his fingertips against the man's lids and slowly drew

them over his dry eyes. The lids moved up again when he released them, giving the dead Indian the half-lidded look of a cha-
meleon. He positioned the hat over his chest, tried to cross the
stiff arms, but gave up that battle. Inside the grave within a few
hours, the corpse would relax and take a pose known only to
God.

Ambrose pulled the corpse into the grave and let it fall. He
climbed in, stepping carefully around the body, moving the
sheet, positioning it, straightening the hat. Had the Indian died
but forty years earlier, Ambrose imagined, the air would be filled
with great keening, prayers said over him, perhaps women cutting their skin, perhaps a funeral pyre burning. Now, nothing. A
lone white man doing what was right. He folded over the sheet
so that it covered the head and body, crawled out of the grave,
and began to shovel the dirt back in. Every time a shovelful hit
the body it made a sound like nothing else in the world. Every
time, that sound fiddled with something inside him. The soul
is nothing but the innards of the finest watch, ruined before the
watchmaker's hands even touch it, by its exposure to air.

Iris heard heavy footsteps on the stairs, a slow, deliberate thump-
ing. She turned up the flame in the lamp and went to the door.
Opened it on Ambrose, whose face was dark in the hallway. She
swung the door open wider and he entered, his shadow huge
and lumbering in the room. He said not a word and she was too
afraid to speak. Something had changed in the course of an afternoon. She was glad she had not seen his eyes clearly, afraid what
she would find there.

"Ambrose?" she whispered.

He went into the bathroom and closed the door behind him.
She stood in the room, waiting for him to come out, at the mercy
of passing time. She held the lamp to the clock and read the time.

An hour had passed. She knocked on the door but he didn't answer. She waited, knocked again. Nothing but silence. She pushed open the door. He was sitting naked in the dry tub, in the dark room. She retrieved the glowing lamp from the room and set it on the edge of the washstand. His clothes were piled beside him on the floor. His shoes were next to the clothes. One of them was turned over, the sole worn down. His hands were crossed and resting on his belly. His mouth slightly open. Half lover, half corpse. The sight terrified her. She did not know what it meant, her man sitting naked like that in the dry tub.

She said his name in the hope it would break the spell. He did not blink. Bits of dirt and grass still clung to his face. She knelt down beside him. Gently took his cold fingers and disengaged them from each other so that she could hold his hand. She stroked his face, leaned down close to him, spoke very softly.

"Blue like a feather. Like a boy's biggest marble. Like a sapphire, like sedge grass in the rain, like a newborn crayfish, soul light, wedding flowers, the sea . . ."

49

HE WAS BETTER the next morning, better still the next. He
drank his coffee and she drank hers next to him. She was getting
used to the taste without sugar. One day the war would be over,
and sugar would return. They'd had the first cool night. The
window was closed and the extra blanket was spread out upon
the bed. They had weathered the storm together. He was Ambrose again. The inflections had returned to his voice. His eyes
were clear. He had a bit of stubble on his cheek that she planned
to gently ask to shave, not trusting him yet with the razor.

"It's time to leave," he said. "We've been here almost two
weeks. We're running out of money. And it's not safe here, not
really. We need to keep moving."

"Can't we stay a few more days? I'm so tired, Ambrose. I feel
like my soul is dead asleep. Hibernating like a bear."

"Maybe another day or two. But we have to have a plan. Half
the railroads are out. And I hear rumors of Indian attacks to the
east."

He took a large sip of coffee, winced at the burn. Was silent
until his expression smoothed again. "I spoke to someone in the
lobby the other day. He works on a schooner that runs down to
the Keys and back to Mobile. I can speak to him. See about doing
some work in exchange for passage to Mobile."

"Mobile is to the west."

He shrugged. "War makes you take the long way home." His
hand found hers and held it. She loved it when he broke through

248

with a gesture of strength. Became the man again. Let her be the woman. Let that moment exist.

"Will we go to Charleston?" she asked.

His hand tightened. He shook his head.

"And even if we were able to make it to Winchester . . ."

"I know."

They went out in the afternoon. He walked slowly down the stairs in front of her, his collar folded wrong. She reached out to correct the mistake, neither one of them missing a step.

Clouds were heavy in the sky, dark and swollen. A coming rain. She could smell it. The streets bustling, people going somewhere, women with parasols to shield them from the current sun or the future rain. The place the Indian's body had lain was like any other spot. People walked right over it.

Ambrose turned to Iris and they joined together for an instant, a quick kiss in open air. Shyly, as though their tale could raise a scandal here. He gave her a smile that meant something boyish and pure, and they went in opposite directions. He adjusted his slouch hat. Her sunbonnet was fixed just fine.

She reached into her pocket, touched the coins there. They lightly thumped against her body as she walked. She had seen a jar of applesauce at the trading post, and over the time since she'd spied it, she'd had a craving for applesauce. The craving had died when Ambrose had fallen ill, recovered when he did, and was now upon her full force. As she walked she thought of the jar in her hand, could already feel its weight. She imagined having the applesauce on toast in the morning, time skipping ahead in her mind, a flurry of the waxing and waning of light.

She reached the end of the street and turned the corner. A group of urchin boys crouched on the sidewalk, playing jacks. Hitched horses dropped fresh manure. An old man sold smoked mullet. She glanced across the street and froze.

A face, so immediate and sharp. Impossible. Her heart was unmanageable in her chest. Her breath caught and aching. Lightning through her bones.

Dr. Henry Cowell.

She pushed into the double doors of the saloon and stared at him over the swinging doors. His face was sunburned and his clothes wrinkled. His posture, though, was unmistakable. That same straight back. The familiar long stride. Two guards trailed behind him. Sunlight glinted off his glasses.

She couldn't move her eyes from him. Her heart thumped wildly. Perspiration soaked through the fabric of her dress. So he had come for them. Had probably stopped and searched Fort Myers, then moved on to this bedraggled town.

He turned the corner and disappeared, and she ran out of the saloon, bumping into people, zigzagging crazily, her breath coming fast, her arms pumping, people turning to stare because even in this crazy town full of drunkards and pirates and outlaws and sailors, a woman in a dead run was a sight indeed. Her fists didn't uncurl even when she reached the porch of the hotel. The lobby floor creaked under her weight as she ran across it and took the stairs two at a time to the top of the second flight. She rushed to the door marked "17," threw it open, and slammed it again behind her.

The doctor had come looking for them, and it was only a matter of time before he questioned the right person or turned the right corner. She had made the mistake that all fugitives make, imagining she was free. She rushed around the room, gathering the few things they'd brought or acquired and putting them into Ambrose's worn haversack. She found the remainder of the money in the bottom drawer and stuffed it inside the haversack as well. She was ready to go, and yet could not leave. She had to wait for Ambrose—and what if the doctor had already found him?

That unalterable combination of blue eyes, high cheekbones, and slouch hat could fit a few other men in this town — yes, a few others — but not many. And how about herself? How easily could the doctor find her by asking a few questions about a white woman with hazel eyes and a mass of chestnut-brown hair running down her back?

She untied her bonnet and went into the bathroom to stare at herself in the mirror. Her own reflection seemed too familiar, too striking. She unfastened the pins from her hair, combing it with her fingers until it hung straight down. She'd run across one of the stark handbills posted on a pole after her escape from the plantation. *White woman. Of medium height, hazel eyes, long chestnut hair. In the company of Negroes.* The Negroes were gone, but her height and build were immutable. And the hair. Thick and long and lovely.

She found Ambrose's razor. Went back and stared into the mirror again. Her heart was still racing. Eyes staring back at herself. She grabbed a hank of hair, stretched it out until it hurt her head, and slashed at it with the razor. She opened her fingers and let the hair fall to the floor. It landed curled like a ribbon. She shut her eyes tight and kept cutting, as the hair fell around her legs, occasionally tickling her shins and ankles. The razor grew dull; she had to use a sawing motion on the last of her tresses.

When she finally opened her eyes, her long hair was gone. In its place was the short, rough haircut of madmen and trappers. She stared at herself, her eyes tearing up, as the door to the room creaked open and she recognized Ambrose's familiar steps.

When she opened the bathroom door he was right there in front of her, staring at her, his face suddenly drained of color. He reached for her short hair and then stopped, letting his hand fall back to his side.

"Seth," he said.

His eyes had turned to glass; he stepped away from her, his hands animated now, flying around as though to find something to steady himself. He kept backing up and she followed him, trying to explain that they had to leave, right now, by boat or train or pony, they could not hide themselves, the doctor had come for them . . . but Ambrose did not let her finish. The sight of her new haircut had undone something in him. He turned and bolted out the door.

She ran after him, bewildered, stray tendrils falling from her head and swirling away in the draft her body made as she flew down the stairs. By the time she had reached the lobby and run out onto the porch, Ambrose was nowhere in sight. She looked to the right and the left, scanning for Ambrose, alert for the doctor. Every fiber in her wanted to go back to the room, hide under the bed, and wait for the darkness, but she chose a direction and ran down the street.

Night had fallen. Loud laughter poured from the saloons, but the town was quieter at its edges and corners, the homeless settling down for the night; predators moving through the shadows, their intentions unknown; penniless gamblers leaning against walls; whores not yet in their element, waiting for the men to grow ardently drunk. Ambrose staggered down the street bareheaded, his slouch hat forgotten somewhere. His feet didn't work. The laudanum had run out earlier in the day, before he'd returned to find Iris, wild-eyed and short-haired, in their hotel room. Now the flask of whiskey in his hand was empty, too, and suddenly he fell and stayed face-down, his nose in the dirt, which was ripe with the organic smell at the center of things. Blood and shit and rot and smoke and something sweet that might have run down a child's arm and dripped off his elbow.

Rain began to fall. Still he lay there, resting. Pushed himself up, finally, brushing away the gravel that clung to one side of his cheek. He was unsure of direction. Hotel and shore and east and ground and sky. Just an empty space in which consciousness was dull and yet memory so acute. He could not escape it. *Dig his grave,* the sergeant said, and handed him the shovel. *Dig it deep unless you want it glowing.* Ambrose stumbled away from the memory, in the direction of a saloon, leaving the flask lying in the dirt. He entered the swinging doors, tried to walk straight, found a stool at the bar, and climbed on it. The bartender finished wiping a glass and held it to the light. The glass was beveled; through it the bartender's eye looked gray and enormous.

"Whiskey," said Ambrose by way of greeting, and watched the man pour him out the brown liquid. It looked hot, as though steam might rise from the glass. It reminded him of laudanum and his sudden wistfulness made him drink the glass in one gulp.

"Another," said Ambrose. As the bartender poured, Ambrose looked around the room, his eyes coming to rest upon a big man with long, red hair and a handlebar mustache. The man wasn't just a man. He belonged in a hazy aspic of history that held something evil. Some kind of atrocity. Some terrible offense. What was it?

The bartender put the glass in front of him but Ambrose didn't notice. He was staring at the red-haired man. Then suddenly, there it was in his mind — the clarity of the answer. Ambrose slid off the bar stool and approached him. His feet weren't working. If he remembered correctly, the soles belonged flat against the wooden boards. He stumbled against tables, grabbed onto chairs. He was aware of a turn in the bar din around him, a path of silence stamped out by his route to the table. Finally the red-haired man was right in front of him; if he had been speaking he had stopped. His face came into full clarity. Some sober part of Ambrose's brain, too good for this foolishness, now focused on his face and it all came clear again: stones falling, the smell of the street, the hole in the Indian's head, and the black stream of dried blood leading into his hairline.

"You killed him," Ambrose said.

The red-haired man might have said something but he didn't have to speak; his expression said everything. Fury, indignation. And the pure joy of sudden trouble.

"You bastard," Ambrose said, deliberately, as though naming a species of rodent, and the red-haired man stood up; this meant war, North and South, two sides who disdained synthesis and conversation in favor of murder.

A large, strong hand came into the story from the side and took Ambrose by the arm, and suddenly Ambrose found himself pulled away from the table, so that the red-haired man's face slipped out of focus and became part of the tableau of color and noise and confusion and smoke, just a blurry cloud of tension in an otherwise drunk's-eye view of a saloon at night, and Ambrose tried to say something defensive or appeasing or righteous, but no one wanted to hear it, least of all whoever now pushed him through the swinging doors with brute force and a warning baritone in his ear, *Don't come back,* and he was alone again, reeling down the street, pausing, attempting to balance himself, the sudden memory as crisp as something newly ironed, the sound of the shovel in Pennsylvania's dirt.

Seth lay to the side, in the same position he had fallen, one arm thrown around the other in a position taken only by the dead and children in deepest tide of sleep. Ambrose couldn't look at the boy he'd killed. The muzzle of the sergeant's gun could still be felt as a hard knot below his left ear. He lifted one heavy shovelful of dirt after another, his back aching from the effort.

Not a cloud in the sky, not a dash of color. The utilitarian sky of early October, stripped of all but its purpose.

He was three feet down when the sergeant came back again, scuttling up to him with one last order.

Take his clothes.

His clothes, sir?

His uniform. We need it.

But it's bloody.

Wash it in the river.

And the sergeant was gone, that officer who didn't care about the story of friendship and loss, could not give a rat's ass on this dull afternoon with the war being lost a little more each day, farmland stripped and cattle shot, slaves run off; the South was dying and he did not, repeat, did not give a shit about one coward burying another.

When the grave was deep enough and the mound of dark earth high enough, bristling with the weeds of early fall, jimson and thistle, he knelt next to Seth's body. The blood had half dried in the wound in his sternum. A clot of black blood twitched and proved to be a trio of horseflies. He waved them away and straightened out Seth's arms. Rigor mortis had not set in but was showing around the jaw line. In an hour or two his arms and legs would freeze, then relax again sometime before dawn. Ambrose was infinitely careful as he moved the body, trying to show the only respect available to the boy, now that he'd been shot like a dog and was about to be stripped naked and buried without even his name scratched on an ammunition box, for the final punishment of a deserter was anonymity.

Ambrose untied Seth's shoes and took them off. Privation was evident on his bare feet. They were scaly, covered with sores and insect bites, toenails yellow and flesh white and loose from days of marching in wet shoes. Ambrose unbuttoned the shell jacket and took it off the body. He couldn't look at Seth's face. He pulled off his shirt and the undershirt beneath it and was puzzled to see not a bare torso but a cotton cloth, tightly bound around the chest. Ambrose frowned, sat the dead boy up, and began to unwind the cloth, white in some places, bloody in others, unwinding around and around until the cloth fell away.

Ambrose gasped.

This final outrage could not be true. He let go of Seth and the body fell backward against the ground, eyes turned to the unremarkable sky, and the breasts of a young woman bare in the light.

He could no longer see the reality of the moment, that he was a drunk man under bright stars, on his knees in the dusty street. He saw Seth in that clarity of detail whose invocation he had always dreaded. He saw the outrage of it, the atrocity, and that is the horror of war, that somewhere inside it for every unlucky man is the moment that undoes him, perhaps something simple, perhaps a metaphor that wandered into the line of fire. Something restless inside, never resolved, some quirk of fate and chance, or just those men who fought without hate, handicapped by the fact that they had no quarrel — it was always something, and that's what Ambrose could never figure out, how to extract that something from the body, but there it was, and Ambrose turned around and staggered back in the direction of the bar, his shoulders hitting things, voices in his ears.

He remembered a little long-eared dog that ran out in front of the line before the battle, wagging his tail, not understanding that this was not a game; with a dog's heart he loved both sides; he was shot in the second volley and licked the captain's hand before he died, and later the captain made the entire battalion stand at attention as he was buried, because he was the best man on the battlefield, and Ambrose couldn't take it anymore, the depth of feeling in a war, the steepness of right and wrong, the way deeds echoed, the way that campfires and laughter were undone by musket and diphtheria, and as he approached the bar his drunk's stumble went away, then the soldier's stride took its place as his heart steadied and his shoulders squared; he was Ambrose, a man a man a man, and it was wrong of his sergeant to make him kill that boy, that girl, even in the context of war, it was wrong that gentleness of soul was a punishable offense, and he burst through the double doors back into the bar, heading straight for that table where the sergeant who made him shoot Seth was enjoying a whiskey with all his friends, and the sergeant, who no longer had long, red hair and a handlebar mustache, but was wiry and small, had just enough time to look up before Ambrose was upon him, grabbing him by the collar, *You killed him you killed him you killed him.*

Ambrose didn't see the gun at all, just heard the shot as the bullet entered his chest just below the sternum. In the heat of battle men can't feel their wounds; it is God's way of apologizing for the fact that they never heal. Ambrose's knees buckled and he felt a great warmth spouting from him, running down his shirt, filling his clothes, streaming off his hands, and he thought how Iris, his love, would have to bathe him, but it didn't hurt, it was fine.

He sank to the floor and crawled through the bar, his head bumping the swinging doors as he made his way out into the street. He turned over on his back to look up at the stars, as the air around him flooded with blue light, and a blue sky appeared overhead, and a long-eared dog appeared by his side and licked his hand with a blue tongue, and he did not so much hear Seth's voice as see it. The voice was blue.

50

HIS BODY WAS already bathed by the time they let Iris in the room, but she had asked for permission to shave him for burial. They provided her a towel, some shaving soap, a straight razor, and a basin of water and left her alone with him. She pulled back the sheet that covered his body, staring at the dark hole in his chest just below the sternum. It was bloodless, the skin slightly blue around it. She dragged her eyes away and looked into his face, finding there the Ambrose she knew, not from the war or the asylum, but from a time when he belonged to himself.

She wet the shaving soap and worked up the lather between her hands, spreading it across his face, over the jaw line, up to the ears, down to the hard knot of cartilage at the bottom of his throat. She had closed his eyes with the tips of her fingers. The purple hue of his lids stood out in contrast to the white lather, his long lashes coated with it. She dipped the razor into the water and used one hand to angle his face to the light from the window as she worked, pausing to dip the razor in the water, leaving floating rafts of lather and suspended whiskers. So black, so white.

Her hands were cold. Lips shivering. Forehead wrinkled in concentration. She finished his face and started on his neck. She pressed too hard with the blade, and a tiny slit in the skin appeared but did not fill with blood. She scraped his throat smooth, dipped a corner of the towel in the water, and wiped his face clean of lather.

She combed his hair and was finished, able to study his body one more time, touching the clusters of freckles, the stray moles, scars from unfelt wounds in the heat of battle, shadows around the eyes, smooth line of the brow, narrowing of cartilage at the center of the nose, flesh of the earlobes. Ridges of the throat, shoulders, arms, chest. (Ignoring the bullet hole. Ignoring it.) Bones of the rib cage, the dark, flat nipples. Yielding chill of the belly.

The penis, stretched flat and cool on the palm of her hand. Bare, smooth skin on his upper thighs. Downy hair beginning midway to the knees. Hard muscle on the calves, knots of the ankles, cords along the top of the foot, arch of the sole, the way each tiny fifth toe was tucked toward the others.

51

ON A QUIET Sunday morning, Iris followed the wagon bearing Ambrose's body through the town. She had found someone who agreed to bury him out by the creek with the last of the money left over from the sale of the bag of sugar. A dog crept out of a yard and barked at the horses or the wheels or the scent of death. The bark sounded strange to Iris. Muted. And the rising sun. Its borders were fuzzy and it seemed to be in the wrong place in the sky. Weeds and treetops moved, and the sheet covering Ambrose flapped, but she felt no breeze against her face.

She had failed him utterly. Stolen him from an institution that had, at the very least, kept him alive. Taken him for herself and killed him in less than two weeks. She was the strangler fig. She did not deserve the feel of the breeze, or the colors of morning. She had condemned the doctor for his hubris without noticing the monstrous pride of her own.

The wagon wheels creaked. A hawk flew overhead. A distant church murmured a hymn.

Iris looked back and noticed a motley group of children following the wagon. Wondered why they weren't in that church. Wondered where their parents were. The wagon wheel hit a pothole; the sheet moved and exposed Ambrose's bare feet. A small exclamation came from the children and Iris stumbled forward, catching up with the cart and pulling the sheet down. The effort exhausted her, and she breathed heavily as the wagon rolled past familiar crape myrtle bushes. Weeds broke through the dirt road.

The children followed them. The tableau of the woman with the man's haircut and the dead man and the wagon was just another toy the war had made for them.

The man she hired wouldn't dig the grave by the creek. "Too many roots," he said, and finally they agreed that he would dig at the edge of the meadow. He was knee-deep in the grave now, and some of the children had wandered away. Others sat in the grass and watched pensively, as though something more exciting would happen any minute. The wagon horse waited patiently in its traces, flicking its ear against the tickle of a blue fly and bending over to nibble at the goldenrod. Iris stood, arms folded, watching the dirt fly out of the grave.

She was not surprised to see the tall man entering the meadow, wearing the same clothes as the day before, walking in that familiar, stilted gait. His two guards trailed him. Yesterday, the sight of him had sent her into a hair-slashing frenzy, but now she simply stared with dull eyes as he made his way toward her.

Two shocks to the system — first, the news from the hotel clerk that yes, there was a man and woman matching the couple's description in the hotel, but the man had died during the night and was now being buried in the field at the end of the road. And then, the sight of her. Iris Dunleavy, arms crossed, her shoulders no longer high and proud, her hair short under her bonnet, eyes downcast. Standing before her lover's grave.

He'd tried Fort Myers first, gained passage through the Union guards by declaring himself on neither side, but a British doctor on official and extremely important business. The guards had burst into laughter at the thought of this strange-talking fool who smelled like roses, chasing two lunatics through the war.

"Of course," they said. "Have a look around, Doc," and

laughed some more. The search of that dusty coastal town had proved fruitless, and so had another, and another, and here he was in the fourth, sunburned and exhausted, tobacco juice on the soles of his boots, yellow pollen collected on his glasses. He motioned to his guards to stand back as he approached her. His grief at the news of Ambrose retreated, briefly, as he let the sight of her fill him. He'd spent so much of the last week hating her, delighting in the thought of her humiliating recapture. But the woman before him was broken, nothing proud left to conquer. And the man they had pulled back and forth between them like a prize lay dead under a sheet.

Her eyes were utterly hollow. He stopped a few feet from her, removing his hat.

She looked away, looked back at the grave. Behind them, the children were quiet. "I failed him," she said. "I failed."

"His chances weren't good to start with, Mrs. Dunleavy," Dr. Cowell said. His words were bare and bleak and soft and true. "You mustn't blame yourself."

She shook her head. No color came to her face to warn of the coming tears.

"I made him worse."

"He was worse to begin with. I imagine you made him as happy as he could have been."

"I believed I could cure him."

The digging continued. A dragonfly circled low and then arced away toward the bonnet of a girl. A night crawler wriggled out of the sod that was piled up near the grave.

"I suppose it's human to believe you can help the ones you love," Dr. Cowell said.

Iris glanced at the guards, who still hovered in the distance. "Let us finish burying him, before you take me back." Her voice was barely a whisper. Her hair wasn't fixed right. The bottom of her dress was torn. As the doctor noticed these things, he felt a deep and flushing regret. He had considered himself a man of peace, disdainful of both North and South for their tendency to use blood as a palliative, but he had fought for love with just as much ferocity, and now he could see that love for the sad, stumbling, prideful, hopeless thing it was.

He put on his hat. "Go home, Mrs. Dunleavy."

52

WHEN SHE HAD left her house for a new life on the plantation, the cat had been sleeping on the porch in a patch of sunlight. Apparently the patch of light had never moved, and the cat had stayed faithful to it.

The state of Virginia was a wreck, blackened fields and empty storehouses. Pigs rooting up severed body parts, and the Sunken Road at Sharpsburg filled with blood again every time it rained. Yankees and Rebels alike were buried in flower gardens. The hospital in Winchester was filled with the dead and dying. And yet certain constants remained. Like the cat. And the snake fence that ran between the house and the fields beyond it, covered in yellow jessamine vines.

Dr. Cowell had given Iris money for passage on a steamer to Mobile. From there she went east on a rickety wagon owned by a Mennonite, who got her as far as northern Georgia. She hitched rides from kindly strangers on wagons and spent two days side-saddle on an ornery mule that bucked her off while fording a stream. She ate what people gave her and occasionally pilfered the rest, stealing from corn bins as she had as a runaway from the plantation.

She was an anomaly. A woman returning from war among all the broken men. She was not wounded. Her body was whole and she had the use of her arms and legs. But she had the same far-away look in her eyes as the returning soldiers. They all had seen things that would compromise their sleep, their posture, manner of praying, enjoyment of music and cool water. Forever they would notice the bloody parts of the setting sun.

Iris stared at the cat, imagining that the creature had spent the war licking at a patch of yellow light on a cedar board. She envied that cat for which the war meant nothing but strange sounds at odd hours. The cat raised its head as she approached the porch, stretched out a paw, and then fell back to sleep, making her walk around it. She paused before entering the house, fearful that her parents would not be inside, that something had happened to them. She had borne many things, but this she knew would kill her. She had carried her story all this way with the intention of letting it fall into her father's lap. He could not abandon her now.

They weren't in the parlor. The kitchen was empty, the pots and pans in their places. A cheesecloth sat neatly folded on the table, and the air smelled vaguely of grits.

She looked into her parents' bedroom and then climbed the staircase to check the other rooms. As she'd approached Winchester, rumors had reached her of typhoid outbreaks in the city, yellow fever, gun battles. Somewhere in the five and a half years that had passed since she left the town, she'd lost the belief that she could alter events by bracing for them. God didn't favor the stoic, necessarily. This she knew from experience.

Her heart began to pound, and the soiled places in the armpits of her dress quickly grew moist again. The house was empty, and with a feeling of dread, she forced herself to go out onto the back porch and look across the yard. There, at the edge of the property, her parents worked in their vegetable garden, crouched together, bent at their work, hats shielding them from the cooling sun of autumn. They both had spades, and a pile of sweet potatoes sat between them, piled up like the eggs she'd seen in the nests of loggerhead turtles. They didn't look up as she walked slowly toward them through the yellowing grass.

She stopped. She had to watch them for a few minutes, loving to the point of tears how familiar and ordinary they seemed at their task. Their spades moving in the dirt. The sweet potato pile growing. That familiar white bonnet on her mother's head. The tuck of her father's chin when he bent toward the ground, as though in prayer. Weeds had sprouted all over the garden. Through war, through peace, weeds took over gardens and she loved them for it. Her parents were alive, doing ordinary things. They, no doubt, had blown gently on their coffee and prayed over their grits. The coffee, perhaps, without sugar. The grits, perhaps, without butter, but these privations could not kill the rituals. Could not end the prayers.

She came closer, wondering which step they would hear or which breeze would carry her scent. One step, two steps, three steps . . . She stopped and waited again. Her father noticed her first. He had bent to retrieve a sweet potato and had halfway straightened before something made him turn his head. He dropped the potato. His mouth moved to form her name. His eyes widened. The war had turned him into an old man, but the sight of her made his face light up like a boy's. Her mother saw her, too, and they dropped their spades and rushed toward her, arms outstretched, the sweet potato pile a tiny, forgotten hill behind them.

They didn't push Iris for her story but waited for her to tell it in her own time. Her mother immediately set to motherly tasks, scolding her gently for her sunburned face, rushing into the kitchen to cure her thinness with her cooking, snipping the ends of her terrible haircut with a pair of shears. Showing her in every action that no matter what happened, mothers went on baking and sewing and fussing and cooking and nursing, forever through time.

Her family had been spared the worst of the war, although their larder was low and they had been ordered by the provost marshal to take on a wounded Yankee soldier whose leg had turned gangrenous. They had nursed him diligently, their nostrils stuffed with cotton balls soaked in camphor to drive the smell away, until he finally died and was buried in the back. Iris kept looking at her parents. They had grown frail. Her father's prayers sounded different when they rose through the gravity vent. More uncertain, weaker, as though they were night creatures almost too old to make the climb. She wondered what changes they could see in her. It was all too much to comprehend, so during the day, she pushed her story out of her mind, filling the hours with chores and idle conversation, never venturing far from home, just taking in the flowers and leaves of the fall, watching the seasons change.

But in the middle of the night, her dreams would insist on what her parents didn't, bringing up the past in the shocking ways that dreams do, with a picture or a face so vivid that she would be startled from sleep, and lying awake looking at the ceiling she would remember those she hated and loved. Her story was insane. The story itself should be dosed with opiates and kept in an asylum and made to listen to a man in authority until it straightened itself, became reasonable. But it never did. Its craziness was its defining feature, like the color of a house, and it could not be painted over. And so, rather than trying to change it, she remembered it, little by little, in the safety of her father's house.

The birds began to abandon the feeder outside for the warmer climates of the South. Ripe cantaloupes sat on the porch. Squash piled up in a bucket. Apples turned red in the orchard. And finally, the day came when Iris and her father sat together on the cedar swing. One slat had rotted and been replaced with a new one that was lighter than the others. She had grown stronger over the days since she'd come home, restored by fresh fruit, beef stew, boiled potatoes, and ordinary moments.

Now she was ready to tell. How she had not appreciated this small life and now found herself nearly weeping at every ordinary thing. How she had started her marriage with such optimism and pride and then found her husband to be a monster. She told him about the baby, her voice breaking, the swing losing its rhythm, and of her guilt over insisting on joining the slaves in their flight, and choosing the path that would lead to their deaths. She spoke of her time on the island, and of Ambrose, and how wrong she'd been to believe love could save the beloved.

The loss of him staggered her now. Anything would bring him back, his face in sharp relief, and she would have to stop what she was doing because the love for him denied simple tasks, spilled the water in mop buckets, and mismanaged the fluted edges of dough. And his spoken name would make him come alive again, make his eyes open and his fixed pupils retreat into dots and blood fill up the cut she'd made in his skin when she shaved him with the razor.

She even told her father something she wasn't expecting to, because she didn't know it herself, but rocking on that cedar swing, her greatest dread expressed itself in words: That Ambrose had not died because of what she had or hadn't done. That, in fact, she'd had no bearing whatsoever on his life; she was simply something insubstantial floating through its inexorable arc, as disenfranchised as the broken wing of an insect in the path of a storm. She was at the beginning again. She was lost, and she needed his absolution and his wisdom.

Their teacups emptied and a red-tailed hawk came to roost on the branch of a nearby tree. Her father listened. When at last she had finished, he said to her, "I don't know what to tell you.

I've made mistakes. I believed in Virginia. Believed in secession. I thought if I made my words eloquent enough in God's ears that the South would win His protection. Now I don't know what to believe. You thought you could control a man. I thought I could control God. So I can't give you any wisdom. But I can sit here with you and serve as your companion. I can do that just fine."

This was acceptable to her. She'd drunk some milk that morning and vomited it back up while it was still cold. Beneath where her clasped hands lay on her stomach, something grew in her, a miracle just beyond her awareness. But for now, just the rocking. Just the silence and the smallness and the remembering. The moments floating by, a horse whinnying for peanut brittle from the darkness of the stable, a ripe persimmon falling to the ground, a coon dog making its way over to the shadows made by their swinging legs.

During the passage of those same moments, far to the south, on an island of sand and breeze and lunatics, Wendell crouched next to Penelope's grave. It was still covered with shells, but in the center sat the junonia shell his father had given him. Wendell took the junonia in his hands and held it to the light. A drop of perspiration ran down his face. His pet lamb, who was now nearly twice as big, had been wandering the tiny enclosure and came over to sniff the shell. Wendell polished the shell on his shirt pocket, then put it back in its place. He rested his hand on the lamb's back.

Out on the beach, an old woman who loved her dead husband with a lunatic's passion danced with him as the surf frothed up around their feet. She was late for her appointment with the doctor, but she didn't care. Her husband's embrace was too inviting, his heartbeat too real, and his body too warm.

Dr. Cowell came out of the double doors into the asylum

courtyard, looking for her, slapping preemptively at a buzzing mosquito. He called her name when he spied her dancing at the edge of the surf, but she seemed not to hear him, and with a great sigh, he slogged off after her, his lace-up shoes sinking in the sand. And any human would see what the doctor saw, a lunatic swaying alone, embracing herself. But the birds saw lovers of equal density, two bodies moving together, two sets of footprints disappearing in the waves.

Acknowledgments

This book would not be possible without the following people who willed it into being: Henry Dunow, rock star agent and friend; Wendy Owen; and Jenna Johnson of Houghton Mifflin Harcourt, editor extraordinaire, whose faith in this novel was unwavering from the very beginning.

My mother, Polly Hepinstall, as always lent her incredible eye for detail in going over the manuscript and finding countless small mistakes. I'd also like to thank Bird Weston, Betty Anholdt, Jenny Evans, Simon Mainwaring, Johnathan Wilber, Michele Wilhite, Rachel Johnson, Jess Vacek, Ed Godwin, Lynn Branecky, Barbara Wood, Julie Thompson, Michaela Sullivan, Adrienne Brodeur, Tim Hanrahan, Cai Emmons, Deborah Morrison, Lisa Glover, Ayesha Mirza, Summer Smith, Melinda Kanipe, Sheri Peddy, Greg Byrnes and Kelly Beck-Byrnes, Dallas Jones, Darcie Burrell, Milo, and Sandy Jordan.

Susan Hoffman and Mark Fitzloff at Wieden and Kennedy were very generous with their support during the rewriting of this novel.

Certain story lines, characters, and scenes were made possible by the imagination and research of my sister, Becky Hepinstall Hilliker. She will have her reward in graduate school or heaven, whichever comes first.

Ro, key's in the wall.